LIFE'S RIVERS
Cross

GLENROY SOLOMON BURKE

Order this book online at www.trafford.com
or email orders@trafford.com

Most Trafford titles are also available at major online book retailers.

Printed in the United States of America.

ISBN: 978-1-4907-1854-5 (sc)
ISBN: 978-1-4907-1853-8 (hc)
ISBN: 978-1-4907-1855-2 (e)

Library of Congress Control Number: 2013919888

Trafford rev. 09/05/2014

 www.trafford.com

North America & international
toll-free: 1 888 232 4444 (USA & Canada)
fax: 812 355 4082

CONTENTS

PREFACE

After finishing high school and starting to work for myself, I took the time out to look deeply into my past, analyzing the life I had lived as a poor boy growing up in rural Jamaica. I discussed it with a number of people I'd met over the years and would always mention to them that someday, though just when I could not say, I would write a book about my life.

In 2003, I told a friend that I would write my book after turning forty because by that time I should be fairly comfortable in life and would have the spare time to do it. However, I was compelled to start writing before that. The inspiration came on a Sunday morning, February 22, 2004 as I was driving back from Boston after spending the night there at a friend's house. When I arrived in Plymouth, I suddenly saw my entire past appear before me and tears started to pour from my eyes, enough to soak a good portion of my shirt. It was as if a voice said to me, "Get some sheets of paper and start writing." I drove straight to a store and did what I'd been told. The tears did not stop falling until the last words were written.

This is a true story, the life of one who has come a great distance. It is my hope this story might enlighten reader's minds and open their eyes to the fact that it is not where we came from that is important in life, but that we should always take part. The road to success is long and hard but we must never be afraid to travel it.

INTRODUCTION

Mother was alone in the house, giving birth—until the midwife showed up—on March 6, 1973. I am the fifth child of a poor woman who worked at a banana plantation, struggling to take care of her children. Arlene was the oldest, then the one that followed her (who will remain unnamed), followed by Paula and then my only brother, Tony. I was next and then there were my two younger sisters, Davine and Natasha, making seven in all. Since Natasha was the youngest, we nicknamed her "Little." My father had two other daughters, Patricia and Judy, who were living with our grandmother before he met my mom.

Arlene, the one that followed her, Paula and Tony all had different fathers who were scattered over the island, not near enough to be found. I still cannot remember seeing any of those fathers ever coming to visit except for one. Being a man living in today's world and knowing the pain and hardship that life can bring, I am proud of my dad, to have seen him father those children as if they were his own.

John's Hall District was then and still remains, one of the most rural parts of Jamaica. It is a district of hills and valleys, with a then population of about three hundred people—situated about five miles from the main road, with no driving road, electricity, or running water. The closest hospital or clinic was about fourteen miles away. The district was a very friendly one; everyone knew each other's business. The main business of the district was farming and that's what nearly everyone did. Most of the men, including my dad, planted bananas and they would compete to see who could have the biggest farm.

In those days, Jamaica was exporting bananas to Europe and this was one of the country's major sources of trade revenues. "Banana Days," when bananas were harvested and brought to market for shipping, were Monday through Wednesday and on Thursday and Friday the farmers would go to the field to reap other crops, mainly wild yams, two types called *renta* and St. Vincent, which grew in some parts of the island. The farmers' wives or girlfriends—my mother included—would take the produce to the market, to be sold to people from other parishes, hoping to make enough money for food and household necessities.

Most of the women in the district worked on one of the biggest banana plantations in the area. On Thursdays and Fridays, they would also join their husbands or boyfriends to help them reap the crops they would take to the market.

The only way of transporting crops to where they could be loaded onto market trucks was by mules and donkeys. Children would have to be in the field with their parents from a tender age, as soon as their parents thought they were ready and strong enough to start carrying a few pounds. Being a child growing up in one of those households, carrying your few pounds could start from as early as nine years old and it was very hard and a heavy burden for a child to bear.

CHAPTER ONE

THE BOY WHO SAW A GHOST

This book is the story of my life. In 1977, fifteen years into independence, Jamaica was facing economic problems and circumstances were very difficult for the poorer class of people. Most of the families in those days lived in one and two bedroom houses. However many there were in a household, they all would have to live in a small cluttered house until the eldest daughter or son grew up and moved out to start a life of his or her own.

Growing up in rural Jamaica, I was one of a family of nine and we lived in a small two-bedroom house. We had no electricity, no running water and sometimes barely anything to eat; life was hard.

As a child, I remember hearing my parents telling my older sisters and brother that when children reach eighteen years of age, they become men and women and by the sweat and tears shed growing up in that house, my parents would strive to prepare us for that passage into adulthood.

At four years old, I can remember sitting with my siblings on a bank in front of the house every evening, waiting for our mother to come home from work. She would always bring home one banana for each of us. After that I used to sit there by myself, waiting for a little old man who walked home from the bush every evening with his little dog. I would call him and sing this poem: "Oh, Mass' Charley, him have a bulldog in-a him backyard and when him get bad, chain have to chain him and when him get bad, chain have to chain him."

During those days, I would play with my sisters Davine and Natasha while our eldest sister Paula watched over us. There was a mango tree in our yard that we played under every day, until one day when my sister Paula told me to watch over my two younger sisters until she came back from the toilet.

While under the mango tree playing with them, I heard bottles rattling in the house. When I raised my head and looked through the window, what I saw there lives in me to this day. The window was very dark and a ghost was standing there looking at me. It had a bald head and a jet-black face with a white beard and from the neck down, it was just a skeleton. I ran down the hill, crying and shouting, "A ghost is in the house! A ghost is in the house!" While shouting, some neighbors grabbed me and asked me what was wrong. In the process of telling them about the ghost, I saw two of my sisters, Arlene and the one after her coming down the road carrying a board on their heads, with my brother Tony following behind them. They put the board down and held on to me and the people who had caught me when I was running told them what had happened. They then took me back into our yard, along with the people who were there. On our way up, we met my sister Paula coming down the hill with my two younger sisters. I was so happy that they were still alive but was still so afraid that I couldn't stop crying. They asked me to show them where I had seen the ghost. I did and then they went into the house and looked all around. They were calling me to come inside but I told them, "No!" and started crying again. I could tell that my sister Paula was also afraid because when they asked her if she would go into the house when they were gone, she said no.

My two older sisters then took all that they knew we would need from the house, such as my younger sister's nappies and our food and put them on the verandah so that we wouldn't have to go back inside until our parents came home.

The moment Arlene and the others walked out of the yard to start carrying boards again, Paula took the supplies off the verandah and put them on the bank in front of the house, where we sat for the rest of the day. My older sisters would stop to check on us after each trip to pick up another board because Paula was only nine years old.

When my father came home from the field that evening, he saw us all sitting on the bank in front of the house, with all the things that my sisters had taken out earlier. My dad looked at us and said, "What are you all doing out here?" My sisters and brother answered at once, "Glen saw a ghost today." My father asked in surprise, "What?" They all repeated, "Glen saw a ghost today." I was sitting in the middle of everyone, saying nothing, just looking into my father's face, hoping for rescue, but he didn't seem to understand what was troubling me.

My father then told us all to go inside and then asked me to show him where I'd seen the ghost. I showed him where it had been standing and he went over there with his machete, cursing and swearing profusely. He then asked me what the ghost looked like and when I told him, he said, "He was your granduncle who was born and raised in this same house and when he grew up, he moved away to another parish and died at some point." My father said that perhaps he had come to look for his sister and must have wanted someone to know that he came.

The day after I saw the ghost as a boy, life continued as it had been before. Mother went to work, Father went to his farm, Arlene, the one after her and Tony went to carry boards again and I was left at home with my two younger sisters and Paula to watch over us. For them it was an ordinary day but for me, home wasn't home anymore. I was so afraid of having that same experience again.

The house we were living in at that time was my paternal grandmother's and most of the people living in the countryside were migrating to a more urban area, not far away but close to the driving road. This would make it easier for them to go to the town and buy their necessities and in case of emergency they could get to the hospital in due time. My grandmother was one of the first to leave the district, along with her loving husband, Mass' Mardy. (Mardy died in 2009, old and blind.)

When they moved out of the neighborhood, my father moved our family into their house so he could tear down his own house and have it rebuilt in a more urban area where he had purchased half an acre of land in 1977, in a district called West Retreat.

Back then, the only means of transporting the boards to the main road was on my family member's heads. As I watched my parents and older siblings carrying the lumber for our home, I could see that they worked with pride and were very happy when dripping sweat, passing by their friends and companions because they knew that sweat was making a new road; a road that would take us to our new home, one that I hoped would take away some of the fear from me and lighten the load that I was carrying in my little heart.

Sometimes I would fall asleep on the bank in front of the house while I watched them and Paula would take me inside to sleep on the bed, but it wouldn't be long before I would wake up. I was so afraid of that house.

After all the boards were transported, my older sisters would take turns going to school so that at all times, someone would be at home to watch over me and my two younger sisters while Mother and Father toiled in the fields. Whichever sister was watching us on a given day was also in charge of carrying enough water from the spring for the household's daily use.

The spring was about half a mile from our house and every afternoon, when my younger sisters were sleeping, one of the older sisters would get up to carry water and I would follow her back and forth with my little bottle. When Mother came home in the evening, she would always check the water drum to make sure it was full and then she would cook our dinner while I was always outside on the bank, waiting for the old Mass' Charlie, to trouble him.

By the time Mother finished cooking dinner, it would be night and she would light the lamp and put it in the middle of the table. She would then send us all to go out and wash our feet then come inside. It was impossible for everyone to have a bath because the water was limited. However, she would give my two younger sisters their baths every evening to ensure that even though she wasn't at home during the day, they were still getting the best of care.

Father usually came home from the fields at dark and he would take a bath behind the house in a little yellow tub before Mother dished out our dinner. Then we would all sit and eat as a family. Some of us would have to sit on the floor as there were only four chairs around the table and the tradition in our household was that my mother, my father and my two older sisters would have the chairs.

Today I can say that I was proud to watch my loving mother, after dinner each evening, take my sisters who were going to school, sit with them around the table and look through their books to make sure they were learning in the few days that they were going to school. Like all the mothers in the district, even though they were working very hard on the plantation, they still found time to show love to their children. It seems to me that kind of love isn't found so much in today's world and I consider us lucky.

Because the district was so small and the men were very neighborly, they would team up and hunt for wild pigs, which was the cheapest way of having meat in our house. Their hunting ground was a piece of forest far away from home, a place called Stony River, which shared a border with a neighboring parish (St. Thomas). As I grew up, I learned that Stony River embodies a large piece of Jamaican history, as a path of battle in the war between the British and the Maroons in the seventeenth century. St. Thomas is known best for its mineral bath, a running spring with hot and cold water which was discovered by a runaway slave whose wound was healed by walking across the water. It is also known for one of Jamaica's national heroes, Paul Bogle, who led the Morant Bay rebellion in protest against the British occupancy, fighting for the rights of his people. He was eventually captured and hanged by the authorities. However, his statue is now a standing image in the Morant Bay Square as evidence of is great work. The mineral bath is also a tourist attraction in Jamaica.

The men's hunting days were Saturdays and Sundays, setting rope traps and hunting with dogs. They would set ropes one weekend and check them the next; my father would usually come home with a wild pig and he would also carry boiled meat and dumplings for us. I usually looked forward to that most Sunday mornings. Mother would be home from the market also and we would always get an orange before breakfast.

There was no electricity in the community, so storing meat was a very tricky problem. The only ways of preserving it was by a method they used called corning the meat. They would cut the meat into small pieces, then place them in a keg and then they would get a lot of peppers, mainly a famous one that is grown in Jamaica called Scotch Bonnet, lots of pimento berries and lots of salt. Then they would grind it all together and rub it into the meat and cover it and it could be kept for months.

There were some parts of the pig that couldn't be corned, such as the intestines. These would be washed in the rivers, then put into a big pot and boiled for a while, then they would be taken out of the water, salted and placed on a piece of mesh wire that was placed above the cooking fire. Named *cran cran* by the natives, the meat would stay preserved on it from the penetration of the smoke.

The men would also team up to work on their farms. As children, we always looked forward to these gatherings. Those men worked together with lots of fun. I can remember walking around the farms watching my father and his friends work; Tony and I would have to keep up with them as they dug the earth and we threw plants to them to be planted while mother and a few of her girlfriends cooked lunch.

The men would often be served rum by one of the girls. Each of them drank it out of a bamboo joint that they kept in their back pocket, waiting for the next shot and it wouldn't be long before some of them started whistling and singing their own songs to make each other laugh. In the evening when we were going home, I used to walk with the Men. Most of them were drunk and stumbling all over the place but mainly I walked with one of them by the name of Sabat. Today, he and I are still very good friends.

Sundays were always fun for all the children in the community. We got a chance to go with our parents to the nearest river or spring to wash the dirty clothes that had piled up over the week and we kids would play in the water. There were a lot of rocks on the riverside, which the women used to trample the soaped-up dirty laundry until most of the dirt was out.

Rinsing them was the next step and then they'd take them home to hang on their lines. You could tell it was Sunday in the community by the sight of clotheslines full with laundry in all the yards. *However, from the tough, scary memory of seeing that ghost, I was hoping that my clothesline would soon move to our new home which my father was urgently preparing.*

Time went on and I noticed some mornings that, when my father was going to work, he wasn't wearing the same field clothes as he usually did. Being an inquisitive child, I asked him, "*Baudon*, why are you wearing different clothes this morning?"

"Glen, I am going to West Retreat to work on our new house," he would reply.

Then I would ask, "*Baudon*, can I come with you?"

"Not yet, Glen. Not yet."

Patiently he put his machete under his arm, jumped on his mule and rode away.

I would then go to all my sisters and brother and tell them, "*Baudon w*ent to West Retreat today." This made us all happy and we would ask each other if we thought he would bring home anything new for us; however the that gift we had all hoped for would only be encouraging words that we were a day closer to moving.

Sometimes my sisters would ask our mother, "Mama, when are we going to move?" She would tell them to ask *Baudon* but warned them not to ask him when he had just come home and to wait until he had rested, otherwise he would get mad.

As those questions continued to be asked, my mother suggested my father start taking me with him some days when he was going to West Retreat. That day finally came and I was a very happy five-year-old boy. That morning, my mother gave me a bath and dressed me nicely; my sisters and brother were all happy to see me go because they were all depending on me to tell them how far the building of our new house had progressed.

7

My father placed me behind him on the mule and we rode out of our yard heading to West Retreat, or so I thought. On our way, we stopped at a house that belonged to my loving grandmother, Persha. She came out to greet us and was very happy to see me, as I was to see her. My father then said to her, "I am leaving Glen here with you today. Some men will be working with me on the house, so I won't have the time to watch over him."

My grandmother said, "Yes," and then Father rode away, leaving me with her. She gave me something to eat and we started talking. I asked her about my sisters Patricia and Judy; she told me that they were at school. While talking, I asked her about the house my father was building, but she didn't know much about it, nor did she know the pain her little grandson was feeling from seeing that ghost. After a while, I asked her if I could live with her and she said, "Yes," and then we started playing. I was so happy that someone was listening to me and playing with me.

The day went on and my sisters came home from school. We were all very happy to see each other because we hadn't been together in a long time. We played all afternoon and I could hold my head up and look at all of her house windows without fear of seeing that ghost again. This happy feeling did not last for long and the fear returned when my father returned and it was time for us to go home.

On our way home, sitting behind my father on the mule, I remember looking at all the buses and trucks that drove by. Those were the major modes of transportation in the rural part of Jamaica, rather than private cars. When we got to Windsor District, where some of his friends lived, he stopped and started drinking rum with them. Later that evening, when we got home, my mother could smell the rum on his breath. She took one look at him and said, "John, you have been drinking?"

"What's the matter with that? Am my own big man," my father replied.

"You have no money to finish the house but you can go to the rum bar."

"Going to the rum bar again" are words that I would constantly hear my mother repeat to my father throughout my entire youthful life.

My father used to sleep a lot on Sundays, like most men in John's Hall District. That was the only day they had a little time off from the field, so he would make sure he got enough rest; he didn't want to be disturbed.

As time went on, I saw him start riding away on Sundays after breakfast. My sisters and I would ask our mother, "Why is Father going to work on Sundays now?" and she would say that he was going to West Retreat.

"Is the house finished?" we all asked. And she finally said, "I think so."

As our hopes to move grew higher and the furniture in the house started to decrease, my young tears began to quench my thirst as they fell from my eyes, until the day we moved into our new house in West Retreat District.

The front of the old board house built by my father in West Retreat District to which we moved into in 1978.

Moving to West Retreat was fun for all of us; my mother and father got married around the same time, so it was a completely new life. The wedding took place at my grandparent's home, in the same district where we moved to live. Their home was about sixty meters from ours. I remember seeing many people at the wedding and my sister Davine and I were circulating the tables, eating crumbs from the cake.

At that time, my aunt and her children were living in that house because my maternal grandparents, Mammy and Dada, were residing in England. My siblings and I were happy to meet our cousins and glad that we were now living close to them; however, the biggest excitement for us then was to stand at the side of the road and watch all the cars, trucks and buses go by. It new and exciting but we would soon realize that the past was still living in the present.

Located in a Blue Mountain valley is the small community of West Retreat, three and a half miles from Port Antonio, the capital of Portland parish. This was where tourism first began in Jamaica. Tourists in those days mainly came from Europe, Asia and the United States.

Most of the families in West Retreat were living at a different level from what my family was accustomed to. Our new house was a two-bedroom, still with no electricity and no running water, but this time the spring was a little closer to the house. For our new neighbors, it must have seemed pretty strange to see us carrying water from the spring to the house every day, since this lifestyle was new to the community. Being awakened at the break of dawn and not seeing my father in the house and going to bed at night when sometimes he would just be coming home from a long hard day in the field told me not much had changed. The streetlights at night were a joy to look at and so was listening to the sweet sounds of cars and trucks passing by. However, the fear of seeing that ghost again still haunted me day and night and the hope of a better life seemed far away. It made me start wondering if where I came from was where I belonged.

My older sisters and brother started attending their new school immediately and things became harder on us as a family. My two younger sisters and I were a major concern for my parents. The discussion around the dinner table at nights was who would babysit us during the daytime.

The answer was my aunt who was living in our grandparents' house. However, my parents were also worried about the pressure they were putting on her to take care of the three of us. Because of that, my father would take me with him sometimes in the mornings when he is going to the field but would leave me to stay with my great-grandfather Dom, who was still living in John's Hall District. Dom would later teach me a lot of things about life before he died in 1986 and his body was laid to rest at a community cemetery in Windsor District, Portland, Jamaica.

Beginning a new school year in Jamaica requires a new uniform. For girls, it was a starched, pleated navy blue uniform and for the boys, it was khaki suit. Sometimes I would watch my mother help my sisters and brother get ready for school in the mornings. Their uniforms looked so beautiful on them; mother plaited their hair so nicely. But one thing had not changed: there were still no shoes on their feet and the tar on the road burned very hot. I would always follow them to the gate and when they were gone, I stood there and watched other kids walking by, waiting for my mother to get my younger sisters ready to leave us with my aunt.

She was now able to spend a little more time with us in the mornings because we were living closer to the banana plantation where she worked. This was about four miles for her to walk and with shortcuts, a bit less. Sometimes if she was lucky, she would get a ride from a passing truck that was going to the same plantation.

Staying home with my aunt during the day was pleasant enough. The most enjoyable time for me back then was to watch the other children going back and forth to school. A lot of them were my size and I would ask myself, "Why wasn't I going to school?" but soon realized that my turn to go would be the coming September, when the new school year would begin.

My sisters and brother would get out of school at two-thirty in the afternoon, pick us up from our aunt, go home and then start getting ready for our parents to come home. We would carry enough water from the spring and would also make sure there was enough firewood to cook our dinner and to cook the meal for the pigs afterward.

Arlene was older now and she would cook dinner some evenings, which made it easier on our mother when she got home from work. Some evenings, she would come home very late because now that we were living in this new community, Mother had to start buying a lot of the crops that she took to the market from the same plantation she was working; mainly she got rejected bananas, not qualified for exportation but still good enough for human consumption.

Though we were now living in West Retreat District, my father was still farming at the same place as when we were living at John's Hall District, which meant we would have to walk about twenty-four miles round trip on field workdays. The twelve miles back home would be with loads on our heads. For my older sisters, it was two days per week and for my brother Tony and me, as we grew, it was four days, sometimes five.

The marketplace where my mother went to sell her crops is called Coronation Market and is located in the center of downtown Kingston, the capital of Jamaica, where gunshots rang out regularly in the ghetto areas surrounding the market. My mother would go to the market every Friday night and we would all stand with her at the roadside, waiting for the market truck. I remember the first night I saw her climb up the steps of the truck. She took a seat on a piece of board that was laid across the back of the truck for passengers. By the time the truck drove away, I could tell it wasn't a good life for my mother. Today some of those trucks have changed and some of the drivers are dead but the memory still remains of that piece of board, my mother's rough, uncomfortable seat, as she rode off to work for our survival.

The journey to the market in Kingston was a four-hour drive but with stops to pick up crops and passengers on the way, it would take much longer. By the time they got to the market and unloaded the truck it would be Saturday morning, time to start selling. She would spend all day Saturday at the market and return home at night. My siblings and I used to sit on the verandah every Saturday night, waiting for Mother to come home and we could hear and tell the sound of the truck from miles away. When it arrived, we would run out to the gate to meet her.

It was hard to watch my tired mother climbing down the steps of that truck, loaded down with her bags. She couldn't spend much time at home with us because we were so poor and she had to make a living. I rarely saw my father; he was working so hard to take the shame of being so poor out of our eyes and being a little boy, I couldn't do anything to help the situation but the days were counting down for me to begin school.

CHAPTER TWO

CATCHING UP AT SCHOOL

September 6, 1979, was a bright Monday morning. I was quite excited; instead of watching my mother help my sisters and brother prepare for school, I was putting on my first school uniform. My sister Davine also began school that morning. As I was about to leave the house, my mother held my schoolbook in front of me and said, "This is for you to write in and you must learn." She then handed it to me along with half of a pencil that I shared with Davine. I took them from her with both hands and said, "Yes, Mother," then walked out of the house and waited outside for the others. As soon as everyone was ready, we took off for school. The journey from my gate that morning took me to Fellowship All-Ages School and that journey would show me better things than I had been seeing with my young eyes.

Walking to school that first morning, I was noticing how everyone was carrying his or her books. The smarter students held them up against their sides; when I asked my sisters why some students had book bags and were wearing shoes and we weren't, they told me it was because their parents had money. Some boys would roll up their books and put them in their back pockets and again I asked my sisters why they did this. They told me not to do it because those boys were not learning, so they didn't even bother to carry their books the proper way. Today some of those same boys are sitting on those rough, tough walls in Jamaica every day, without an education, still rolling papers and hoping for a better life.

When we got to the gate of Fellowship All-Ages School, I noticed my sister Paula walking away with Davine, so I asked, "Where are you taking her?"

"To the basic school," she replied and suddenly I wasn't so happy anymore because my best friend was gone. I had thought we were going to be in the same class but I was just getting to know how the school system works. Nonetheless, I still wasn't alone because my older brother and sisters attended the same school that I was starting.

When we finally walked into the schoolyard, they took me to grade 1 and said, "This is your classroom." I looked around for a while, then asked if I could sit anywhere. They said that I could and then my sister Arlene wrote my name on my book cover, told me not to lose it and I nodded my head.

"Come," they said, "let us show you around," but before they could even finish, the school bell rang.

We all gathered in the auditorium for devotion, which was conducted by the principal. After the devotion, Arlene walked me back to my classroom, introduced me to my teacher and for the first time that morning, I lost sight of my sisters and started to feel very lonely. The teacher then told us all to take our seats, said "Good morning," and taught us her name. She then asked us all to tell our names, but by the time she got to me, I just sat looking at her, not saying a word; I was so shy. When that moment came to an end, I realized that I wasn't alone. There were a lot of other children who did not say their names, and those were the ones to become my friends.

The morning session in class went by slowly; instead of paying attention to the teacher, my eyes were constantly set on the classroom door, waiting for my sisters to come and get me. At lunchtime, we went home for lunch. My siblings were all asking me if I liked school; I told them, "Yes," and we had lunch, then went back.

When I got back to my class, I changed my seat from the middle to one at the back of the class. This was because during the morning session when the teacher was asking questions, she had started at the front and now I didn't want her to ask me anything.

In those days, three students would have to sit on one bench, with a shared desktop for writing. The bench was only about four feet long and the other two boys sitting with me were total strangers but to this day one of those boys, Albert Thaxter, remains one of my best friends. Albert is now working on a cruise ship. He called me from St. Thomas in the Virgin Islands in January 2004. While it was nice to talk to him again, it brought tears to my eyes when he mentioned the past and how far we had come, as was always our dream.

That first evening when I got out of school, I was so excited that I couldn't wait for my parents to come home from the field so I can tell them about school but as the week went on, the excitement wasn't there anymore. I did not understand most of what was going on in class: the teacher was writing on the chalkboard and asking lots of questions; many of the other students were responding to her and getting ticks, or check marks, in their books. Immediately I realized that those children had started basic school three years ago and were some of the same faces that had passed my grandparents' gate in those days when I wondered why I wasn't going to school.

A tick in a student's book was all that was used then to show parents that a child was learning. I did not show my parents one until about six months had passed at school. That day, our teacher asked us to draw a cow. When I drew mine and took it to her, I did not know what to expect because previously, when I thought that I had finished my class work on any given subject that she was teaching, she would just look into my book and hiss through her teeth. However, that day she gave me a tick and said, "Very good." As soon as I got out of class, I ran to all my siblings' classrooms, opened my book and said, "See, I got a tick!" When I got home, I was still very excited, went to visit all our neighbors and showed them my tick. My parents were also happy for me when they came home and I showed it to them. But all through the first grade that was the only tick I got in my book; however, I did not stop carrying it in the proper way and I was looking forward to grade 2.

When school started again, I felt more at ease, because grade 2 was divided into levels A and B. I was placed in B because of my poor performance in grade 1 but by the end of the term, I was doing a lot better in class. My teacher, Mrs. Hanson, understood me well and she gave me a great deal of love and support in times of need, both in education and in others. (This is to be explained later on in the book.)

Meanwhile, there was a new challenge at home for me in the evenings. My brother Tony was now eleven years old and was already going to the field with our parents some days during the week. It was now up to me to boil the hog's feed some evenings and my water jug was also getting bigger and heavier.

During the third year, I was able to answer a lot more questions in class and because of this, the teacher called on me frequently. However, as I got older and my school days started to decrease, my teacher would sometimes ask, "Why don't you come to school every day?" I told her that it was because I had to go to the field with my parents. At the time, I didn't know why she was asking, but I would soon find out.

One evening after school, I went home and set about looking for some wood to cook our dinner. Because of the ghost I had seen when I was four years old, I was afraid to go into the bushes by myself, so I choose to look for wood by the roadside. In those days, the teachers walked home from school in the evenings. As I was heading down the street with my little machete under my arm, approaching a corner, I could hear the sound of the kids and teachers coming and immediately recognized the voice of my third-grade teacher talking to the others as they walked. She was telling them about a little boy in her class who was learning a lot but who couldn't come to school every day.

Another teacher asked, "What's his name?"

"Glenroy," she answered. As I popped around the corner, she saw me and said, "Here he comes." My teacher's concerns made me feel happy and encouraged to work harder in class.

That night, when my parents came home, I told them what I had heard my teacher telling her colleagues, hoping they would send me to school every day. Instead, my days in the field increased and the load on my back was growing heavier and heavier. My only hope was to do my best on the three days a week that I was in class. At the end of that school year, the result of my teacher's encouragement was clear in the final examination, as I placed third in my class and moved to grade 4.

My grade 4 teacher wasn't just a teacher; she was also like a mother to me. I was getting close to ten years old and starting to understand a lot of things about life and was feeling ashamed my family's poorer circumstances and of the way we lived at our home. Sometimes I would sit in class and listen to some of the kids talking about their homes and the many things they had; I would just sit there and wonder if only I could be in their position.

At times, they would ask me about my home and I would have to tell lies. I couldn't tell them that I had been sleeping on the floor all my life; I couldn't tell them that sometimes when I went home for lunch, I had nothing to eat. I couldn't tell them the distance that we had to walk to the field on my absent days or that there was only one toothbrush in my house for everyone to use. But I was able to tell them that my parents were two people who refused to quit on their children and that if I had the will and strength they had when I grew up, I would be proud someday.

Most of the boys in grade 4 were getting involved in sports and it was up to me to fit in. The time for us to play would be during the one hour lunch break but because I had to go home to eat most days, I could not participate. So I started looking for empty beer and soda bottles in the evenings to sell to local shops in the area to make enough money so I could pay for the school canteen lunch, which was about forty-five cents. Sometimes I would share my lunch with my friend Thaxter and when I didn't have any, he would share his with me. That was the way he and I lived through our school days as friends.

Some evenings, I went looking for bottles but couldn't find any and would wonder what I was going to eat the next day for lunch. However, I always remembered my mother telling us as children, "Don't steal people's things" and that lives with me until today. Some of those mornings in class, the teacher would ask me if I had any lunch money and when I said I didn't, she would call me aside and tell to come and join the line at lunchtime. She would always call my name, even if I didn't pay. My teacher gave me lunch in those dark days. I did not know why she was doing it, but in time I have come to understand and now I share the same love that I believe she had for children in their innocence.

By 1983, most of the families in John's Hall District had moved to better neighborhoods. This included my great-grandfather, Dom, who came down to live with our aunt at our grandparent's house. One of my cousins and I used to gave him his bath every Sunday morning under a pipe which served as a shower fixture. It was fun for us to listen to him curse about how cold the water was and we would laugh at him and say, "Dom, you don't want to take a shower. You are nasty, ha-ha!" He used to get mad and say, as he often did, "From the time I was born out of my mother's womb, I have never seen a set of kids so rude!"

Nonetheless, by the time his shower was over, he was just a gentle, friendly old man again. Sometimes he would call me and say, "Glen, go and get me a piece of fire stick to light my tobacco pipe." When I gave it to him, he would then say, "Sit down boy," and start talking to me while smoking his pipe. He would tell me many times, "Glen, take your education seriously in school. Show respect to your parents. Do not steal people's things because they will go to the four-eyed man about you." I would ask him, "What is a four-eyed man?"

"Men who can see out of four eyes," he would always say. He wouldn't make it any clearer for me to understand. When I asked my father what four-eyed man meant, he told me they were men who people visit to practice voodoo.

Dom's final words to me after every conversation were always the same. While pointing his finger at my forehead, he would say, "Boy, when you grow up and start working for yourself, save your money, because once a man, twice a child." I did not know what he meant then but in the months leading to his death, he was on his sickbed at home, with my grandmother taking care of him. She would change his diaper and he could only be fed with a baby bottle. Sometimes he would complain at my grandmother but she continued to take care of him, until one day he just slipped away from us. Even today, long after his death, his words are still alive in me, a legacy that I think I can hand down to other young people in this world.

Our grandparents were recently home from England, on retirement. It was like having two special guests in the house. All of us kids wanted to be beside them at all times, so it was like a competition even to sit beside them. They had a big living room with a television but we could only watch it when they were interested and their favorite time was when the news was on, while most of the kids wanted to see something else. I would often sit there with my grandparents, asking them lots of questions about England.

I still remember something my grandfather said one Sunday night in the living room. I was ten years old and the entire family was there watching television and sharing conversations. At one point, my grandfather called me to sit beside him on the sofa. I was wondering why he wanted me to sit there with him, but it wasn't long before I found out. He asked for everyone's attention and then said, "Since I came back from England and have watched all of you grandkids and your behavior, I can say that the only little one in this house tonight who is going to be like me is Glen." Everyone laughed but I was sitting there wondering why he said what he had said. He then took me aside, gave me some money and told me not to tell the rest. I was very happy and when I went to school the following day, I told my friend Thaxter what my grandfather had said and he replied, "That's nice."

Starting grade 5, I was now among the brightest students in my class and with four more years left to complete Fellowship All-Ages School, I made a decision one day regarding what I would like to become when I grew up. However, the reality of what I chose was shadowed by seeing my sister Arlene complete school without a skill and return to the same plantation where our mother had worked most of her life. With no chance of success, Arlene had started traveling around Jamaica, looking for a better life but all that she brought back home with her was a baby boy, Duwane and the plantation became her only means of survival.

In the 1980s, tourism was very strong on the island. Lots of white people were passing my gate every day in big pretty buses, going to a river called Rio Grande, where river rafting as a tourist industry first began in Jamaica. (*The Spanish, who occupied the island after Christopher Columbus discovered it in 1494, named the river.*) Seeing the buses full of tourists every day, I asked my family where on earth all those people were from.

"They're from abroad," they replied.

"Where abroad?" I asked. America, England, Canada and lots of other countries overseas were the responses.

I immediately started thinking to myself that those people looked as if they had lots of money and that certainly they must eat and I decided that I wanted to cook for them when I grew up. At the time, my sister Paula was attending Port Antonio Secondary Vocational School. I asked her if they taught cooking there, she said yes, there were cooking classes.

Anxious to pursue the dream that I now desired, one day in class I asked some of my friends what they would like to become when they left school. Each one stated what he would like to be and I told them I wanted to be a chef and why.

Most of them at that time, had their minds set on the grade 6 achievement examination, which was conducted by the Jamaica Ministry of Education. Those who passed that examination would start high school earlier than the rest and many of the children who sat in that exam room had parents with money to pay for additional classes after school in the evenings. I could not afford those extra lessons but nonetheless, I had my mind set on Port Antonio Secondary Vocational School when I finished at Fellowship All-Ages School.

During that time, my mother and father weren't getting along very well at home. They were arguing a lot and sometimes it would be loud. Now that my father had to pass the plantation where my mother was working on the way to and from his farm, it started causing problems because most of the arguing was based on the plantation where my mother spent most of her time.

I remember one evening my brother Tony and I were on the plantation helping our mother and at about 4:30 p.m. my father passed by, coming from his farm. To me, that seemed a little bit early for him to come home. He didn't stop to help us as he usually did and he wasn't riding his mule, which also seemed strange. Nonetheless, Tony and I were very happy that he would be home before us so that he could boil the pig feed. Instead, that evening, my struggling father became a shameful man in the eyes of his companions.

About an hour after my dad passed us, we finished helping our mother and were heading home. Most of the other employees were also heading home. There was a stretch of open road which was about two miles long and we were walking it. My mother and some of her colleagues were walking together in a group. As we were about halfway into the stretch of road, I saw my father rush out of the bushes and have a fight with my mother and he walked away, swearing and embarrassed.

We arrived home not knowing what to expect; my mother and father started fighting again and that resulted in my mother leaving home. She moved into our grandparents' house with my sisters and brother, who weren't supporting my father in the argument. Davine and I were the only two left to live with him.

The first night after mother moved out, my father opened all the windows on our house and I went to bed with them that way. I did not sleep well for fear of seeing that ghost again and could tell every movement my father made. He wasn't normal; he was deeply hurt but I couldn't help him.

At home without our mother, things became tougher on my father. He would have to make sure that Davine and I were all right and ready to go to school in the mornings. Davine, however, would have to get her hair done at our mother's house and I used to follow her to get some additional breakfast because being so poor and not knowing where the next meal was coming from, we had to fill our bellies whenever we could.

Sometimes when we got back, my father would ask me if our mother had asked us anything about him. If she had, I would tell him.

But my mother would mainly ask us if we had eaten and sometimes we hadn't. With all that pressure on my father of taking care of Davine and me at home, he couldn't spend the amount of time he would have liked working on his farm, so our older sister Patricia came to live with us to do some of the women stuff in the house.

When my mother moved out, she took most of what she had bought for us, including clothing and said to my father, "You take care of them now." I was left with limited amount of clothes and there wasn't much to begin with.

I remember one Sunday evening when all that I had to put on was a T-shirt and briefs. The kids in the community would always gather at the roadside close to our gate to play games and I had wanted to go play with them. I looked at my father and asked, "Can I put my khaki pants on and go play? I won't let them get dirty." "No," he replied.

"And don't go up there in your briefs and let anyone see you like that." I sat down in a corner inside the house and started crying but the moment my father shouted at me, I knew I had to stop or he would beat me. At one point, I came out of the house and when no one was looking down into the yard, I ran toward a huge grass root that was halfway between the gate and the house and watched them playing from there.

Time went by and I noticed my mother started coming to spend nights with my father. It continued like that for some time until she eventually moved back in with my sisters and brother. However, for as long as she was working on that plantation, the fighting and arguing continued.

By the time I went to grade 6, four days a week in the field, sometimes five, became the routine. Wednesdays and Thursdays were the days we reaped wild yams; Fridays, we would reap bananas; Saturdays, Tony and I would have to go and find enough firewood to last for the week cooking and on Sundays, I would have to go to the pasture with my father to make sure the cows were okay.

In 1985 our school changed principals; we were all looking forward to the change and a change was just what we would experience as the result of bad behavior. One day, when our teacher was absent, we were gambling in class. With a limited number of teachers that the school could afford to employ; we could sometimes do whatever we wanted. In the process of the game, our new principal walked in and caught us. He then walked us to his office and picked up an object we were not used to seeing at school—a thick leather strap—and gave each of us four slaps on the palms of our hands. Then he said to us, "You come to school to learn, not to gamble." I left his office in tears, but I still thank him for doing that. He showed me that gambling in class wasn't important because when you are broke, the game is over for you, but a good education will never decay.

Gambling wasn't the only thing I was doing in grade 6; I was also getting attracted to girls in class, as were most of the boys. However, the girls would not talk to me because of my poor circumstances. Consequently, I did not have my first girlfriend until I was eighteen years old. But that did not break the spirit of the little boy in me who was growing up; instead, it made me stronger in life. With my tough situation at home as a child, sometimes I felt like running away, but there wasn't anywhere to run to. The closest refuge was my grandparents' house, where I would go occasionally when I was tired of sleeping on the floor, just to have a chance to sleep on a bed. If I stayed at my grandparents' house the night before I was to go to the field, the precious time of sleeping on the bed would have to be cut short because of the early hours we would have to wake up.

The distance to the field was a very long walk and some mornings were cold. It wasn't pleasant walking in the mud barefooted, with the animal feces and urine in it. Eventually I realized that it was affecting me when I felt a burning pain between my toes; when I looked at it, I found that I had athlete's foot. I showed it to my parents but they just looked at it and said, "Everyone has it." I lived most of my life with athlete's foot. At one point, I thought I would have it until I died, but fortunately a friend recently introduced me to a medicine that took care of the problem.

Early in the mornings—as early as four o'clock—we used to wake up (my father, Tony and I) so that we could get to the field by 8:00 a.m. We would also take our mule with us to transport most of the crops we harvested back to the house. On our way to the field, we would leave the mule at a place called Long Hill. This was the location from where he could carry the load. The condition of the road beyond that point was too rough, even for animals. (Charlie, whom we named the mule, was injured in 1986 and my father had to sell him. However, he did purchase a donkey to replace him.) He named him "Spree Boy," but I didn't think that name fit him—he was so slow. Ha-ha.

We would start digging yams until my mother and sisters arrived with our breakfast, then they would stay to help with the work. Everyone would have to dig the amount that he or she could carry or what our parents thought we could handle. To find and dig the yams was very difficult work. It is a root crop with a vine and lots of small leaves; that's what we used to identify where the yams were. However, it gets very tricky when all the leaves and vines are dry and have fallen to the ground. In this case, the only way to locate a yam bank was by sticking our machetes into the ground until we found the yams and then dig them out.

Sometimes there were many different families in the forest looking for yams, so in order to find enough quickly, we would all have to spread out. No one wanted others working beside them, competing for the yams they were trying to dig.

For me, there was another challenge, as the fear of seeing that ghost again was taking on a new manifestation in my life: I wouldn't leave my father's side. He would sometimes get upset and ask, "Why don't you go somewhere else to look for your own yams?"

I would softly say, "*Baudon*, I am afraid."

"What are you afraid of, did you kill anyone?"

I would shake my head. "No."

"Make sure you find your amount of yams before we are ready to leave," he would reply.

Inside, I was crying out loud, but if my eyes brought forth tears, he would beat me badly. Not even my mother's voice could stop him when she shouted at him and said, "John, are you going to kill the boy?" He would just kept on hitting me and repeating, "What are you afraid of, did you kill anyone?"

I used to scream in pain, hoping for rescue but no one felt my pain. Sometimes when I looked at my body and saw the welts evident and knowing of no one who could help, I wondered how long it would last; I was pretty young when the beatings started and they lasted until I was almost eighteen years old.

When we had finished digging as many yams as we could carry, we would all gather at one spot to pack our bags. The women carried their bags on their heads and we men carried our loads on our backs. The method of carrying the load on our backs was by tying a rope at both ends of the bag, shaping it like a half moon, so that it would rest against the lower back, as it hung by the rope from the top of one's head, cushioned by a "cotta," a sort of a padding rolled from dried banana leaves, to protect our heads from the pressure of the rope; we would also pad our backs.

If it rained on a day when we were harvesting yams, there would be a major problem—something we dealt with many times over. Wherever the dripping from the bag of soaked yams touched our skin, it would itch from the time we started carrying the bag until we put it down. In that case, instead of using dried banana leaves to pad our backs, we would use green banana leaves and somehow that would help.

(*Yams of African species must be cooked to be safely eaten, because various natural substances in raw yams can cause illness if consumed. Excessive skin contact with uncooked yam fluids can cause the skin to itch. If this occurs, a quick cold bath or application of red palm oil to the affected part of the body will stop the itching*).
http://en.wikipedia.org/wiki/Yam_(vegetable)

Sometimes when I got home late those evenings, my back would be aching and swollen and if I showed it to my parents, they would barely look at it, then make comments like, "How come your back is so soft?" Then they would compare me to other kids around my age group and tell me that I wasn't a man.

Davine, my sister who followed me, was now ten years old and started doing a few things around the yard; she would mainly carry water from the spring but just enough for our mother and father to use. I would sometimes ask Mother, "Why doesn't Davine carry enough water for all of us to use?" She would just became irritated and say, "Is she your servant?"

"No, Mother, but I can go to the field with you every day to look for crops to make money for everyone." I would then go to the spring, not liking what my mother had just said and while I would never lose my respect for her, I started to acknowledge that she was not fair regarding a lot of the household work that she wanted me to do. The moment I decided not to do everything she asked, she started to single me out as a bad kid, saying I didn't have any manners and that I would never turn out to any good in life.

By the end of my school year in grade 6, I was one of the smartest and best-educated members of my household. However, at night, when I was doing my homework, there were still many questions to which I had trouble finding answers. If I asked my father to help me, he would send me to mother if she was available but she usually did not know much about the subject. Nonetheless, these difficulties could not overcome my youthful determination.

In grade 7, now wearing a pair of shoes to school, I started to wonder if my days there were going to be of any help to me when I grew up. My older sisters Arlene and the one who followed her had both started families and were working on the banana plantation. Paula was in her final years of school with not much to look forward to. My brother Tony wasn't the smartest kid in school either. Seeing all this, I started to really hate going to the field but could always lean on God's help for rainy days so we could not cross the rivers; then I would get a chance to spend an extra day in school.

To get to the field, we had to cross three rivers—one of them twice—but whenever it rained really hard, they would flow high, making it impossible to cross. The first one we called Back River. My father used to judge how high the rivers were running by a special stone on the riverbank. When the water was flowing over that stone, he wouldn't try crossing because he couldn't swim.

As a boy going to the bush on some of the rainy mornings, I would run in front of everyone whenever we got close to Back River, just hoping that the water would cover the stone so we would have to turn back and go home. Sometimes I would be lucky and get a chance to go to school but sometimes I would be disappointed. Those lucky days for me, however, would mean the hardest time for my family at home. My mother could not go to Coronation Market to sell crops to feed us for that week.

So on Friday nights, I would see my mother and father sitting at the dinner table, facing each other. My mother used to tie her hair up in a piece of red cloth, then she'd put her hand at her cheek and start talking to my father about how we as a family were going to survive for that week. The conversation was usually about how much money they had in the house for her to take to the market. I was there; I knew it wasn't much.

Mother usually had a notebook in front of her and she would ask one of the kids to lend her a piece of pencil. She would then turn up the lamp to have it burn brighter. It usually burned so black that you could see the soot on the zinc roof. She would start writing all the items we needed and their prices. Sometimes Mother would write a certain amount on a specific item and Father would say, "No, cut that down." I would wonder why my father said that. But when my mother finished writing, calculated the total, then asked him for money, sometimes what he gave her wasn't even a half of what she needed.

Mother would then say, "John, what did you do with the money you were supposed to have?"

He would look at her and ask, "What money?"

"The money that you spent at the bar; what are the kids going to eat next week?"

"I wasn't the one who made the rain fall," he would reply. Then he would scratch his head and hiss through his teeth. I still enjoy seeing him doing that in my memories. They would start to argue and my father would either go to his bed, or soon we would hear his two friends at the gate calling him to go to the rum bar; very rarely would he say no to that, but I love my father.

Our mother would then look at us and say, "Pickaninnies, we don't have anything to eat next week," but somehow she would find enough money. She would either borrow it from a friend or she would have some hidden in the house that my father didn't knew about. Those days were hard and scary, but somehow we got through them.

In those tough weeks, I used to go to my friends' houses close to their dinnertime, so that I could get something to eat from their parents. Then when I returned home, I would go sit in the kitchen and watch what mother was doing. Our kitchen was outside, apart from the main house. It was made from old zinc and bamboo. There was a fireplace made of three stones on the ground, on which the cooking pot was placed. Many evenings I sat there and watched my mother put wood in the fire to cook our dinner. She would then put nine plates on the ground to serve us dinner; there was no table to put them on. She used to serve my father first and then the kids, that was the tradition. Sometimes all seven children would be there looking at what was going on our plates. I could tell at times she was troubled because of the little amount she had to feed our hungry mouths; my mother's cooking was very nice, especially her fried dumplings, but at times there just wasn't enough.

Looking at the conditions of our life, I would always say to myself, "I am going to make a change. Someday my mother will have a nice house to live in and someday she will have a nice kitchen to cook in. Someday she will have running water, someday she will have electricity and someday she will have enough food to put on her plate." I would then look at her and say, "Mother! Someday I am going to America, and I will get you all that you need in life." She would always say, "Yes" and laugh. I understood why she did, seeing that most of her seven children were grown up but unable to give her even a dollar. The ways of life and the expectations of young men in our community were far from what I hoped for myself. Yet I could still see the reality of a better life and although I tried to explain this to my mother, I think she could only laugh until I could prove it to her.

With two years remaining at Fellowship All-Ages School, I was going into grade 8, as the pain and tyranny of day-to-day life continued. The teacher in that class was someone who understood me well, since she had also taught me in grade 2. That morning of September 6, 1987, when I walked into the classroom, it was much different from grade 2 but one thing hadn't changed: Mrs. Hanson's loving, caring face. It was a joy for me when I looked at her and I remembered the compassionate love that she had rendered to me when I was in need of it. Above the chalkboard was a new sign made of letters that she had cut out of papers. It read "**Only the best is good enough**," and that was the first thing I wrote in my book that morning. To this day, I remember those words wherever I go.

In that same year, I went to my bed one night and had a very special dream about a hero of my country. I dreamed that I was standing by my gate with the great Marcus Garvey. I was asking him questions about his time on earth and how it was that I didn't know him. He told me that he had died young and did not get to finish his work on earth. He then told me where I should go and what I should do to get a full understanding of his life and teachings. Then he disappeared from my dreams but not for long, as he reappeared when I was seventeen years old.

I dreamed again that we were standing in the same spot, he was wearing the same suit as before; he had four stones in his left hand and four prepared for me in his right. This time we were throwing stones at some breadfruit on a tree. With every stone that he threw, he would hit one, while every one of my throws missed. I was just looking at him and saying, "Yeah, I know that you are great. That's why you are hitting all of them."

He then took one step to his right, tapped me three times on my right shoulder and said, "One day you will hit them too." Then he disappeared. Those two dreams I still remember every day that I tread the earth.

Mrs. Hanson encouraged me a lot in grade 8; during reading classes, she made me the leader of my group of students. This wasn't because she had known me from grade 2 but because of the tremendous effort showed in my class work on those three days each week that I sat in front of her. She was preparing us for the road ahead, though many fourteen-year-old students didn't think that way. I did and I would even be more aware of life's challenges due to a mistake I made in class one day.

I was in charge of a group; three other students were also in charge of other groups. The leaders were reading the same story to the other students. When I got to the word "uniform," I mispronounced it and said, "aniform." The class started laughing at me and my teacher said to them, "Don't laugh at him—anyone can make a mistake. We are all here to learn—it could be any one of you." I thought she would take the book from me and give it to another student but instead she said, "Continue!" and I did without fear and without feeling embarrassed because if that sign above the chalkboard meant anything to the others, then it meant more to me. Along the road to success, one can make lots of mistakes many times over. But, if you strive to do your best and believe that you are good enough, you can make it to the end.

My fourteenth birthday was one that I had hoped to celebrate in School, but even of that, my parents deprived me. It fell on a day when I usually went to the field. That morning, I didn't say anything about it to anyone and no one said anything to me. The first voice I heard calling me was that of my father's, not saying, "Happy birthday, son," but rather, "Get up, come on! It is time to go to the field." Still, this did not surprise me: if throughout my childhood neither of them ever hugged me and said, "Son, I love you," why would they bother to remember my birthday?

We got to John's Hall District and my father sent my brother Tony and me to one of his farms to cut plantains. He described it to us and told us where on the farm the plantain trees were located. Then he said, "Make sure you don't cut the wrong ones."

We went, cut the plantains and then returned to join them where they were digging yams. When my father asked Tony to describe the location of the plantains we had cut for him, we instantly realized they were the wrong ones. My father started cursing, then looked at my brother and said, "You don't have any sense. Why don't you use your instinct?" My mother looked at him sadly and said, "John, it's animals that use instinct. Humans use senses." But he just continued cursing. I was just laughing, maybe because I was happy that it was my birthday.

On our way home that evening with about thirty-six pounds of yams on my back, we were climbing Long Hill, close to where the donkey would take over carrying most of the load. My mother was in front of me; suddenly she stopped, turned around and said, "Glen, do you know what today is?"

I said, "Yes, Mother."

"What is it?" she asked.

I replied, "Today is my birthday."

She just said, "Oh," and kept on walking. My birthday present was the sweat that was dripping from my face.

With now only one year remaining at Fellowship All-Ages School before I started secondary vocational school, my dream of becoming a chef was getting closer and closer and I knew someday I would be able to celebrate my birthday.

Cricket, track and field and soccer were the three most popular sports played in school. I loved playing sports but didn't get a chance to excel at it because of the few days each week I was able to attend school. Even if I participated in my schoolhouse color team practices in the evenings, I couldn't complete it but would have to leave early to go home and boil the hog feed before father got home. Usually the leaders of the house teams would pick the kids they thought were the best or the ones who could stay and complete practice. Nevertheless, before I got to grade 9 I made myself a promise, to play for the cricket team before I graduated from that school. I didn't wanted my name to be remembered just as a certified graduate, but also as an athlete and I had one year left to make that mark.

When I began grade 9 in September of 1988, I was quite excited—all that I had struggled for those hard days in school was soon to be on a piece of paper and I was looking forward to it. However, I would have to work harder if I wanted to be in the graduating class. I did get the opportunity at that time to attend school more days, a privilege that was the result of considerable pain.

One Thursday evening, we were coming from the field, tired and hungry. When we got to the yard where I had seen the ghost years ago, we stopped to rest and to wait for my father to catch up. There was a tall coconut tree in the yard with lots of coconuts on it. My mother told me to climb it and get some coconuts for us to eat.

I said, "Mother, I am not going up there. The tree is too tall."

"Climb it, I said," she replied.

I obeyed her and climbed the tree with my machete to cut a bunch. When I got up there and positioned myself to cut it, I raised my hand with the machete and brought it down with full force. The machete, however, slid on one of the coconut limbs and struck the big toe of my right foot, cutting it almost into two pieces. I immediately dropped the machete and shouted, "Woo, my toe is cut off!" and started crying, slowly coming down the tree with blood dripping. I can still hear the voice of one of my sisters, saying to my mother, "The boy told you he did not wanted to climb it and you forced him to. You see what's happened now."

She replied, "I sent him up there to cut off the coconut bunch, not his toe."

My father arrived there soon after and saw me lying on the ground crying, with my toe bleeding. "What happened?" he asked. My mother told him and they started to argue, with father saying, "Why did you let him climb the tree? You should know better than to force a child to do dangerous things. Where are you going to get the money to take him to the hospital?" My father then bandaged my toe with a piece of cloth and cut a piece of stick for me to walk with. I could barely walk, and he couldn't put me on the donkey until we reached level land. The donkey was carrying a huge load and the road was very bad. I fainted three times that evening and each time, I recovered and continued to walk slowly in pain.

When we got to Back River, where the road condition was better, my father put me on the donkey. As the donkey walked along a short distance, I felt myself leaning to one side and remembered seeing my father running toward me and then I didn't know anything else until I woke to cold water pouring over my face. As I opened my eyes, my mother and father were kneeling over me, emptying the last drop of water onto my face. My brother and sisters were also standing there looking frightened and when I stood up on my feet, they were all happy for me. My father put me back on the donkey—I was able to stay on for the rest of the ride home and my sister Arlene took me to the hospital for treatment. Today those pains are just memories that live within me, but my toe still carries the scar.

Cutting my toe stopped me from going to the field for a while but gave me more time in school. I could not participate in sports but it was good that the coaches knew I was there every day to support my teammates. As my toe got better and the track and field season began, I represented my school all the way to the parish championship. My best event that day was the four-by-one-hundred-meter relay, in which my team was placed third. At the end of the race, my coach tapped me on the shoulder and said, "I thought you couldn't run."

I laughed, sharing in her happiness, yet knowing that third place wasn't good enough to get me to the national championship which took place at the National Stadium in Kingston. Nonetheless, I left there that evening a champion and walked into my community a proud winner. I had just represented not only my school, but also the entire Rio Grande Valley. That winning spirit didn't stop there. By the time the cricket season came around, I didn't just make the team but was also named captain of my schoolhouse color and led those boys to victory many times on that cricket field. My success on the playing field was also matched in the classroom but at home, my family condition had only changed a bit.

My two older sisters, Arlene and the one who followed her, were in and out of the house with their boyfriends and could contribute a little from what they were making on the plantation. Dad could now afford to purchase a new mule and was lucky enough to obtain a piece of property from one of his cousins to farm. This place was much closer to home than John's Hall District but was still about a seven-mile walk, with bad road conditions. There was also a small river which we had to cross about nine times before we got to the property.

Birdie, the mule (above), had carried most of the crops to
feed my family from 1988 until 2009, when she died.

The new property and the mule were a big help for us. However,
they did not reduce the number of days I had to go to the field and
they would make it harder for me in years to come.

Father planted lots of bananas and plantains at this new property
and they were also enough wild yams we could dig for mother to take
to the market in Port Antonio whenever it rained hard and we could
not cross the big rivers. She could still make enough to feed us for the
week.

It wasn't long after he got the property that we started depending
on it as a part of the family survival. It was right there, one week in
the pouring rain, where I almost lost my hand. The machete handle
was very slippery; at one point I was digging a yam and when I stuck
the machete into the earth, it landed on a tree root that was growing
near the yams. My hand slid down the blade of the machete and I got
a huge cut in my right palm. I remember screaming loudly, "Woo,
woo, my hand is cut!" When my father ran to my rescue, I was holding
my bleeding right hand in the other and started trembling. My father
cut off a piece of his shirtsleeve and bandaged it, then tied a piece of
banana bark around my neck as a sling for my wounded hand. With

such a huge cut, I thought my father would say, "Let's go home," but instead he sent me home alone and told me to go to the hospital.

On my way, a lot of things were going through my mind. I remembered the day I had cut my toe and fainted three times because of lost blood. My hand was still bleeding and if I fainted this time, I could die, with no one around to help. Nonetheless, as I got to the main road, luck came my way: one of my friends was passing on his motorbike and offered me a lift. He took me straight to the hospital, where I got my hand cleaned and dressed. That injury kept me out of the field again for a while and this happened at the right time too because my final exam at Fellowship All-Ages School was just around the corner. It was also nearing the time when we would be visited at school by representatives from Port Antonio Secondary Vocational School to lecture us about life and our next step to attend that school.

One morning in class, our teacher told us there would special guest to talk to us in the afternoon. They would give us a clearer idea of our career choices and provide us with printed forms on which we would indicate our chosen professions. She also mentioned that those who had not made up their minds yet had the whole morning session in which to do so. I was just waiting for the time to come because I had already made up my mind from back in grade 5 and those tourist buses were still passing my gate; nothing had changed. I asked my friend Thaxter if he already knew what he was going to major in but rather than answering, he repeated the same question to me. I told him I wanted to become a chef and he replied that he also was considering going into the catering business.

We broke for lunch and came back to class all excited. A few minutes later, two gentlemen walked into the classroom. They introduced themselves and started talking to us about secondary school and some of the things we should expect when we get there. They also advised us that doing well in our upcoming exam would help us a great deal. They then took some forms out of their bags and handed them out to us. When I took mine, it felt good in my hands; it was the beginning of a journey that I had dreamed of four years ago but for now, it was the farm that held my future.

They then told us to fill out the forms and to indicate the skill that we would most like to learn and a second choice in case the class for our first choice was full. I filled mine out, giving catering service as both my first and second choices and then I handed it to the taller gentleman. He looked it over, then said, "Glenroy, you made a mistake here: you wrote the same career for your first and second choices."

I replied, "Sir, I don't have a second choice, I want to become a chef."

"Okay," he answered. "Let's hope the classroom is not full when you get there."

His reply was true, but I had a long-time dream to pursue and a struggling family in need of help.

I went home that afternoon feeling very happy—I told my parents what had taken place and that I was going to study catering services in secondary school. They didn't knew the meaning of catering services but gave their consent anyway, as the final days at Fellowship All-Ages School continued.

My khaki pants weren't in the best shape anymore; nonetheless I tried to accept the situation, hoping for better days. A young man from my community used to stare at it constantly to embarrass me. One day on my way home for lunch, he was sitting with his friend in front of a girl's house and as I was passing, I greeted them as I usually did. On my way back to school, they were still sitting there. When I walked by, one of them started laughing and said to the other, "Look at the seat of that boy's pants, how it looks like dry trash."

I acted as if I hadn't heard them, but when I got home from school later that evening, I took a good look at my trousers and I saw that they were right, the material was very worn. It was what my parents could afford and every time it was torn, my mother would sew it by hand, mainly around the pocket and now there were too many repairs. I felt there was no choice but to wear those old khaki pants until the evening I came home from school and told my parents I was going to graduate. I had done well in my final exam; nine years of struggling had paid off. There had been days without lunch, days when I felt like running away, but instead my ambition to succeed kept me running to Fellowship All-Ages School. Nine tough years were coming to an end.

Telling my parents that I was going to graduate was one thing—getting them to buy a graduation suit was another. It would cost money that they didn't have but nevertheless, they found it and I couldn't thank them enough.

My graduation suit was very nice, consisting of gray trousers, a vest, a white tuxedo shirt and gray shoes. That was the first time I ever wore a suit and it couldn't have been for a more worthy occasion.

On that special day in 1988, I walked to Fellowship All-Ages School feeling proud. The journey there was the sweetest of them all; People were passing by in buses, cars and trucks, shouting out, "Are you graduating today?"

It was such a good feeling to answer "Yeah, man." Even the people in my community, who had always stood in their yards and watched me coming home from the field those hard evenings behind the mule, were looking at me that afternoon as I walked toward every child's dream. I felt very proud.

My mother and brother Tony attended my graduation. It was a joyful moment to be sitting at the front of the auditorium, looking out at the attendees and knowing that I was one of those they had all come to see. The only picture I have today of that great moment is the one that lives in my mind. My family could not afford a camera but when my name was called to collect my certificate, I did not miss the flashing lights. My diploma was handed to me by an official of the school's board of directors and it was as bright as sunlight in the hands of a little boy who was growing up into a man. Nine years in Fellowship All-Ages School had become memories, with a great reward and now, the two most challenging years of my school life lay ahead at Port Antonio Secondary Vocational School.

CHAPTER THREE

THE CHOSEN PATH

During the two-month summer break, I decided to look around for extra work to make money for my school uniform. I was expecting to look as good as any other boys attending school in the town. However, in a third-world country with very few jobs for young people, my only choice was to turn to Golden Vale, the banana plantation where most of my family worked. My days spent there would be Mondays, Tuesdays and Wednesdays. The rest of the week I would be in the field with my parents as usual.

The morning I started working on the plantation, I didn't know what to expect, since I had not worked for money before. Even so, my school uniform was more important than my expectations. I was put to work with a crew and in charge of cutting and packing bananas for the tractor to transport to the main plant, where they would be boxed and shipped overseas. The manager in charge of my crew, I learned that morning, was from another parish in Jamaica. I didn't knew him and he didn't know me but the first time we had a conversation, I knew we would get along.

He looked at me that morning and said, "What's your name?"

"Glenroy," I replied.

"How old are you?"

"Fifteen."

He then said, "Glenroy, are you still going to school?"

I said, "Yes, sir, I just graduated from Fellowship All-Ages School, and I am going to start Port Antonio Secondary Vocational School in September."

"Glenroy, what are you going to major in when you start there?"

I said, "Sir, I would like to be a chef."

"That's nice," he replied. For his parting shot, he said, "Glenroy, when you go back to school, learn all you can so when you finish, you may become an example in your community."

As a young man of fifteen that morning, what he said meant a lot because most of the crew were older people. The manager seemed to be in his early twenties and I could see that he was already an example to others there.

As time went by on the plantation, I developed a good relationship with him. We talked a lot whenever got a break; he would tell me about his days in agricultural college and would ask if, when I finished vocational school, whether or not I would be thinking of going to college.

I would have loved to but I could not afford it; my ambition, however, was to make America my university someday and my immediate aim was to save enough money to buy my school uniform.

There was one entry test before the start of the school term, which would determine student's eligibility for grade 10 A, B, C, or D. The test took place during the summer break. While taking it, I was intensely focused because I wanted to place in either 10 A or B, as was every student's dream.

By the time September came around, I had achieved all that I wanted during that summer break. The days on the plantation had been very tough but I got a lot of encouragement from my manager. Most of all, I was able to get my school uniform and for the first time, I was going to begin a school term with a bag over my shoulder to carry my schoolbooks.

September 6, 1988, the first day of school, was much different from previous first days. Instead of walking to Fellowship All-Ages School, with books in my hand, I was heading into the opposite direction in a new khaki suit, the gray shoes I had worn to graduation and a nice red bag for my books. I was looking good and feeling excited as I stopped the bus that would take me to school.

Lots of my friends from the old school were on it—we talked and were all hoping to be in the same classroom. However, when we arrived at school and received our entrance exam results, we were all placed in different classes. I was placed in 10-B while my friend Thaxter was placed in 10-C. I would miss him, my friend since the first grade, but we were learning the same skill and would meet every day in catering class.

The new school had two shifts, morning and afternoon. The morning shift runs from 8:00 a.m. until noon and the afternoon shift was from twelve-thirty to four-thirty. I chose the evening shift for my first term, trying to eliminate some of the work I had to do at home.

By the time I got settled into my classes and got to know all my teachers, I realized that as a student in the school, I was pretty much on my own. My classes consisted of students from all over Jamaica and they were some of the smartest ones from their parishes. Some of them had lots of attitude problems but the teachers treated us all the same. If we wanted to learn, we could learn; if we didn't want to, we didn't have to. However, if you showed interest in your class work and respected your teachers, they would render it back to you and that's what I did.

The school was highly competitive and keeping up with the rest of the class while attending school just three days per week would be difficult. However competition proves greatness and I had come too far to quit.

Now that I, a poor boy from the countryside, was attending a good school located in the town; my friends would sometimes joke with me, saying, "Glenroy, you are seeing the light now." However, the townspeople weren't the only ones seeing the light. Around that same time, my parents ran electricity into our home. They could only afford to wire the living hall, one bulb, one switch and an outlet, which we hoped would be used so that we could stop buying ice from local shops and neighbor's homes to cool our drinks and also stop sitting on neighbors' verandahs to watch their television when our grandparents turned theirs off. Moreover, you could see the joy on all of our faces, we didn't have to light the lamp anymore but just flip the switch. Even my school uniform could be better maintained now that the lamp was off the table because my mother had more space to spread it out for ironing. She was very good at ironing. She kept my uniforms clean and pressed throughout my school years, with or without threads hanging from them. We didn't have an electric iron, but a steel one that we had to put into the wood fire to get hot. Then she would use a special piece of cloth to clean it so it wouldn't leave any dark streaks on the clothes.

As things were changing a little for my family, a huge disaster hit the island. On September 12, 1988, Hurricane Gilbert struck Jamaica. It was the most destructive hurricane in our nation's history. It slowed down the country for some time, numbers of businesses were closed, many citizens lost their homes and we were out of electricity for weeks., A few sheets of zinc were blown from our housetop and we had to move in with our grandparents for some time until my father could make repairs. For us as a family it was very hard, as conditions prevented my mother from going to Coronation Market and most of the crops my father planted were destroyed. Agricultural crops suddenly hiked up in price and only the hagglers who had that type of money to invest could go to the markets when the roads were cleared and repaired.

It was hard on my parents to find money to provide for us until things returned to normal. On Wednesdays and Thursdays, my father would still harvest the wild yams and sell to the rich hagglers. I would join him on Thursdays to dig yams to make my school lunch money for the entire week.

The hagglers were paying twelve dollars for every eighteen pounds of yams, which was about seventy-five cents in U.S. money. I would have to carry about fifty-four pounds to make close to the forty Jamaican dollars I needed to get me through the week, even living very frugally.

In the beginning, catering classes made me wonder if I had chosen the right career. This occurred the first time our teacher tried to get us familiar with all the equipment in the kitchen. I didn't even have a stove at home and had never turned one on before; however, I didn't give up or feel left out I was the only person in that class who knew the secret of my home and my family condition, there is a first in everything especially when they are for a worthy cause. most of all was meeting the challenges as the other students in my class, so I knew I could accomplish what I was there for.

My first test at that school was in social studies; four students in the class passed it, me included. After that, I developed more confidence, no longer feeling that the rest of the students were brighter than I was. I became more comfortable among them and I just kept on doing my best.

As the weeks passed after the hurricane, things became normal again on the island. My mother returned to the market and again, my time in school was cut back to three days a week. During that time, my friend Thaxter became even more important to me. I was missing my catering classes on the days I was absent from school. The day after, I could always depend on him to tell me about the topic our teacher had covered and to copy from his notes. However, if an important event was planned in my catering class, I risked the anger of my father and went to school instead of to the fields.

Around that same time, I got a chance to go to the market with my mother. On the way there, she was telling me that Kingston was going to be much different from what I was used to in my hometown.

"Different in what way?" I asked.

She said, "If you see anyone stealing from another, don't say anything—act as if you don't see."

By midday, what she had told me became a reality in front of my eyes. While in the market beside my mother selling, I saw a young boy stealing money from a lady's apron while she was attending to her customer. I quickly turned my head away and acted as if I hadn't seen anything, then took another quick peek out of the corner of my eye. The thief was done and gone and the lady did not find out until she put her hands into her apron to make change—all of her money was gone. She started looking around and was asking people, "What happened?" But everyone stayed silent, acting as if nothing had happened; they were all scared to point out the thief.

For the rest of that day, I wondered at what had just taken place in front of my eyes. Could people rob you just like that while nobody sees, nobody knows and nobody cares? I couldn't wait to get out of there and was very troubled over what my mother had to deal with on a week-to-week basis.

On our way back home, I quietly asked mother if that happened every Saturday she went to the market. She replied, "You haven't seen anything yet. That was just one person."

I then asked her, "Mother, do you like going there?"

"No," she replied, "but I can't do any better."

Hearing this, I felt sad, knowing that she was going there to feed my siblings and me. Three of my sisters and my brother had grown up in front of my eyes. They were now adults and couldn't put a stop to it. Instead, they were still depending on some of what she took back to help take care of their children. I was next in line to leave school. That evening, riding home in the market truck, I told myself that I would not leave Port Antonio Secondary Vocational School without mastering the skills needed to become a chef. I wanted to see my mother stop going to that dangerous place.

After that week, I wasn't interested in going back to the market with her and I worried about her every Friday night when she would leave home to go to that place. Nevertheless, all of that worrying just gave me more courage to work harder in school. It was my only hope and I was dreaming of that day when I would finish my studies and walk into that old board house and say, "Mother, I have gotten a job in a hotel." There was still a long way to go; I hadn't even taken my first practical test as yet, but it was soon to come. One day in catering class, our teacher gave us a project that we all would have to do at home. The assignment was to cook a fish in any style. The teacher suggested that we go to the library to research cookbooks for recipes. After class, my friend Thaxter and I walked to the library and looked through a few cookbooks. I was looking for something easy, knowing that I didn't have a stove at home or a refrigerator, but I also wanted to choose a dish that could get me a passing mark when I took it to school the following day. I searched until I found one that fit my criteria, a dish called Escovich Fish. The recipe that I read that day called for one whole fish, carrots, onions, hot peppers, vinegar and butter. The method was to first fry the fish to perfection in hot oil. Next, sauté thinly sliced carrots, onions and peppers in butter, add the vinegar, and simmer for a minute or two. The vegetable mixture is then spread over the fish.

After the library, I went to the fish market and bought a small Parrotfish. I also bought a small carrot; there were peppers and onions at home. Next was the supermarket, where I bought a small roll of aluminum foil and a small bottle of vinegar. When I got home that evening, I took the fish to my grandmother's house and put it into her refrigerator. I went to bed that night thinking about the task ahead of me for the following day, knowing that I didn't even have a proper frying pan at home in which to cook the fish. The few pots in my house were all big deep ones that mother used to cook the family meal, but I would have to work with what I had.

The next morning I woke up, ate my breakfast and everyone went his or her own way, leaving me at home to deal with my project. At about ten o'clock, I gathered my wood together and started the fire; I then cleaned and seasoned the fish with salt and pepper. Afterward, I chose the pot closest to what was needed, set it on the three firestones, and then added some oil. When the oil was hot, I put the fish in—I bent down on my knees over the pot with a little fork, hoping that it would come out perfect. As the fire burned low, I put in more wood and blew on the embers to raise the flames. When it was time to turn it over, I was very worried, knowing that it could stick to the surface of the pot and break apart. However, when I pushed the fork under it a few times and lifted, it turned right over and looked perfect. I continued to blow on the wood, thinking about my poor mother and father out there in the fields, working so hard trying to make ends meet, while their son was at home on his knees, trying to cook a fish perfectly. A proper frying pan would have made the task a lot easier. But nothing worthwhile comes easily in life. I knew that when I took my dish to school, if I got a passing mark, that would be a step closer to my dream and if that dream were to come true someday, my parents would be able to spend fewer days in the field and things would be better at home for all of us. Once it was finished cooking, I was happy with the result—I wrapped it in the foil paper and was laughing to myself on the way to the spring to get water for a bath before school.

Later that morning, when the bus picked me up at my gate, I was carrying two bags: the red one with my books and a plastic one with my tightly wrapped fish. I held it securely, not wanting even the breeze to blow on it. In catering class that day, I could see the intense looks on some of my classmate's faces, not knowing what to expect. The teacher told us all to unwrap our dishes as she walked chair by chair, inspecting them. In the end, most of the class got passing marks and I was very happy and relieved. She then went around and tasted some of the fish dishes and told the class to do the same, to get a feel for the different recipes. It was a good experience to taste the different recipes, not just to fill my belly, but also to make note of the ones I liked.

I went home and told my parents about the success of my first practical test; they were happy for me. However, my mother's only question to me was, "Which one of the pots did you use?" I told her, and she replied surprisingly, "That one can be used to fry fish?" I said, "Yes, I did it." I guess that was the time she first realized I was heading into a new direction and that nothing had been provided at home to help me with what I had to do—nothing to make my journey a little bit easier. It still didn't ring a bell in their heads, the realization of what I wanted to become and how well I was doing in school.

I was now approaching my final year in school, but my parents blinded their eyes to this. I was still expected to spend more and more time working in the field—more than I could handle sometimes. Still, I didn't quit on them nor did I show any lack of respect. At times I cried silently, so they would not hear, knowing that they were taking away precious days from me, days that I could never relive. My responsibility as a student was to prepare for a career and after finishing school, if I were to walk the streets every day doing nothing, people would look at me and say I didn't make good use of my school days. I heard it said of others many times and didn't want to be in that situation. My parents took away some of my school days, but they left me with three and I was determined that the success from those three days would dry my tears someday and that my parents would be proud of their son.

After the hurricane there were a lot of landslides in Jamaica, mainly in the country areas and most of the roads were broken up. This was also true in the hilly pastures where my father and other family members raised their cows. At that time, my father had two cows that were soon to give birth to their calves. He didn't want to risk leaving them so far away, in case the calves should become separated from the mothers before they got strong.

One day my father and I went to the pasture to get those two cows. We were taking them to one of his friend's pastures, closer to our home, where they could have their calves safely. On our way with the cows, we came to a part of the road that wasn't suitable for animals to walk across because of a huge landslide. The farmers instead started using a new road when they were traveling with animals. On the new road, one of us had to lead the cows and one had to drive them. I was told to lead; everything was going fine until we reached the intersection of the trail and the original road. At that point, instead of the cows continuing to follow me down, one of them turned the opposite way and started running. By the time my father had tied the cow that he was leading to a tree and finally caught up with me to help, it was too late. The cow had already gotten to the part of the road where the landslide was and while trying to go across, had fallen down the precipice, a drop of about twenty meters. As she landed, I heard my father behind me utter some curses and say, "Boy, you killed off my big cow."

I said, "*Baudon*, I couldn't hold her back," knowing that I was likely to face a beating or some other punishment. Nervously, I was standing there looking over the precipice, hoping that the cow would get up and walk, with him beside me swearing. Exactly what I was hoping for happened. I saw the cow shake her body and then she stood up and started feeding from the grass that was around her. I was still shaking because the cow weighed eight hundred to a thousand pounds with a calf in her stomach and was due to give birth in three weeks.

I couldn't imagine her falling from that height and surviving. But as a boy growing up, I always heard my parents say, "Everything in life happens for a reason." I didn't know it right then, but five years later, the reason the cow had survived the fall would become clear and I knew had she died that day, perhaps the dreams I'd pursued since I was a little boy would have died with her.

My father and I went down to the bottom of the precipice and led her out. We reached his friend's pasture with the cows looking fine and we left them there. After that evening, he told my brother Tony and me to go there some evenings when he couldn't make it and see if either of them had given birth. One evening, as we entered the pasture, we heard a strange grunting sound. We both looked at each other and said, "What is that?" As we inched closer to the sound and looked behind some big grass roots, there she was, lying down in pain, giving birth to a bull calf. We stood there and watched her clean her calf, then we made sure they were safe. We then went home and told my father.

"What kind of calf did she have?" he asked.

"A bull," we replied.

He smiled happily because a bull calf for a poor man in Jamaica those days was like a piece of gold. It was much easier to sell a bull to butcher than a cow, so most farmers would rather see a few of those in their pasture.

Attending school on the evening shift at first gave me extra hours to sleep in the morning on school days, Mondays through Wednesdays but even those extra hours of sleep were taken away from me. It was now months after the hurricane and most of my father's crops were back and ready for harvest. He started taking me with him early in the mornings to the new property to reap bananas and plantains and I would have to be back home in time to catch the eleven-thirty bus for school.

Around that same time, my parents purchased a small refrigerator. It changed a lot of things at home. We now had cold water to drink any time of the day. Most importantly, we had a freezer to store our meat. It was a joy when my sisters made flavored icicles on Saturday nights and froze them for Sunday evening, when we would all sat on the verandah after dinner and eat them.

As those early mornings of going to the field before school continued, I remember one morning I came home very hungry. When I walked into the kitchen and opened the pot, it was the same as usual: two cold plain fried dumplings. I shook my head and said to myself, "No, I can't eat plain fried dumplings again this morning." I was home alone, but if anyone had been standing outside the kitchen, they could have heard what I said—that was how much it hurt.

I walked out of the kitchen and went into the house, hoping to find something in the fridge to have with the dumplings, or at least to change the taste of them. However, when I opened the fridge and looked, there was nothing but a small head of lettuce which I first thought was a head of cabbage. I proceeded to steam it and when I finished steaming, it didn't looked like mother's steamed cabbage, nor did it taste that way. Though it wasn't very appealing, I ate it and was satisfied; I had at least created something to change the taste of those cold fried dumplings. I then left for school, unable to tell anyone what I'd eaten for breakfast but happy with myself for trying to create a new dish and knowing that the field I was heading into, professional cooking, was a creative art. Catering training was going smoothly. I was learning a lot and now had my next practical test to be done at home. This was even more challenging than the first test had been since it required an oven, which I didn't have.

We were told this time to bake a plain cake from a recipe provided by the teacher. When she read the method to us and reached the part that said, "Put in the oven," I thought, "Hmm, what am I going to do now?" Nonetheless, I kept on writing and thinking about how I was going to find a way to complete that project. Before the class was over, I remembered, the previous year at Christmas, I had seen how one of my friends' grandmothers had steamed a cake on a wood fire. Instantly I told myself I was going to try the same method.

After class I went to the supermarket, got all my items together and then went home knowing that if my cooking method didn't work the following day, I would have no other choice than to pull my teacher aside and let her into my poor life. But first I was going to try my best, and if I tried hard—as I had seen that old lady doing—then tomorrow it would be good enough.

In the evening when I got home, I tried to find enough wood and dry bamboo to make the fire. I told my parents about the task ahead of me for the following day and that I could not go to the field before school. Luckily for me, they did not object.

The following morning I woke up early, gathered all my ingredients, and started my cake mix. When the mixing was finished, I lit the fire, then got one of the deepest pots. I added the required amount of water, then put some stones into the pot and placed it on the wood fire. As the water started boiling, I poured the cake mixture into a baking tin, sealed it with aluminum foil, placed it on the stones in the pot of boiling water and then covered it. The stones were placed into the water pot to prevent the baking tin from sinking. I was also careful not to put too much water in the pot; otherwise the tin would float too high.

I stayed there for hours putting wood and bamboo into the fire as needed, trying to keep the temperature of the pot very high and not opening it except to add water. The water I was adding had to be hot, so I made another fire and kept a separate pot with water boiling. The trickiest part was to judge when it was ready; in that case, I lifted a part of the aluminum foil to take a quick look now and then until I decided that it was done. I took it out of the pot and it went straight into the refrigerator to cool. It sat there until I was ready to go to school. I cut it into four pieces, wrapped it in aluminum foil and took it with me in a plastic bag.

On the way to school in the bus, I was concerned about what the teacher's reaction would be when she saw my cake. The method used to cook it was far from baking in an oven but in life I had learned that no failure is worse than not trying at all. I had tried very hard that morning and could only hope to be rewarded with a passing mark.

I walked into catering class that afternoon and the teacher told us to open our baking projects. I opened mine on the desk and sat there, watching her coming through the rows. When she got to mine, she looked and said, "Very good," then she moved on to the others. To this day not even my friend Thaxter, who was sitting beside me, knew how I made my cake. Most importantly, however, was that I got what I was looking for—a passing mark.

I left school that evening a happy man and was now headed for greater heights. My first end-of-term exam was just around the corner, and I was ready to compete against the other students from the different parishes. I was ready to see if some of their attitudes matched their educational skills; I was ready to see if the five days a week they were attending school meant more to them than my three days meant to me. Most of all, I was ready to retain my seat in grade 11 B or move up to level A if I worked hard enough.

During the week of examinations, I left home each morning dressed the same as on any other school day, but my frame of mind was much different. There hadn't been much change at home. We now had electricity and a refrigerator but there was still no running water in the yard. Mother was still cooking on the ground in that old bamboo kitchen. None of my sisters or brother were looking for work in the town areas but were all on the plantation. My promise to my mother—getting her a better life someday—continued to rattle in my mind and every day in school was a step closer. When I finished the exams that week, I left school for the summer break of 1989 with strong thoughts that I had done well, but I wouldn't know the result until the next school year began.

Before the break, I did ask one of my friends if he could help to find me a holiday job in the hotel where he was working. He was one of two young men from my neighborhood who were working in hotels. He was also the same guy who had been sitting in front of that girl's gate a year ago, ridiculing my well-worn khaki pants. I didn't hate him; instead I had made him my friend and was now depending on him to get me my first desirable job. It did not work out for that summer break; nevertheless, he promised to keep his eye open for a position.

I went back to Golden Vale Banana Plantation to work for the two months, knowing that I only had one more year remaining in school and that after those 365 days, I could consider myself a man.

The hard days spent on the plantation this time tested my physical strength even more because I could choose either to do "job work" and be paid for the amount of work I could do or to be on the clock and get paid hourly. I chose the "job work." The supervisors would just show us a piece of property, tell us what needed to be done and price it before we start working. We would then decide if the job matched the money. If it did, we would work hard to finish it quickly and move on to another. I did make some good money during that summer break because working hard wasn't a problem for me.

There are still some mango trees on that property, close to the main boxing plant, from which my kids might eat mangoes someday and I will be able to look at them and say, "Daddy planted those."

That job was given to me and two other workers. The task was to cut down bushes, clear the land, then dig the holes and plant the mango trees. I remember one Friday when we were there working with the sun burning our backs, we took a break and purchased some frozen boxes of juice to quench our thirst, sat under an orange tree and drank them. They were so refreshing that when we finished drinking, we got so lazy, we couldn't start working again. I just looked at my friends and said, "Yow, that's it for me, men, I am done for the day." I just couldn't go on anymore. It was also payday, so we walked to Rio Grande, relaxed in the water for a while, then went to the main office and waited until our pay was ready.

The money was good, but it did not encourage me to stay there. I bought all that I needed for school and couldn't wait for the new term to begin, to carry on with the journey that had started ten years ago when life had seemed impossible to me, watching my family struggling for survival. I had walked barefooted to Fellowship All-Ages School, seeing it as my salvation, with one thing on my mind; to achieve all that school has to offer. So there I was, on September 6, 1989, starting my senior year in school and all I needed to do now was to keep my focus and get it done.

The start of my final year at Port Antonio Secondary Vocational School came quickly. That day when I left home, I reflected on the journey that was coming to an end. I had always looked up to the seniors at school and respected them, but this morning when I walked into the morning devotion service, I was one of those whom the younger kids would regard as an example.

The year began on a positive note, as I was placed in grade 11 B because of my good performance in the final exams from grade 10. I was now on the morning shift, which meant I had to get there by 7:30 a.m. and classes would end at twelve-thirty. This left me with lots of spare time in the afternoons that I would have loved to have spent with my friends, to join in some of the things they were doing. However, there was a new schedule at home written for me, though it wasn't hanging on the wall. My parents had plans to change those afternoons from childhood fun to stains on the palms of my hands.

Most afternoons when I left school, I had to join my mother at the plantation to help with her work. In those days, she did mostly "job work." Her duty was to cut the bad leaves from acres of banana trees. It wasn't easy keeping my head tilted upward all afternoon; sometimes my neck would become tired and when it got painful I would take a rest. While sitting, I used to watch my mother working, knowing that this was what she had been doing all of her life. I was so sorry for her when I looked into the palms of my hands, black with stain, the way hers had been all of her life since becoming a mother. I looked at her one afternoon in that field and said, "Mother, if I don't get a job in a hotel when I leave school, I am going back for an extra year."

She replied, "Do what you want to do, son."

My father didn't knew how well I was doing in school, nor did he knew my aim in life but he did know I was in my final year. I could tell from some of the things he was now telling me to do whenever I went to the field with him.

He looked me in the eyes one day at the new property and said, "Glen, you are leaving school soon. Clean up a piece of the property and start planting some crops for yourself." This didn't interest me at all but it was hard to say no to him. I obeyed his words, cleaned up a piece of the land and planted some crops for myself. I took care of them just the way I watched him taking care of his crops and even though I wasn't interested in doing it, I lived to reap my own crops that were planted by my own hands. By doing this, I also learned that in life, you do what you have to do until better things come. For me, of course, the better things were going to school and learning all about the catering service.

By then we were doing lots of practical lessons in catering class. We were also covering many different topics, including food and nutrition, food preparation, food service and food safety—everything that we needed to know about the industry. We also had a chance to visit a dairy farm to learn about milk processing. The trip was very good for me because I got a chance to travel in one of those big pretty buses that were carrying the tourists all over the island. The dairy farm was located in the parish of St. Thomas, about three to four hours' drive from the school. My friend Thaxter and I shared a seat; it was fun traveling in the air-conditioned bus, to which I was quite unaccustomed and to look out at the sugarcane plantations along the way.

It was even more fun when we reached there and the tour started; it was the experience of a lifetime. When I returned home that night, I was happy and eager to tell my family what I had learned about milk and how much fun I'd had. However, this piece of happiness would all be for nothing if I could not answer a lot of questions in catering class the following day, when our teacher would test us on what we had learned. The test turned out well, as I was able to answer every question. It was also getting close to the time when all the students in my catering class would be sent out for on the job experience.

From the day the teacher mentioned this, we started talking among ourselves regarding where we would like to go for training. Everyone wanted to train at a hotel, but there were a limited number of resorts in Portland—we would have to settle on wherever the teacher placed us. I was placed at an agricultural college, in a town called Passley Gardens. My wish to train at a hotel hadn't come true. Nonetheless, that did not discourage me from performing well, nor did it break my resolve to someday get the kind of job I really wanted. For now, I was still going through the school system and had to respect it.

The Monday morning, my job experience started. I was happy—so happy! I boarded the bus at my gate and paid the conductor the fare. He asked where I was going. "Passley Gardens," I replied. However, the reality of my mission that morning didn't hit me until I reached Port Antonio Secondary Vocational School's gate, when most of the students got off the bus and I was still sitting there. I then realized I was going into a real kitchen to cook for people to eat and it was going to be the test of all times for me. However, by the memory of poverty empowered with courage, strength, determination and pride, I knew I could meet the challenges.

When I walked into the kitchen, I introduced myself as Glenroy Burke, the student here for job experience. Another one of my classmates was also there. We met the supervisor and she showed us around, introduced us to everyone in the kitchen, then told us about our duties and gave us some chef uniforms. Later that morning, I was standing by a stove with a notebook in my pocket, doing what I dreamed of since I was eleven years old.

The first thing that amazed me was how fast the chefs used their knives and their speed around the stove. By asking them lots of questions, I immediately realized that speed was something I had to develop if wanted to be good in the kitchen. For every question asked, the answers were immediately written down in my notebook.

At twelve o'clock, it was time to start serving lunch. I was placed on the service line in the midst of things. I showed the chefs my willingness to work and learn and they were giving me things to do. It was buffet style service; we put the food on the line and made sure it stayed hot.

When it was time for us to eat our lunch, the supervisor told me and the other trainee we could have whatever we wanted. I didn't know how to handle that, not being used to a lot of food at home, and this was the first time in my life I had seen so much cooked food. Every kind of meat that was available found a place on my tray. We then walked to the cafeteria, sat together and ate. With every bite I took, I remembered my family and their needs. I ate until my belly was full and then went back to work.

By then it was time to start preparing dinner—this time to see the menu being prepared from scratch—and into my little notebook went more and more information. As the afternoon turned to evening, I was happy with what I'd learned on the first day and eager to return to my neighborhood to tell my family and friends how great my first day was working in a fully equipped professional kitchen.

Before leaving the kitchen for the day, I had another meal; when I reached home, my belly was so full that I didn't even check to see if there was any dinner cooked. I was just feeling happy and was waiting for my parents to come home from the field to tell them what I learned. I also wanted to tell my mother how the chef had prepared the food, just to see if she would try something different now and then. First, however, she would have to get a stove, which wouldn't be anytime soon. Still, to this day, I love my mother's cooking. She always provided good meals even when it seemed impossible.

The following day when I went back to work, there was at least one new face that hadn't been there the day before but there were also a lot of things in the kitchen that weren't new to me anymore; the things that I needed to be familiar with, equipment that I hoped to be around for a long time. At times, I would just daydream about working, as I'd always wanted, at a good hotel kitchen, running from the stove into the cooler and back, waiting for the waiters to come in with the next order and satisfying the diners for whom I cooked.

As the days of my job experience continued, I started to feel more comfortable in the kitchen. I was also eating more, so much that the supervisor warned me about it. She told me that people in the kitchen were talking about the amount of food I had been taking on my lunch tray—this couldn't continue, she said. I was embarrassed in front of her but still didn't think I'd done anything wrong. I was just a growing young man who had just gotten a chance to fill my belly. After that meeting, I started taking less food on my tray but continued learning more and more.

The job experience lasted for three weeks. I even learned how to bake properly and couldn't wait for Christmas to come to make my family their holiday cake. First, however, I needed to get a good mark from my supervisor to prove what I'd learned and to make my teacher happy. When the Day of Judgment arrived, the only thing I was worried about was the eating incident—whether it would take away a few points from my performance but it did not. Hard work had paid off for me again and I left Passley Gardens Agricultural College as happy as I could ever be. The experience I left there with could be used to perform successfully in any local restaurant around town.

My sister Arlene had rented a house and was now permanently living on her own. She purchased a gas stove, which I used in 1989 to make my family Christmas cake. That was the first time my parents realized that I was truly learning well what I had gone to school to study for. I was proud to see my mother wrap pieces of Christmas cake and give them to friends and family in the community—she was proud to tell them that her son Glen had baked it.

After the job experience, I felt more like a senior in school, with the fact that I could take what I had already learned out into the world and get a job. To have that backed up by a diploma to show my achievements was a prize waiting for me and if I kept good relationships with my teachers and continued what I had been doing for the past ten years, it would soon be in my hand.

In our English class, Mr. Heinz was teaching us how to write an application so that when we left school, we could apply for a job in the correct way. This was very important since school days were coming to an end. The words I had heard as a growing child from my mother and father telling my sisters and brother that when a child reaches eighteen years old, they are men and women, were now ringing like a bell in my head. I was getting close to that age and every time I saw my friend who was working at the hotel, I continued to remind him about getting me a job there. Despite asking over and over, I still hoped he wouldn't gave me a positive answer before I took my final examination, the most important one in my life. Its purpose this time wasn't to get me into the next grade but rather to take me successfully out into the world and my chosen profession.

The Sunday evening before my final exam week started, my entire family was sitting on the verandah after dinner. Mother and Father were having a conversation. I was surprised when I heard the plan my father had for me when leave school. My mother looked at him and said, "John, the boy will be leaving school soon. What plans do you have for him?"

My father answered, "All I can give him is a file and a machete." I didn't want them but I still respected him, for these were the tools with which he had worked all of his life. Sorry, Father, I didn't want to become a local farmer. That Monday morning when I walked into the exam room, the thought of what he had said encouraged me to work harder. I knew then, if I failed, that my entire career had failed. I took a seat beside Thaxter when my thoughts returned to my parents and the life we had lived. I took one deep breath with my eyes closed and told myself I was doing it for my family and for each day sat in that room, I motivated myself by remembering our suffering.

At the end, I could tell I'd done well and now it was just a matter of time before knowing if I was going to be in the graduating class. When that time came around and the names were announced, mine was on the list and I was the happiest kid leaving school that day. The moment I got home, however, it all turned into sadness. It never excited my parents one bit; their only concern was to know how much money it was going to cost. I gave them the figures and their answer was "No, we cannot afford it." I thought they didn't understand the life that lay ahead of me. I couldn't afford it on my own; consequently what should have been the greatest day of my life went by with me sitting at home.

It wasn't hard to tell the time students were marching to the selective song, since I had the schedule. I immediately recalled my graduation from Fellowship All-Ages School and how exciting it had been. This time around, I could only imagine the other students walking up into the bright light to collect what they had worked for all their lives: their graduation diploma. After that, I started wondering if

I would still get mine without attending the ceremony. However, when I asked around, I was told that those who could not attend would still be able to pick theirs up at a later date. I began to feel encouraged again.

The following week, Thaxter and I went to the school to pick up our diplomas. A senior member of the school board handed them to us and bid us farewell. I walked away from the school feeling very happy and satisfied that I had achieved what had set out to do eleven years before. But now I needed a job.

My diploma from Port Antonio Secondary Vocational
School in 1990

From the school gate to the bus terminal uptown, Thaxter and I stopped at every restaurant, looking for jobs. There was no success to be had that day. I went home, showed my parents what I'd achieved out of school, then put my diploma away in a safe place and started to wonder what I was going to do next with my life. As for my friend Thaxter, he went his own way in search of success.

With the lack of jobs in Jamaica for young people, finding work was critical. Many ended up choosing the wrong roads, ones that can lead to the wrong places and doing the wrong things—young men and women who were just getting out of school, struggling to get by, often without help or encouragement from their elders. The island news was saddened by violence most mornings I listened. That road was an easy one to take, but I chose to take the one more difficult.

The first Monday after leaving school, I woke up, ate breakfast and wandered around the yard for a while, then went back into the house and started listening to the radio. About nine o'clock that morning, I walked to the front door; the sun was shining bright in the distance and I could hear the whistling sound of bamboo trees as the wind blew. Everything that morning was beautiful, except for my life. I held on to the doorjamb, looked up at the sky and said, "Lord, what next? If I was still going to school, I would be there now and not even one building in town had a Help Wanted sign posted."

I walked out of the house with a little bit of pocket change and headed to the gambling house which was close to my gate. This place had became my new hangout when I wasn't going to the field. At that time, I knew how to gamble, but I didn't know how to win. By later that evening, I was asking mother to lend me some pocket money when I wanted to go out again.

The following morning when I woke up, the mountains around the house looked the same: the sun was shining a little brighter and I was still at home, not knowing where to turn for help. I continued to ask my friend to get me a job at a hotel and I could only hope that something positive would happen soon. Nonetheless, while waiting, I was trying everything I could think of to put my life in the right direction. I left home that Tuesday morning and went to the house of a young woman I knew who had two brothers that were working on cruise ships. In the early nineties the cruise ship industry offered some of the best opportunities for young men in Jamaica. I asked her if she could have her brothers get me a few ship companies' addresses. Before the week was over, she gave me four addresses and I sat at my old dining table one morning and wrote a résumé and cover letter, which I sent to each of the addresses. In writing them, I had only what I had learned in school to depend on; there may have been mistakes but I did my best and could only hope that they would reply. This is what I wrote that morning:

RÉSUMÉ

Name:	Glenroy Solomon Burke
Age:	17
Date of Birth:	March 6, 1973
School:	Port Antonio Secondary Vocational School
Qualification:	Secondary School diploma
Skill:	Chef
Hobbies:	Work

West Retreat District,
Alabama P.O.
Portland,
Jamaica W.I.

Cruise Line
28 NWn Boulevards
Miami FL, 111364
United States

Dear Sir/ Madam

I have been informed that there is an existing vacancy in your establishment. I hereby submit my application to your consideration of filling that space.

I am willing to cooperate within your system, your organization and the many different aspects which enhance the development of your establishment.

Enclosed please consider my résumé, which gives full details of myself.

Thank you.

Yours truly,
Glenroy Burke.

Later that day, I mailed them off.

I could have applied for positions all over Jamaica but it was hard to get employed that way. You needed what we referred to as a "godfather," someone who was working at a specific place and was looking out for you—whenever there was a position open, they would try to fit you in. That was exactly what I was depending on my friend to do.

While waiting and hoping for better days, life in the field continued just as when I was in school. I could now choose not to work with my parents but I would have to find my own place to live. After a few weeks, when everything seemed hopeless, I decided to join the defense force. When I took the entry test at Titchfield High School in Port Antonio, I failed it and left the room that Saturday evening feeling sad and thinking, "What next, where next?"

The roads led me to the gambling house without luck or experience. However, I was now learning a few tips from the owner, so I started surviving longer in games. Eventually I went broke again and I often went to look for one of my female friends. We would sit and talk on the wall at her gate.

We were sitting together at about six o'clock one Friday evening, in August of 1990, a few weeks after leaving school, when I heard the voice of my friend (the one who worked at the hotel) calling out to me from a passing car. He said the words I had been waiting to hear all my life: "Mama, your son will be working in a hotel."

CHAPTER FOUR

ON MY OWN

My friend shouted to me, "Glenroy, I got you a job at the hotel. I am going home to change my clothes. Be right back." In about ten minutes, I saw him walking back to see me. By then my friend's mother and her cousin had joined us on the wall. In front of everyone, he told me the job was to wash pots and plates.

I laughed with happiness and said, "I don't care what I am going there to do, I am happy that it's a hotel." I asked him when I could start; he said that I would have to go and see the manager first.

"When?" I asked.

"You can go there tomorrow," he replied, then gave me directions and told me which bus to take and where to get off.

That evening, I became the happiest man on earth. When I went home, I didn't tell anyone in my household. I started searching through the boxes in my room to see what I could wear to the interview. There wasn't much to choose from but I recalled that in my final year at school, the teachers always told us that whenever time we were to go on a job interviews, we should always dress properly, so I chose the best from what I had. That same evening my sister Patricia was visiting us from another parish. I told her that I was going somewhere the following day and asked her if she could give me my bus fare. She did without even asking where I was going and what for.

The following morning was Saturday. I went to the spring—got water for my bath, got dressed, took my graduation diploma and headed out of the house, holding it tightly in my hand. When I reached Port Antonio, I boarded the nine-thirty bus heading east. I wasn't confident enough where to get off, so I told the conductor the name of the hotel I was going to and asked him to keep an eye out. Then I took a seat at the front.

We drove for about thirty minutes and I saw the sign of the hotel; the driver stopped the bus and I got off. I didn't knew where on the property to look for the manager, so I stood in front of the gift shop until I saw someone in the hotel uniform. I told the person I was there to apply for a dishwashing job and that I would like to see the manager.

"I will tell him you are here waiting," he replied, then walked away. I stood there for about one hour that morning until I saw a tall white man walk toward me. He asked me if I was the guy there to apply for the dishwashing job.

"Yes," I replied and followed him to his office.

He sat me down and started telling me about my duties as a dishwasher and my salary. My weekly pay would be one hundred and fifty Jamaican dollars, which was about ten American dollars at that time. Before the end of the conversation, I told him I had just left Port Antonio Secondary Vocational School and showed him my diploma that I had majored in catering service. I didn't have much experience as yet but I was willing to learn while working as a dishwasher, I told him. I also mentioned that I would love to stay after my shift to learn more of what the chefs were doing without extra pay and if there was a position for a cook to open at any time, I would be interested. He asked when I could start and I told him as soon as possible. He said to come to work at eight the next morning and asked which day I would like to take off each week. I thought for a while about which day to choose because I wanted to stop going to the field altogether. Eight and a half years of carrying loads on my back was enough. It was time for the man, no longer a little boy, to show his true colors to the world. Finally, I decided Monday to be my day off—there wasn't much to do in the field on that day. We then shook hands and I left his office and headed home.

When I got back to my neighborhood, I went straight to my female friend's gate and told her and her mom that I had gotten the job. We sat and talked for a while, mainly about the local transportation problems and how was I going to get to work on time in the mornings. My female friend's mom decided to lend me her granddaughter's bicycle to ride until I could afford one for myself and I couldn't have thanked her enough. I took it home and maintained it properly since it was a seven mile ride to and from work each day.

As the evening got later and the island turned to darkness, my life at home was about to turn around and I still had not told anyone in my family. I just took a bath and went to the gambling house where I hung out—waiting for mother to come home from the market. As the truck arrived, I walked to my gate to help with her baggage. While my body unloaded the truck, my mind was on the following morning. I didn't even bother to go back out on the street; I just went to bed and I still did not tell anyone, not even my mother. She didn't knew that her son's dream was about to come true.

The next morning I woke up early and as usual, went to the spring to get water to take a bath, this time before going to work. I then went into the house and started putting on my clothes. My mother was cooking breakfast and my sisters Davine and Natasha were polishing the floor. Still no one had a clue that this Sunday wasn't like the past ones for me and the first time I was going to say no to my father and not care about his reaction.

Most Sunday mornings, we would go to the pasture to look after the cows, which was my father's intention. At about seven o'clock, I was in the bedroom getting dressed. There was a window through which I could see straight into the kitchen and I could tell my father had finished eating his breakfast. He picked up the cow rope and said, "Glen, come and eat your Breakfast; we are going to the pasture this morning."

I poked my head through the window and replied, "*Baudon*, I am going to work this morning."

He said, "What! Where are you going to work? What work are you going to do? Come and eat your breakfast now. We are going to the field," and started cursing and swearing. My mother said to him, "John!

Leave the boy alone. He said he is going to work. Let him go."

I got on my bike and rode away, without telling them I was leaving, thinking of my father's reaction to me starting my first job. I thought he would be happy after spending my boyhood carrying loads on my back for him. But rather than congratulating me at that moment, getting my help with the cows was more important to him. His words that morning just made me stronger in life and they also told me that I was on my own. There was still a roof over my head at their house, but I was responsible for the circumstances and direction of my life. I did not want to accompany him every day to the field with a machete and a file in my hand.

Riding to work, I kept thinking of how I was going to greet everyone who worked in the kitchen. What was I going to say to them? How should I present myself? But thinking of where I had come from to arrive at this point in life, the worries subsided and I just kept on riding. A few miles along the way, it started raining. I stopped to seek shelter under a shop's awning, hoping it wouldn't rain for too long—I didn't want to be late for work on my first morning. After waiting a few minutes, the rain hadn't stopped and I had to ride off in it. When I got to the hotel, I was soaking wet. I parked my bike and walked into the kitchen. As I entered, I said a big good morning to everyone and the response was good. The head breakfast chef was a woman. She asked me if I was the new wash-up guy. I told her, "Yes."

"Why did you ride a bicycle in the rain?" she asked.

I told her it was because I did not want to be late. She then asked the assistant storeroom keeper to give me a work uniform. At that time he had only shirts that would fit, so I had to wore the rain-soaked pants.

He walked me through the kitchen and showed me the sinks for washing pots, plates and glassware, then the garbage house in front of the hotel, which would have to be sanitized later that day. Both sinks that morning were filled with dirty dishes, some left over from the night before. There weren't any dishwashing machines in the hotel; I had to wash everything by hand. Some coworkers would ask if I thought I could handle it. I told them that I could. They didn't know how easy this work was compared to what I had been doing since I was nine years old. When I had finished washing the glasses and the plates, I moved to the pot sink and was having fun, saying to myself, "If that's all the work they have for me to do, this is going to be easy." By later on that day, everyone was impressed with my work and was telling me how well I was already doing. Inside, I was laughing. They were praising me for my work, which meant I wouldn't have to go to the field anymore. All the bruises on my back would someday fade away, but the hard work I had been used to doing all my life, I would continue to do, if that's what it took to keep my job for a long time.

As the day moved on, the waiters were in and out with their orders. I was paying lots of attention to what was going on, knowing that I was at the right place, where I'd wanted to be all my life and there was no stopping me now.

A little after midday, one of the cooks told me I could have lunch; I was very excited to eat my first meal out of a hotel kitchen. The menu was rice and red beans, with chicken stew and a small green salad on the side of the plate. They showed me where I could go to eat, in the dining room where the guests were served in the evenings. That was my first meal in a real dining room and it was a dream come true. I finished eating, went back to the kitchen and cleaned up both sinks again and then I washed the garbage house.

By then it was about two-thirty and there wasn't much in the kitchen for me to do. The head chef turned to the pastry chef and asked if she would be making banana cake for the next morning. She said that she would and asked me to cream the butter and sugar. In those days, the hotel didn't had a mixer; we would have to mix by hand, which could be hard on the arms. However, in a few minutes, I was done and everyone was impressed again. Some people were saying that it was the fastest they'd ever seen someone cream butter and sugar by hand. At about three-thirty in the afternoon, some new workers arrived; I was told they were the night crew. About four o'clock, the head night chef came in and my coworkers introduced me to him. When he finished writing the menu and changed into his chef uniform, I walked over to him and told I had taken the catering service course in school and that I was interested in learning about everything to do with cooking. The chef asked me when my shift ended. I replied that I was scheduled until three-thirty but I would like to stay until they had finished preparing the menu.

"That would be fine," he said and then he asked if I knew how to use a knife.

"No," I replied.

That was the first thing he started teaching me. I stayed until about 6:30 p.m. watching the chef and his staff prepare the dinner, except for the dessert, which he told me had to be made to order. The hotel back then was serving a six-course meal for dinner. Guests would pay one price for the entire menu, served to them by very friendly professional waiters. The menu that Sunday night in August of 1990, as I remember it, was as follows:

MENU

Appetizer:	Citrus cocktail
Soup:	Pepper pot
Salad:	Tossed garden salad with lemon vinaigrette
Fish course:	Grilled petite fillet of snapper
Main course:	Garlic encrusted pork loin, served with duchess potatoes, carrots, and green beans
Dessert:	White wine sabayon

When I left work that evening, I was in a hurry to get home. I rode straight to my friend's gate and told her about my first day at work and how much I'd loved it. From her gate, I went home and told my family about the job; I also told them that I was not going back to the field. This I had wanted to tell them for a long time, but now the right time had come and it made me very happy. The following day was my day off. I didn't let my parents know, for fear that they would find something for me to do in the field.

By Monday evening when I went to the gambling house, it was already a major topic of conversation that I was working in a hotel. In those days in Jamaica, when you could be talked about like that, you were an example to your community. Only a few of the gossipers, however, remembered where I'd came from. They now saw me as a kid working at a hotel but I never let the way others saw me shadow the reality of the past. It is something I can never forget, which has made me stronger in life.

On Tuesday morning, my second day at work, everything was the same as the day I started; I continued to work hard and impress people and was also talking a little more, mainly to the guys in my age group. As most young men love talking about girls, that was the main topic. They would ask me about my girlfriend and I would make up stories for them to believe since I still didn't have one. However, being in their company now, I hoped I could stop lying about my love life soon.

The head breakfast chef worked from 7:00 a.m. to 2:00 p.m. Oftentimes when she left, there were still lunch orders coming into the kitchen. From the first evening I noticed it, I wanted to be the person to fill in until the night cooks arrived. I started carefully watching everything she did and now when she left in the afternoons, I started hoping the orders would continue to come in so that I could prove myself to them from early on.

About two weeks later, it started happening. One afternoon after she left, the orders were still pouring in. I decided to take up the challenge, and I told the waiters I could make them. By the following day, the biggest talk in the hotel was about how fast I was learning and what I was doing; even the food and beverage manager was congratulating me. From that evening on, when the chef finished her shift, she started telling me I was in charge until the night crew got there. I was gaining a lot of recognition on the job and could only hope that it continued until a cooking position became open.

There was a gentleman who used to set the main dining room every day for dinner. I started to spend most of my free time watching what he was doing. I watched how he was setting the utensils and glassware for different courses and how to fold napkins in many different ways. Within a few weeks working, evidence of my success could be seen by the way I started dressing for work each day, as I was wearing lots of brand-name clothes that people in town area were wearing. Suddenly I started looking like a young man who worked in a hotel.

At the gambling house in my area, I was also getting better at the Games; I now had money to pay to learn the tricks of winning. Also, a few girls in the area were noticing me but I still wasn't having any luck with them. There was one in particular, who had moved there from the parish of St. Thomas. I was in love with her—I did all that I could to impress her, but she wasn't looking my way. She was in love with another. It's been so many years and I still feel the pain of unrequited love.

By then it was getting close to Christmas of 1990; I was happily anticipating the holiday. There was always a Christmas party on the plantation where my family worked and I was looking forward to it—to see some of my old friends and have a good time. After leaving work on the evening of the party, I went home, got dressed in the best clothes that I owned and went there. I had a blast—I got so drunk that I could barely walk home. When I got to my gate, I was still staggering all over the place. My father was sitting on the verandah watching me coming down into the yard.

As I entered the verandah, he asked, "What happened to you now?"

I said, "Nothing."

He then went behind the house for a piece of rope and started beating me on the verandah. At one point, I remember asking him how he could beat a drunken man, but he just continued hitting me. My mother then entered through the gate, approached us and said,

"John, why are you beating the boy like that? Don't you see that he is a man now?"

My father then raised his hand and gave me one more hit across my back, then he looked at my mother and said, "That will turn him into a man now." That was the last beating I got from him.

As 1991 approached, things were looking good for me. I was doing well at the hotel and was ready to start cooking for the guests. I also started working some night shifts to get a feel for the kitchen at dinnertime. It was just the right move because my wish of becoming a chef would soon come true.

One evening, I went to work and was hit with the news that the head chef was leaving. He had an opportunity to work on a cruise ship and had to leave immediately. His position was to be handed down to his assistant; however, before that could happen, the assistant had quit as well and there were now two positions open. That night, the food and beverage manager brought me two chef jackets and told me to be at work at eight the following morning and that I was promoted to the position of cook. Another dishwasher was also promoted and he was placed on the night shift.

When I started working as a cook, it was a little challenging. Now that I was responsible for satisfying the customers, it was much harder than filling in now and then. However, the woman with whom I was working was a very good teacher and in a few weeks I had mastered most of what had to be done on the breakfast and lunch shifts. This gained me a raise in pay—two hundred and fifty Jamaican dollars per week, which was equaled about sixteen American dollars. I bought a new bike and could now give my mother some money each week to help with the household expenses. My eighteenth birthday was also just around the corner and I was looking forward to it. The time had come when I could celebrate with cakes and drinks instead of climbing a hill dripping sweat with load on my back.

In life, when we start working somewhere, we develop new friends and sometimes one of them may become very important and a very good friend. One of whom I met was kind enough to tell me that, with a dream like mine, I needed a passport in order to travel. He was telling me about opportunities that could come my way through the guests that were coming to the hotel from all over the world. Someday I could be lucky and someone might want to take me to a foreign country to work for them. My first step, however, was to get my passport, which I had to obtain through an agent, then my police record, which was only issued in Kingston. I didn't knew where the office was located, so my friend took me there one day. I applied for it and was supposed to go back to pick it up in two weeks. Before the pickup date came, my friend and fellow cook got an opportunity to go work on a cruise ship, and I was moved to work on the night shift at the hotel.

Within a few weeks, I was handling the night shift well and was comfortable with the dinner menu. As time went on, I started planning menus and was working with some great chefs from Europe. I was gaining more and more respect in the hotel while my name became more popular in my community. It was time for a lot of my friends to come out and celebrate my eighteenth birthday with me. The only thing that was missing was that I still did not have a girlfriend. I invited the girl that I was in love with, hoping she would be my date, but after the cake was cut and she'd had something to eat, she left. Time went on and I got more involved in menu planning. Lots of things started to be expected of me. I was now feeling the responsibility of a chef on my shoulders and I was handling it well—getting better day by day.

Around that time, the tip policy in the hotel changed. Instead of the workers at the front of the house making all the tips, the hotel manager started collecting a 10 percent service charge from all the guests to be shared among all the employees on a weekly basis. I started taking home some very good paychecks and you could see it by the clothes I was wearing and the things I was doing. My parents had seen the changes in me and were ready to confront me about some of the dangers in life that we all can face at times.

One evening, I got home after going out on my day off. When I entered the verandah, my mother and father were sitting side by side.

It seemed as if they were waiting for me to come home. They took one look at me and said, "Glen, sit down. We want to talk to you."

I took a seat beside them and asked, "What?" They said, "Boy, we were on this earth long before you; we have seen a lot of things happen to people. You are now working in a hotel, and a lot of people in the community are talking about you and some of them will hate you. You need to go to a voodoo man and protect yourself from those people."

I asked them, "Where am I going to find a voodoo man? And if I do, what should I take to him?"

They told me that some people wear their protection in silver rings. A few days after, I went to a jeweler and ordered one silver ring with a hole in the bottom. Then I started asking some of my friends and family members if they knew where I could find a voodoo man. I got an answer from a friend who was living in the town. He decided to take me to see a man in the parish of St. Mary. I put a change of clothes into a bag one evening when I was going to work, intending to spend the night at his house so we could catch the bus early the following morning.

That evening at work, my mind wasn't comfortable; I was thinking about why I was going to a voodoo man. What for? I didn't want to mix up my life in those things. By the end of the dinner shift, I'd changed my mind and decided not to go. The following morning when I woke up, my mother asked me if I was supposed to have gone somewhere that day. I told her that I was all right and that I was not going to get my life mixed up in those things. She then said, "That is all right."

Soon after that, my mother got a chance to go and visit some of our family in England. The trip was for six months. I was happy for her, having this chance to travel after spending her entire life working hard in the field and having to go to that dangerous marketplace to provide food. Nonetheless, I was also feeling sad for my father, who was going to be alone for so long. Somehow he would be okay.

When the day came for mother to depart, they chartered a big van to take the family to the Norman Manley International Airport in Kingston to bid her goodbye. All my siblings were ready and excited, except for me; I was standing at the gate watching them. My mother asked me if I wasn't coming. I responded, "No, Mother, I am not going back to the airport unless I am going to get on a plane." I then bid her goodbye right there and watched her drive away.

During the time mother was away, Father and I became very good friends. We would talk a lot when we were together at home and he was also drinking a lot more. Sometimes he would come home drunk and if I wasn't working and not in the house, wherever I was in the neighborhood, my sisters would had to come and find me. He wouldn't leave the verandah until he saw me. Then from the moment I walked up to him, he would start talking to me about life. Among all the things we talked about those evenings, there is one specific lecture that stood out in my mind, though I still cannot understand why he said it to me. That evening, he was very drunk, sitting on the verandah, humming his favorite songs. As I walked up to him, he looked me in the face and said, "Glen, there is one thing I have to tell you: In life, don't get married." Then he bowed his head. I made sure that he was okay and that he got into bed, then I left again.

There were two bars in my neighborhood where most young men would hang out to drink. Young girls were always tending bar there, and the guys would do whatever it took to impress them, which would sometimes lead up to big competitions. However, in the end, it was always the ones who were spending the most money that got the girls. One night after work, I stopped at one of those bars to have a drink with some friends. At the end of the night, we were told there would be three new girls working the following day; we were all looking forward to seeing them. The next day, as soon as the bar door opened, I was one of the first to arrive and there really were three new girls in town. I went in and ordered a Red Stripe beer and as the bottle got low, I ordered another. In a short time, the bar was filled with young men who were all after the same thing. At about one o'clock that afternoon, some of us started gambling. I did win some money out of the game, but that wasn't all I wanted to win. I was hoping to win one of those young ladies.

At about 2:00 p.m., I left the bar and went home to get ready for work. Later that night, after I finished working, I stopped there again. At some point during the night, one of the girls came over and asked me my name. I told her and she said that one of her friends liked me.

"Yeah," I said and asked which one.

She pointed and told me the girl's name. I immediately went over and said hi. However, the bar was so busy, we couldn't find enough time to talk, so she told me to come back the following day. On my way home, I told one of my friends what was going on.

He replied, "Yeah, that sounds good, man."

The following day I went back, this time to speak with her; we had a chance to talk the first thing she asked was, "Where did you go yesterday when you left and did not return until later that night?"

"To work."

"Where are you working?" she then asked.

"At a hotel," I replied.

By the afternoon, things were looking good for me; however, it was time to go to work again. That evening was the happiest I ever felt on the job—I now have something to look forward to when I left work at nights. There was a small apartment attached to the bar; a few weeks after we met, I started sleeping there with her. With my mother still in England, I would take her home sometimes to sleep at my parents' home. Everything was going well in my life: at work I was on top of things and the praises continued to come from management and the guests for whom I cooked.

As the year went on, my mother returned from England. The night she arrived, I wasn't home; in the morning when she saw me, she asked, "Where have you been?"

I laughed and replied, "What have you brought back from England for me?"

"Nothing, boy. Didn't you know I wasn't there working?"

I then went into the house and started going through the bags she'd bought back. I found a pair of jeans that could fit me and a pretty bath towel. I asked her for them and she said that I could have them. I then looked on her dresser—I saw a little silver chain with a cross pendant. I asked her for it and she gave it to me. She had not brought back much money but enough that we could have a television in our home for the first time in our lives.

We were all excited about this. Personally, I loved the game of cricket very much and sometimes when the West Indies cricket team was on tour, highlights of the games would be televised at night, so I finally got a chance to watch them. However, with only one electrical outlet in the house and the fact that I didn't yet know about extension cords, I couldn't watch TV, as I wanted to, from the comfort of my bed. The television cord could only stretch to as far as the room's doorway; but it was no problem. I just changed my position.

When my mother realized I was barely sleeping at home, she started asking me questions about the girl. I told her she was working in a bar and that she had two kids.

"Can you bring her home that we can meet?"

Not long after, I brought my girlfriend to meet her. By later that day, my mother was telling me that she wasn't impressed by her and was asking why I'd chosen to date a girl who was working in a bar.

I was just having fun; what she was saying didn't matter to me. She now wanted to choose a girl for me. But she didn't see that, in the days when she was taking me out of school to go to the field, had they given me the chance to learn and achieve the way I should, then maybe she would had liked the first girlfriend I introduced to her. Maybe I would have been in a better position to attract someone who looked the way she expected my girlfriend to look.

The words of my great-grandfather, "Save your money, boy. save your money" had become my motto and by the end of 1991, I had saved a good amount of money and was heading into the coming year.

Natasha was the last of my siblings who was still going to school but still there weren't many changes at home. A few pieces of electrical equipment made us happier and more comfortable but Mother was still boarding the truck every Friday night to go to the market. With that continuing to happen, it seemed there wasn't much improvement in the family. I was trying my best to see us survive and most weeks I would take home lots of the fish heads from the hotel so she could spend less on meat. I was also searching the four corners of Jamaica for an opportunity to go to America, where I could work and help my family. Although that was so hard to find, there was now an educational opportunity opening for me at the hotel. They decided to pay for a food and beverage course, which I would attend for about nine months. The course was through the Jamaica Heart Academy. It was the first program of its kind to come to my parish and I was very fortunate to be a part of it. The class was from 10:00 a.m. until two in the afternoon, and we were covering the topics of food, service and management.

From the first day I attended, I realized it was a good opportunity for me. At work in the evenings, my food and beverage manager started to expect new items on the menu and I was able to offer good suggestions.

As the year of 1992 was coming to an end, I felt I had more knowledge, gained through hard work and respect and I had more money in my pockets. I saved a lot that year and decided to start taking my chances in life, to turn my money over.

Those days in Jamaica, promoting parties with big sound systems and reggae music blasting was a part of our culture. It was a highly popular form of entertainment for the poorer class of people who would come out in numbers to rock to the music. If you could promote a party at the right place and the right time, you could make some money. I promoted one at Christmas time in 1992 and invested all my savings in it. Unfortunately, it did not work out successfully for me and the following morning when it was all over, I had lost almost all of my money and was back to square one again.

At the beginning of 1993, I was getting closer to my twentieth birthday with more understanding about life and how hard it could be. Just a month before, I'd so much money saved from the last calendar year and now, at the beginning of that new one, I was almost penniless. My first love which had started so sweetly was now bringing pain to my heart. This was because many evenings on my ride to work, I would pass one of Diane's baby's fathers going up to see her. And if I ever got out of work early, when I arrived at the neighborhood bar, he would still be there. If I asked her about him coming there and staying for so long, she used to say that he came to see his daughter; I would just act as if I believed her.

Around that same time, the hotel changed management and life became harder for most of the employees. I was no longer making the kind of money that I was used to from the tip pool, yet they still expected the same effort out of me. I started giving them what they were paying for because I'd learned that encouragement strengthens labor, and they weren't encouraging me anymore.

During the early months of the year 1993, my financial situation continued to look grim. I wasn't working with much energy anymore, but physically I was still there. I was now falling asleep a lot on the job; some of my friends were telling me that I wasn't looking the way I used to and that I lost a lot of weight. Some were saying that it was because I now have a girlfriend but that was just man talk and anyway, the job was still getting done.

While I was going through the hardest time of my adulthood as life presented a challenge for me, one of my friends brought me a new idea that would interest me a lot. He asked me if I had heard there were people from a certain cruise line coming to Boston, Jamaica, on Saturday to recruit workers.

"No, I hadn't. I am really interested, what should I do?"

"I will go to the person in charge and register your name, man, because I already registered mine," he replied.

I thanked him and told him that I really appreciated it.

The following day when I went back to work, I asked my friend if he'd met with the recruiter.

He said, "Yeah, man, I registered your name. You are supposed to be at his house tomorrow morning."

On Saturday morning, I woke up early, got nicely dressed, then picked up my only proof of achievement: my catering diploma. It was going to be more important than ever, since it was my reference. I rolled it up and put it in a plastic bag, then stuck it into the waistband of my pants, covered it with my shirt and with my belt tightly buckled, I rode away in search of success.

From my gate to Boston was about eleven miles. My appointment at the recruiter's house was at 9:00 a.m. The town of Boston is a very famous place in Jamaica—known as the place where jerk chicken and jerk pork was originated.

When tourism first began on the island and the tourists were traveling on banana boats back to Port Antonio, Boston Harbor used to be one of their stops and they would all disembark for that island, tasting jerk chicken and jerk pork.

When I reached the recruiter's house, about three hundred young men were there, all for the same reason: an opportunity to go abroad and work to better their lives. I parked my bike and took a seat beside them on the wall. A few of my friends from the hotel I worked for were also there. At about nine-thirty, the gentleman walked out of his house with a book in his hand. He told us he was going to be calling names and if we heard ours, we should go into the garage and take a seat. Those who didn't hear their names should leave but could return for the next recruitment in three months, he also mentioned. As he started calling the names, that wall on which I was sitting was getting quite uncomfortable. I just wanted to hear mine to go and sit on a chair in garage. When he finally called out "Glenroy Burke," I ran in there, filled with happiness.

In a few minutes, he came out of his office and told us where the interview would be taking place and to come inside when our names were called. Meanwhile the applicants who were turned back were all leaving the yard, walking slowly and with disappointment. I can still remember seeing some of those guys wandering around Port Antonio, still waiting for that same opportunity to come their way again.

As the day went by, hour after hour, names were called at long intervals. Guys started getting impatient. Some started leaving and saying it was ridiculous to be waiting so long—quitting on themselves in time of need. I was supposed to be at work by three o'clock that afternoon; however, I wasn't leaving that garage. If there had been a phone nearby, I would have called my workplace, but I just didn't have access to one.

Three o'clock had come and gone and I still hadn't heard my name; nonetheless, the recruiter would have had to tell me to leave before I would go.

At about eight-thirty that night, I heard my name called. I answered and walked into his office, then took a seat in front of him at a desk, where two other gentlemen were also seated—one to my left and one to my right. He took out a form and wrote my name, age and address, then looked me in the face and said, "Are you the one who writes menus at the hotel where you work?" I said, "Yes, sir," and immediately I showed him my catering diploma, stating I had completed the catering service course at school.

He took a copy, then, with a red-ink pen, wrote something on the bottom of the form.

He then asked, "Glenroy, can you afford a two-way ticket to Miami?"

I told him "Yes."

"Okay," he said. "If anything happens, I will get in contact with you." I thanked him and walked out of his office.

That night I rode back from Boston, feeling like I now had something to look forward to. On Sunday morning when I woke up, I told my family what I had done the day before and how that day hadn't been like any ordinary Saturdays for me. At three o'clock that afternoon, I reported to work, not knowing what to expect because I hadn't shown up the day before. However, when I explained my situation to the manager, she understood and it was no problem. The hotel was still my bread and butter and I was still attending the class that they paid for, but I wasn't happy working there anymore.

With all what was facing me at twenty years old, I couldn't continue living the way I had since going out on my own. To put some extra money in my pocket, I would do anything, as long as it was within the law.

After the party which I promoted, I had about two thousand five hundred Jamaican dollars left to my name, which was equivalent to about one hundred and twenty-five U.S. dollars. One Monday, I went to Port Antonio and purchased some Red Stripe beers and some cigarettes for my girlfriend to sell in the bar where she was working. It wasn't the right thing to do, since her boss would fire her if he found out. Nevertheless, sometimes you have to take your chances in life. After that purchase, I was completely broke and depending on my weekly paycheck only.

The following morning was Tuesday; I went home. Mother was still leaving breakfast for me. As I entered the yard, she looked at me and said, "Glen, I had a dream about you last night that I didn't like."

"Mother, you are always dreaming," I replied, then walked off.

She immediately said, "Boy, stand still and let me talk to you. You think you are a man yet?"

I said, "Okay, what did you dream?"

She told me that she dreamed that a man came to her and said, "Mama, don't you realize—your son Glen went to Port Antonio with all of his money and spent it all. The police arrested him and gave him seven days." Then she told me to be careful and I walked away.

After my mother told me the dream, my life continued just as before. That was just another dream of hers, I thought. But by the following Monday night, as the sixth day after her dream was breaking into the seventh, I was in bed and I had a dream.

CHAPTER FIVE

VOODOO

T hat Monday night at about twelve o'clock, my girlfriend and I went to bed at the apartment attached to the bar. From the time my mother told me the dream, I had noticed every night there was a butterfly on the ceiling exactly over my head. I didn't think much of it; for me it was just another butterfly. We made love for some time and after, I was lying on my back, relaxing. At some point in time, I started to hear a loud noise at the barroom door—like someone was breaking in. After the sound continued for about half an hour, I was getting very concerned. I woke up Diane and asked if she had heard the sound.

She said, "No."

"What! Are you deaf? Don't you hear it? I am not sleeping here tonight. I am going home—if that is not someone trying to break in, it's a ghost." I then said, "Are you coming?"

"Yes," she answered.

At about 1:45 a.m., we left the bar and started walking to my parents' house. We got there at about 2:00 a.m. and immediately went to bed. I wanted to make love again but she was tired and just wanted to sleep. At about 2:30 a.m., I hugged her, closed my eyes and started dreaming.

I dreamed that I was coming from work and stopped at one of the bars in my community. There were quite a few young men there hanging out. When I walked onto the verandah of the bar, I saw a slaughtered goat placed on a table before me with a cutting board beside it. I took out my chef's knife and started cutting up the meat. Once I had cut up half of it, the table broke into two pieces and fell to the ground. I immediately walked away from it; meanwhile all the young men were sitting or standing there, watching me leaving.

When I walked to the main road, one of my friends appeared beside me and asked if I had finished cutting the goat meat. I told him no and that I wasn't going back there to finish it. I then walked away from him, heading home. About forty meters up the street, I saw another one of my friends standing under a locust tree, his head held downward, looking sad and his arms hanging at his sides. He stopped me and said, "Glenroy, it is my aunt's granddaughter's goat that someone had stolen and it's happened that you are the one who gets the meat. Consequently, it's the little girl's deceased great-grandmother's spirit that someone had cast upon on you."

I immediately walked away from him, heading home. In a few seconds, I saw a van driving down the street toward me. It ran off the main road and into the bushes. The driver came out and wanted to start a fight with me, saying I was the one who made his van run off the road. I told him I wasn't and that I was coming from work where I earned my honest bread.

As I continued walking, I saw my brother Tony appear beside me and started harvesting flowers that grew on the sides of the road. As he was doing that, I saw a butterfly appear behind me; it was flying in a circle. I looked at my brother and said, "It is you whom the butterfly is coming for."

"No, Glen, it's you," he replied and kept harvesting more flowers.

As I slowly walked, the butterfly was getting closer to my body and I started to feel a terrible pain in the dream. At that time, I remembered my mother always telling us when we were kids that if we ever had an encounter with an evil spirit, we should repeat the twenty-third psalm, and I started repeating it in the dream:

The Lord is my shepherd, I shall not want. He makes me to lie down in green pastures, he leads me beside the still waters, he restores my soul; he leads me in the path of righteousness for his namesake. Yea, though I walk through the valley of the shadow of death I will fear no evil, for thou art with me, thy rod and thy staff they comfort me, thou prepare a table before me in the presence of mine enemies, thou anoint my head with oil, my cup runs over, surely goodness and mercy shall follow me all the days of my life. And I will dwell in the house of the Lord forever.

I continued repeating it over and over. As I was getting closer to my gate, the pain and pressure was getting more and more intense. However, I kept fighting to get home. As I was about to turn into the gate, the butterfly landed on the back of my neck—now I was forcing myself to continue walking. When I got to the tangerine tree that was about halfway between the gate and the house, I started screaming for my parents to hear. As I was about to enter the verandah, a force was pushing me away from it. The butterfly was still behind me, but I grabbed onto the verandah rail and pulled myself onto it; the front door of the house burst open and I walked in—straight to my bedside—and woke up in tears, trembling.

I woke my girlfriend and asked her if she hadn't heard me screaming in my sleep.

She said, "No."

Then I told her I was going to tell my mother about my dream. To get from my bedroom to my parents' room, I had to go through the living hall. My parents' room didn't have a door; there was a curtain that screened it from the living hall, which is what many poor families used those days in Jamaica.

Every morning, my mother would pray loudly before she got out of bed; when I reached the living hall, I called to let her knew I was coming. As I entered her room, she was sitting on her bedside.

"Boy, what happened now?" she said.

I replied, "Mama, I dreamed that I was coming from work." And as I was trying to tell her the rest of the dream, I started trembling and my knees started giving way. My mother immediately stood up and I staggered toward her and grabbed on to her waist with both hands. On my knees, kneeling down and tightly holding on to my mother, I lifted up my head and looked at the ceiling, in tears. I said, "Lord, are you going to make me die in my youth?" I was so afraid and shaking that I could not let go of her. This happened about 5:00 a.m. on a Tuesday morning, exactly seven days after my mother told me about her dream.

By then everyone in the house was aware of the situation and were all standing around me. I heard my mother tell my sister Davine to go and get the Bible. When she got it, my mother told her to turn to Psalm 23 and read it; meanwhile, she was praying.

She then looked at my father and said, "John, I told you about the dream I had last week about this boy."

My father replied, "I wonder if it's anyone messing around with my son?" He was walking around the room, looking confused. My mother then said, "John! We have to do something with this boy. We have to find a voodoo man to take him to."

My father asked me if I had any money and I told him only one hundred Jamaican dollars. He shook his head and asked my brother Tony if he had any and he also had one hundred. My father had five hundred and they gave it all to me. They didn't knew where to find a voodoo man, but someone who was at the house that morning did.

Diane and her mom took me to a place in Kingston, a home that had a church attached to it. We entered the churchyard at about 9:00 a.m. Immediately one of the voodoo men came out of the church and took me inside with him. He did some things to me and then took me back outside and said, "Stay here until I call you." Then he went back to attend to the person he'd been with before I got there.

Later that morning, he called me and I walked in to meet with him. He did some more things with me, then started talking.

He said, "You work with white people, don't you?"

I said, "Yes."

Then he said, "Everyone at the hotel where you work guards him or herself except for you and you have a lot of enemies in your community." I asked him if I was going to be all right and he said, "Yes, when I am finished with you."

He kept me there for about forty-five minutes, doing all kinds of things and talking to me. When the session was coming to an end, he asked if I had done some paperwork lately to go and work overseas.

I told him, "Yes," then asked if I was going to get through with it.
He said, "Yes, but when you do, you shouldn't tell anyone."

He then told me to come back in nine days with a silver ring, that
he could give me a guard to wear. He also said to not take a bath or
have sex for three days and that was the end of the session.

I reached home that night feeling a lot better than how I left earlier
the morning and was ready to face the fact that life is not only hard
but could also be dangerous at times.

Nine days later, I went back to see the voodoo man, bringing
the ring I'd bought almost two years before when mother and father
warned me of the dangers in life. He did something to the ring, then
put it on my finger and said, "You're okay now. Always wear it."

Life went on after that—I was feeling a lot stronger and more
comfortable as I trod the earth and carried on with my day-to-
day routine. However, a few weeks later, I lost my job at the hotel.
They thought I wasn't giving them 100 percent of effort anymore.
Nonetheless, I didn't lose the opportunity to continue attending the
food service and management class that they had provided.

I found another job as a chef at a resort beside Port Antonio, a
place called Navy Island. It didn't take me long since I was one of the
best in my parish.

Around that same time, my girlfriend lost her job at the local bar
and was now working at another in Port Antonio. Jealousy surged in
my heart even more now. I was working the night shift at my new job
and would pick her up every night on my bike and take her home.
Sometimes she would work late, especially on the weekends. Those
nights I would sat there and wait for her. At times, I couldn't even
afford a beer and I would see guys came in and talk to her. Some of
them would even touch her—I wasn't comfortable with some of what I
was seeing. When I couldn't take it anymore, I broke up with her and
was now hoping that something positive would happen, that I could
go abroad and work for that cruise ship company.

On my way to work in the evenings, I had to pass her gate. I
would still greet her and sometimes even stop to talk. One Wednesday
evening, she asked me for some money. I gave her twenty Jamaican

dollars; by the time I got home that night, she was in my bed. But early the next morning, she had to go.

The Friday night of that same week I went home from work, my mother told me there was a certain young man who was looking for me and that he had left a message stating I should check with the recruiter from Boston about the cruise ship position. The following afternoon, I went to his home and knocked on his door. He opened it, shook my hand and said, "Congratulations, Mr. Burke, here is your letter of employment from a cruise line." Then he told me I should return to his house a few days later, when a representative of the cruise line company from Miami would be there to talk to us.

That evening, when I walked away from his door, I was the happiest man on earth and couldn't wait to reach home to tell my parents the good news. When I got to my gate, I saw mother and father sitting on the verandah. I walked down into the yard and stepped up in front of them; their tired faces looked the same. I stood there for a while then said, "Mother, Father, I am going to America."

They didn't believe me and mother said, "Boy, move from in front of us. Go find something to do and stop playing jokes." I then took the letter out from the waist of my trousers and handed it to her. When she read it and got to the part that said I should report to Miami on April 9, 1993, she broke down in tears and started trembling, then looked at my father and said, "John, it's true. The boy is really going abroad."

I saw a big smile break out on my father's face while my mother was still crying. I stood there for a while looking at them, knowing the journey had not yet started, but they were the ones whom I was going to represent. The tears she was crying were new to her: tears of joy, knowing that one of her children were going to make it to America. They then asked me how much money it was going to cost. About ten thousand Jamaican dollars, I told them. They didn't have the money, and neither did I; however, my father did turn to his pasture and sell a bull to a butcher. The bull he sold was the very same one that had been yet unborn in the belly of the cow that fell over the precipice five years earlier. At that time, I had wondered why that cow had survived, along with the unborn calf, after falling from such a height. The calf which she was carrying in her stomach that day was now paying for my plane ticket to America. My father got ten thousand six hundred dollars for him. He gave it all to me and said, "Do what you have to do." And I thanked him very much.

When we met with the representative from the cruise line, he told us what to expect when we arrived in Miami and how strict the company was about their employees' medical condition. He told us that we should make sure we were okay from head to toe before we left Jamaica; I then went to the American embassy and was granted my seaman's visa.

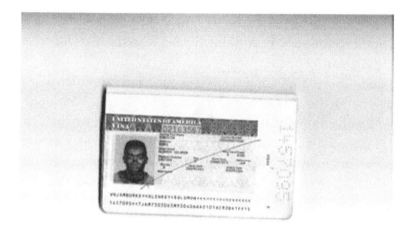

Above, my seaman's visa, with which I traveled on to Miami, in 1993

By traveling around Jamaica, in preparation to go abroad, I spent almost all the money my father had given me. With the little that was left, I went to the bank and buy some U.S. dollars to travel with; thirteen dollars was all it equivalent to and what I would have to take with me to America.

The night before leaving, I was hanging out with friends at the gamble house close to my gate. None of them knew that the little boy who used to came home late at nights from the field—behind the mule, tired and hungry—was spending his final night with them, under the moon that shone so brightly from the skies of Jamaica. The following day I was traveling to a new land, where it would shine even brighter on me.

While standing with them, I wanted to buy a final round of liquor, so I ordered it, plus a grape juice for myself. From where I was standing at the gamble house, I could see mother and father sitting on the verandah and every time I looked down there, I could tell they were looking out making sure I was in their sight that last night before leaving. After a while, my sister Davine came to me and said, "Father thinks you should come home now and to remember you are going away the following day." I did not leave at once and one of my friends noticed I was drinking a grape juice. Out of suspicion, he said, "Shrimpy"—my nickname—"how come you are drinking grape juice and everyone else is drinking liquor? It seems like you are up to something man."

I said, "No, man, I am just chilling out," and in a little while I left them.

As I walked toward my gate, I was thinking that maybe I should talk to someone who had traveled before, to get an idea of what to expect when I arrived at the airport in Miami. I went and talked to a guy who used to work on a cruise ship, He gave me some tips on what to expect, and then I went home.

My family watched me pack my bags; when I had finished, my mother gave me a white coat she had brought back from England and said, "Maybe where you are going will be cold. Take this with you." I put it in my bag, then she gave me a wristwatch, which she had also brought back from England and said, "Wear it. You will to need to know the time." I put it on my wrist and was starting to look better already. My parents then told me to remember where I had came from while on the crew ship and not to go there and get involved with the wrong people or mess around with drugs. She said to work hard and save my money and to remember them, my family, while I was away. My sisters were all happy and laughing and were telling me to bring something back for them. I told them yes and with a joyful mindset, I went to bed.

The following morning I woke up to a sunny Jamaica; the rooster was crowing as usual, the birds singing sweetly in the trees. I wandered around the yard that final morning, thinking of what America was going to be like later that day. My parents also stuck around until I left. The girl that I used to date found out I was going away and wanted to come to the airport, suddenly interested in me again. I told her no. And about eleven o'clock that morning, I left West Retreat District, bound for the United States of America. At the airport, I met up with all my friends who had gotten jobs along with me and we traveled together.

CHAPTER SIX

STARTING MY AMERICAN JOURNEY

When the plane took off and was in the air, I felt that it was taking me into a new world but the old one was still in my memories, which was the fuel to push me to achieve all that I could out of life. As we were flying over Cuba, the pilot let us know but I had already seen it from my window seat. In less than an hour, I started to see buildings in the distance and the pilot told us to fasten our seat belts—prepare for landing. That precious evening when the plane touched the ground, it felt so good that I was finally in America. Next, I needed to clear immigration and customs. I faced several questions when I got to that point and was even brought into a private room for further interrogation. In the end, however, I walked out of the airport into a warm and welcoming country, the place I had dreamed of coming to since I was a little boy—I always heard there was a better life here.

I was first impressed by all the pretty cars, including the taxis. I could choose the one I wanted to travel in for my colleagues and I this was something we had never seen in our country. We then got together and grouped ourselves into different taxis; in all, there were about fourteen of us.

By the time we got to the Budget Inn Motel on Biscayne Boulevard in Miami, Florida, I had already spent three dollars from the thirteen I had to my name. When we checked into the motel, we met other guys there from my hometown in Jamaica. In all, there were about twenty eight of us plus other men from different walks of life, all there for the same reason: to better our lives.

Next morning, most of the crew was in the dining room for breakfast at the same time. We all got to meet each other and shared conversations of our experiences. I learned there were already guys who had failed their medical exams and had been sent back to their country. I asked some of them how long they'd been there waiting on their medical result. Some said two weeks, some said one. At that time, I remembered what the gentleman had told us in Jamaica about the company policy on medical status; however, I was still optimistic about my chances—I did not have anywhere else to turn.

When the day came for our medical examinations at Mount Sinai Hospital in Miami, everyone was intense. I completed my blood work and other tests and was sent to a private room for further examination. A nurse came in and told me to undress; she put her stethoscope on my chest and spent a while listening to my heartbeat with a concerned look on her face. She then went and got another nurse to come and listen. While the other nurse was listening, the first one said to her, "Something is wrong with his heartbeat. Maybe we should send him back to his country and have his doctor check him out."

The other nurse said, "No, it's not a major problem. It's common with a lot of people. Maybe he is just nervous." She was right.

They completed their work, wrote up my medical report and left me in the room to get dressed. When I came out of the room, I was standing in a hallway with lots of file baskets on the wall with our medical report inside. I looked into the basket in front of the room I'd just been in and got a chance to read the exposed top page of mine. There was handwriting by the nurse that read, "All medical test done on this young man. He is fit for employment." I didn't tell any of the guys what I'd seen. I was just waiting for everyone to finish so we could leave and go back to the motel.

By then all the money I traveled with was already gone. I was now at the motel solely depending on the three meals a day provided by the company. Sometimes I wouldn't like the food served at the restaurant but had to eat it. The dining room used to close at 7:00 p.m. and sometimes by ten o'clock I would be hungry again without even a dollar to go to the snack machine.

Five days after I landed in Miami, broke and awaiting word from the company to start working, I took a walk out on the street side one night by myself. I stood in front of the motel thinking and looking at all the pretty cars going by and wondering when the day would come for me to drive one.

As the evening grew darker in beautiful Miami, I was still standing there; however, I would look behind me frequently because the motel gate closed at 10:00 p.m. and seamen had to be inside before that. At one point, I was looking down the street and saw someone coming toward me. As the person got closer, I could tell he dressed like a waiter, in black and white. Both of us started looking at each other in surprise. I immediately thought, "Is this really one of my friends?" Then big smiles appeared on both of our faces. He was someone I used to work with in Jamaica, returning from work.

He stopped and said, "What's going on, man?"

I replied, "My friend, I'm broke man. Give me some money."

We shook hands, talked for a while and when he was leaving, gave me ten dollars.

I went into the motel soon after and straight to the snack machine. I got myself a Sprite and a peanut butter biscuit and then went to bed. While lying there, I was thinking of how lucky I was; however, the real luck still hadn't came as yet. I was anxious to start working because I still could not afford to call my family back home to tell them I was all right.

There was an information board in front of the motel's office, on which the company would post the names of those who were going to join a ship on any given day. We would often check it hoping to see ours. One week had passed and I hadn't seen mine posted, but my hopes were still high.

With very little to do at the motel, my friends and I took a walk down the Biscayne one day. When we came back, I was in my room relaxing. At some point in the afternoon hours, I heard a car outside and recognized from the sound that it was the company van, coming from the office to post names on the notice board. As the van drove away, I went to look at the new names as I usually did. Three names were written there: the name of one of my friends, of a man from India and mine, with a note that we should be ready at 2:00 p.m. the following day to join a ship. I was so happy that I ran straight into the pool, knowing that I'd made it. All of the guys were happy for us and they bid us goodbye the following day.

We drove away from the motel with thoughts that we were going to join the ship at the port in Miami, but we soon realized that we were entering Miami International Airport. I started to wonder if they were sending me back to Jamaica, so I said to the driver, "I thought we were going to join a ship?" "Yes, but in California," he replied and I was happy again.

When we arrived in California and exited the airport, I saw a gentleman holding a sign with the company logo and writing, which said, "Company workers come over here." I walked over to him and he took my passport, then drove us to a Doubletree Hotel in San Pedro. When I checked in and walked into the room, it was as beautiful as I had dreamed of sleeping in—never knowing that my dream would came true so fast.

The following morning after breakfast, the same man came back to the hotel and took us to the cruise ship. On our way there, I was amazed when I saw the ship in the harbor, a big pretty thing. The Indian guy, who was also signing on, turned to my Jamaican friend and me and said, "That's the ship we are going to work on." I was so happy riding the bus, knowing when our ship set sail for the Mexican Riviera that evening, I was going to be on board.

Above, the cruise ship that I started working on, in April of 1993

That Sunday morning when I signed on, I heard guys talking in Jamaican language, which told me that I wasn't going to be lonely. However, there were also guys there from all over the world and I didn't know how I was going to adjust to communicating with all the different nationalities that I would have to deal with.

They brought me to the cabin that was going to be my home for the next ten months. Inside were two bunk beds, one over the other; a locker, which was about three feet wide, to serve two people and a face basin. I put my bag down and turned around and if I had turned with my arms extended, I could probably touch the walls on either side. The bottom bunk was already occupied, so I put my bag on the top one, then went to the mess hall to have lunch. When I got there, the place was very big, with rows of tables and chairs occupied by hundreds of guys, young and old, all kinds of faces, speaking different languages. All of them were there for the same thing, to ensure their family's survival and that day, the little boy from John's Hall District took a seat beside them.

For lunch I had curry chicken, rice and steamed cabbage. As I started eating, I remembered my poor family back home, struggling in a land where opportunity comes once in a lifetime. I could not finish eating. I had to leave some on the plate and before throwing it into the garbage bin, I whispered to myself, "If God could just take it for my family."

After lunch, I went back outside to look around the dock, knowing that I was about to start working for U.S. dollars. I spent a little time out there viewing the place and then I went back on board to get ready for work.

That evening when I walked into the galley for the first time, one of the stewards introduced me to the sous chef and the head chef. They assigned me to the sauce station as an assistant sauce cook; communication was easy because the head sauce cook was a Jamaican.

Prepping that evening for the following day was a lot of work; immediately I realized that the ten months weren't going to be easy. At the end of the first night, I still had very little understanding of what was going on in that galley, so it was a choice between quitting the job or showing how tough I could be.

I returned to my cabin after work and for the first time, I met my cabinmate. He was from Honduras, an elderly man. We talked and got to know each other better; however, he was going to work at 11:00 p.m. Before leaving, he asked me if I drank alcohol.

"Yes" I replied, he took out a bottle of Bacardi White. (What!)

He said, "Drink what you want out of it."

I asked him if he had any writing paper and envelopes and he gave them to me, then he went to work. It was time for me to write my family and let them know I was fine; I hadn't called them as yet and still couldn't afford it. I wrote a letter to my family and drank Bacardi until I was almost drunk. I unpacked some clothes from my bag and went to bed.

At eight the next morning, I went to work. There was a lot to be done and we had to be busy at all times; nonetheless, I still found a way to start writing down everything that happened at my station. We started serving lunch at 12:00 p.m. and ended at about 2:30 p.m. I was told to come back at 4:00 p.m. to work the dinner shift also, which ended at about 10:00 p.m. Those were to be my working hours every day for the next ten months.

That night after work, I wondered if I could endure it. The answer was yes. I decided that it was a lot of hours to work but at least I wasn't going to the field or carrying a load on my back.

On Tuesday morning, I took part in a boat drill, to learn about safety on the ship and international maritime law. The final stage of the drill took place on the top deck; as far as my eyes could see was nothing but blue ocean.

On Wednesday morning at about 9:00 a.m., we were docking at Puerto Vallarta, Mexico. That day when I walked off the ship, the sun was shining on me in a new country. I was with some Jamaican guys who were working on the ship before I joined up. They brought me to a cantina, where we had a few Corona beers. While we were there drinking, I noticed there were a lot of girls hanging out and when I looked around the neighborhood, the lifestyle of the people reminded me of where I am from. It made me think of how poor people feel the same pain all over the world. From the cantina, they brought me to a small motel, where we drank more beer and where more girls were hanging out. There were some pretty ones and it seemed as if we could make a move with any of them.

By later that day, when those Corona beers got to my head, I wanted to learn how to speak Spanish right there and then. I asked one of the Jamaican guys to teach me a few words that could be useful to me right then. I also borrowed some money from him; it was a great time had by all that day, but not something to make a habit of.

That evening, when I went back to work, I was thinking about how wonderful the day was, enjoying myself so far away from home. I hadn't been paid as yet but was already in debt. The following day, we were at another port in Mazatlan. The excitement was the same and put me into even more debt.

At the port in Mazatlan, just after getting off the ship.
Behind me is the trolley that took us to the main road.

Days went by and I was missing the love of my family and started
to experience the jealousy that can lie in the human heart. The galley
had lots of cooks and everywhere you looked were guys in white coats
and black checkered pants—all speaking different languages. Some
of them would do whatever they could to make your life harder.
However, in the end, your experience was all that matters. The good
work you do will defend you and that was all I had to defend me.

Two weeks had passed and I was just been paid. It was two
hundred twenty-six dollars and some cents. I was very happy after
work, going to my cabin with United States money in my pocket. I
took a shower, then sat in my chair, thinking of what I was going to

do with the money. I remembered my poor family back home without running water. I put one hundred and fifty dollars in an envelope and wrote my mother a letter, telling her the money was to get running water into the yard.

The following Sunday, we were at port in San Pedro, California, I saw one of my fellow Jamaicans get fired for breaking a lock off a food rack. It shouldn't had been locked in the first place. He didn't have any choice; he had to use it to do the company work. A guy from the Philippines, who had put the lock on it, didn't face any punishment. That day I realized that it wasn't hard for some people to lose their jobs. The Jamaican was a roast cook and they did not employ anyone to replace him. The next day they moved the head sauce cook to the roast station and I became the head sauce cook, just three weeks after signing on.

The new position brought a lot more responsibility; however, I grew up doing harder work than that and I was going to make it look easy.

A few weeks passed and I received a letter from my parents. They had received the first letter I'd sent but not the second one with the money. They also said that since I left Jamaica, my ex-girlfriend had been sleeping in my bed every night and they also provided the phone number of one of my cousins, who was living in Port Antonio, where they could take calls.

The Sunday after I received the letter, I called Ivey and told her to have my parents come to her house for a phone call. When I talked to mother, I asked her if she'd gotten the money I'd sent them. She hadn't, so I just called it a loss; however, by the following week I learned how to send money safely via Western Union and I sent them another hundred and fifty dollars.

During the conversation, I asked her why they were allowing my ex-girlfriend to sleep at the house. She said, "Because she and you were together."

I then said, "Mother, you knew we broke up weeks before I left. She is coming now because she knows am abroad. Stop her."

"You have to do it yourself," she replied.

Time passed and they hadn't stopped her from sleeping there. I wrote them another letter, stating if they didn't stop her, I wasn't going to send them any more money. They realized I was serious and one of my older sisters eventually stopped her.

By then my sauces on the ship were getting better and better and I was gaining a lot of respect in the galley. Men who had been working with the company for over eight years were telling me that I was the first they ever saw in charge of a station after working on a ship for three weeks. However, with all the progress made, there was no raise in pay and I was struggling to save money from the little I was making. Nonetheless, I still tried to send my mother at least fifty dollars per month. Out of the rest, I had to buy clothes and other necessities, plus I was caught up in the excitement out in Mexico.

While I was having problems saving money, greed took over my heart and I started dealing drugs to make some extra money. Week after week, I would walk close to the prison door but was lucky enough not to step inside. Sometimes when I took it to where it was going, instead of me making money, I would get taken. Lots of times, it would be a delivery for a promise and the week to get paid would never come. But I kept pushing myself to do it.

As life on the ship was getting tougher and tougher, my days in Mexico were getting sweeter and sweeter. However at times I would wonder if, after I take my vacation, the company would take me back. This was based on my job report that the chef would send to the office. I was doing my best on the sauces and the results were still there but I was facing a lot of pressure from those in charge because of the color of my skin and where I am from. Many mornings I started waking up scared to go to work, knowing the hard times I was going to have with the chef. Still I never let them overcome me, knowing the life I lived as a boy.

My Jamaican friend who had signed on with me was facing the same pressure as I was. One Thursday evening after a fine day in Mazatlan, I was in a small bar on a mountainside, drinking and looking out at the ocean, with señoritas all around me. I was having fun, which would turn to sadness when I returned to the ship and went to work.

As I started doing my sauces, one of my friends went to the restroom; on his way back, he saw my name and that of my Jamaican friend posted on the notice board to be transferred to another ship, along with others. I just gritted my teeth and geared up to sign off the next Sunday morning in California.

I signed off the ship after seven months with three hundred and thirty dollars to my name; nonetheless, I was still happy knowing every month I had sent my mother some money. They took us to Los Angeles International Airport at about 1:00 p.m. In all, four of us were transferred all for the same reason: because of who we were, we were not their favorites. Our flight wasn't until 10:30 p.m. and we were traveling to Puerto Rico to join another ship the following day.

When we arrived there, we checked into a hotel in Old San Juan. At lunchtime, we ate at the poolside and then we geared up to join the ship later that evening. We went to the port at about 7:30 p.m. As we attempted to go aboard, the food and beverage manager in charge told us he had only received two persons' names from the office to join the ship. They were to be the galley steward and the assistant food and beverage manager. My friend and I were left standing there, wondering what to do. At that time, a lot of my friends from back home were working on the ship and while they were going off to have fun for the night, I was struggling to get on board.

The food and beverage manager asked my Jamaican friend and me why we had been transferred. We replied that we didn't know. He then called the chef in charge of the galley and talked to him about the situation we were in. The chef told him that his gallery was full and that he didn't want any more cooks just then. The assistant food and beverage manager who was transferred with us was from Spain, the same country where the food and beverage manager in charge was from. He saw the desperation on our faces and knew that the transfer wasn't a justified one, so he called his countryman aside and talked to him in their language. When they finished talking, the food and beverage manager came to us and said, "Guys, I am going to do something special for you." We bowed our heads and then he said, "Right now we don't need any more cooks on this ship. We don't even have any cabins available for you in your quarters, but I am going to put you on the upper deck, in the officer's quarters, for one week. Please don't let me down." And we thanked him.

The following morning we went to work—all the stations in the galley were full. However, I was placed on the vegetable station as a third person. I also learned that morning that one of the guys were going on vacation the following week and it was already planned for me to become the assistant vegetable cook. I worked that station for three weeks, then moved again and was put in charge of the soup station. Still, I didn't get a raise in pay. Nevertheless at that point, securing my job so I could work with the company for a long time was all that mattered.

By then, I was managing my money much better than before. I would often think of the amount that was left back in the streets of Mexico and that what was tied up in drugs when I got transferred. I would had loved to have it back, I had already squandered. Even if I were to become wealthy and died leaving a million dollars, I would knew it should have been that million, plus what I'd wasted and lost.

For the rest of the contract, I dedicated myself to saving but at the same time putting at least one article of new clothing in my suitcase for each member of my family, as well as some very nice ones for myself to look good when I went home on vacation; I was also thinking of getting a gold chain. However, shopping for it in downtown Miami was too expensive. I asked a few friends where the best places were to shop for a good but less expensive gold chain. They suggested the flea markets were the best places to go. One Saturday, a friend and I took a taxi, went there and I bought myself a ten-carat gold chain with a big pendant.

Back on board the ship that evening, I was feeling good; I didn't had a lot of money, but I'd at least gotten some pretty clothes and a gold chain out of my first contract at sea. I was also gaining back the respect that I'd been getting at the beginning of my contract when

I was on the other ship. This happened at the right time—it would ensure my position on the ship after returning from vacation.

In the nine months already completed, I had learned a lot more about life and was becoming a tougher competitor. The thoughts of my family and where I was from never left my mind and that's what kept me strong through all of those difficult times.

When I was about to go on vacation, my Jamaican friend who had signed on with me was asking to stay on longer in order to save money. I guess both of us got caught up in the same world of enjoyment, but some figured things out before others. I did had seven hundred and fifty U.S. dollars to take home with me. I also had my three pieces of luggage full of things for my family and a nice red bicycle for myself to ride around town.

During the hard days on the ship, I was always engaged in conversations with my fellow Jamaicans. I often heard them talking about their visiting visas to America. I asked the difference between that and a seaman's visa, they said, "It gives you the opportunity to visit the United States at any time." I asked them how I could obtain one. They said that the easiest way for a seaman to get a U.S. visitor's visa was to get a letter of reference from the ship company and take it to the embassy; however you had to be working with them for at least two years. Despite that being my first contract, I still asked the company for that letter, just pushing my luck—trying to better the life of my family. They told me that I had to be working with them longer and that I was willing to do.

January 15, 1994, was the day I signed off the ship for vacation, I had all the necessary documents that were required for me to return in six weeks' time. I went to the Miami International Airport that afternoon to board a 7:10 p.m. flight to Jamaica, so as to arrive at home in the early evening. I wanted to surprise my family—I didn't call to say I was coming. However, the flight was delayed and when we landed at Norman Manly International Airport in Jamaica, it was about 10:00 p.m. When we got to baggage claim, I was informed that most of the luggage had been left behind in Miami and was to arrive on the 12:38 a.m. flight. I decided not to leave the airport until that flight arrived.

By the time I got my luggage and cleared customs, it was about two o'clock on Sunday morning, which raised the question of whether I should go home or stay at the airport until daylight for my own safety. Moreover, I was longing to see my family. I couldn't wait; so I joined up with two other guys who were also going to Port Antonio, got in an airport taxi together and took our chances home.

On the way, it was raining and that took us a lot more time than usual. As the journey got closer to Port Antonio and we started to see the town lights, I could tell the clubs were still open. When we got to the center of town, we told the driver to stop for a little. We went to one of the most famous clubs and I bought myself a cup of "mannish water," as I was longing to drink a cup of my favorite goat head soup.

Some of the guys that I'd grown up with were hanging out there, and they all greeted me saying, "Shrimpy, you coming home?"

"Yeah, man." I replied, smiling.

They knew then that I was coming from a different direction, not the one they were used to. I was coming from America.

I arrived at my gate about 4:30 a.m. The place was still dark and the neighborhood asleep. Before I could tell the driver to blow his horn, I saw the curtain at my parents' bedroom window move. They realized I was home and was soon to learn that I was coming from a battlefield, where the only weapon I could use was the mental toughness they'd put into me from the time I was a little boy.

My father walked out onto the verandah and by the time the driver took all the baggage out of the van, my entire family was awake; they came up to the gate to meet me and I didn't even got the chance to carry my own briefcase. They welcomed me that Sunday morning as if I was someone special.

When I walked into the old wood-framed house, my mother was sitting at the table; she stood up and walked toward me smiling, then she spun me around and when both of our faces met again, she was crying. I hugged her—the first time in my life that I could remember hugging my mother. It certainly wasn't because she never loved me but just that I didn't grew up seeing a lot of parents hugging their kids. Such physical affection seemed not to be part of the culture in Jamaica. But could this expression of love that exists in other parts of the world really be unknown to some countries?

I did not slept for the rest of the morning and most of my family stayed up asking me lots of questions about America and other parts of the world I'd been to. The first thing I told them was that there on the cruise ship, it was not easy; it was a battlefield but there were also good times. The experiences and pleasures had been sweeter than what I was used to but the greatest pleasure was in returning home and standing in the middle of them as they all said I looked fine, with U.S. money in my pocket and gifts for all of them.

At some point during the conversation, my father pulled me aside and asked where the money was that I'd brought home. I told him I could only afford to save seven hundred dollars. He said, "Okay, that's better than nothing."

About 6:30 a.m., I went out onto the verandah to look around. The community was the same as when I'd left it ten months before. I then walked to the side of the main road and called one of my friends out of his bed. The moment he heard the voice, he knew it was me. As we greeted each other he said, "Shrimpy, you are looking good, man." I said, "Yeah, man, I am coming from the promised land." We got so loud that a lot of the neighbors heard our voices and were looking from their verandahs. It felt good the way some of them greeted me later that morning.

By midday that Sunday, I put my new bike together and took a shower—this time under a pipe with running water. It was such a great feeling knowing that my family had stopped carrying water from the spring. Later that afternoon I got dressed; it was the best I had ever looked in my own country: my gold chain was shining around my neck when I looked in the dresser mirror. I then took a walk through the neighborhood with two of my friends and my nephew, Dwayne. As we walked slowly down the road, there was a lot of attention—I could see and feel it.

That evening, I had dinner with my family. The way we sat together and ate and the old-time conversations we were having took me back to reality—this was the ground I had come from. I stayed home with them that night and the following day went to Port Antonio with my mother. There, I opened a bank account in both of our names that we could use in case of emergency, I also kept some in my pocket for enjoyment because for the six weeks that I was supposed to be home, I wasn't planning on working; not because I was lazy but because there weren't many jobs available.

After the bank, we went to a furniture store; I bought myself a new mattress and a piece of carpet and then we went home.

The Monday evening after dinner with my family, I was on the verandah relaxing. At some point, I saw the girl I used to date before went to work on the cruise ship walk by the gate, back and forth about four times. A few minutes later, one of my friends came down into the yard and told me she wanted to talk to me. I told him to tell her that I didn't want to. After she left the area, I went to the street and hung out with my friends for a while.

The following day, I decided to hang out in the town but I first went to visit some friends I used to work with at their workplaces to tell them about my experiences abroad, both good and bad.

Later that afternoon, at about five-thirty, I was standing in the town square in front of the courthouse where I met a beautiful young lady by the name of Veron. The following day, I rode about twelve miles to visit her at her workplace in Summerset Falls. We talked, got to knew each other better and during the conversation, I learned she was ten years my senior. However she was so beautiful, I told her I was twenty-five, though I was only twenty.

Days went by and I started spending time together with her and as a result, she became pregnant. With this news came responsibilities I would have to face as a man. It also put me in a position where I was truly dependent on the opportunity to go back and work with the ship company when my vacation was over.

While having fun on vacation, I ran into a friend of mine in town one day. He mentioned that another friend, who had asked for extra time on the ship at the time I was leaving, had been fired and was back on the rocks. The next day, I went to visit him and to ask what had happened. My understanding from what he told me was that the pressure got to be too much for him and he just couldn't dealt with it any longer. Some coworkers were constantly giving him a hard time. His complaints to the chef didn't help, so he got into a fight with one of them and beat him up badly; the result was a plane ticket back home. I felt his pain and knew I was going to be extra careful when I went back to work for the ship company.

My vacation was going according to plan; the time to have my medical exam done was near, but this time it was going to be done in Jamaica instead of beautiful Miami.

After my first contract at sea, the company had changed their medical policy and we started doing our medical examinations in Kingston, Jamaica, before flying to Miami to join a ship. On the eve before I was to have mine, I ate dinner at home with my parents, then I took a shower and got dressed. When I walked out onto the verandah, Mother and Father were sitting there. Mother looked at me smiling and said, "When the doctors see you tomorrow, they should just give you your employment letter and let you go back to work. You are looking good, my son."

I told them goodbye and before walking away, Mother said, "Glen, be careful. The Lord goes with you tomorrow." I then rode away with all the documents needed to take with me the following day.

I stayed at my girlfriend's because she was living just about a mile from Port Antonio, where I was going to board a bus early in the morning. That night in bed, we talked about what the relationship was going to be like when I left and also wondered what kind of baby she was going to bring into this world of struggles and whether I should shop for a boy or a girl after shipping out. I had already known what it felt like to be heartbroken by a woman, but I didn't yet knew how it would felt to left someone I loved behind for so long. That was also something talked about and fell asleep memorizing the few weeks we'd already spent together. How nice the time had been, yet if everything went well the following day, it would be coming to an end for the next ten months.

The next morning I woke up early, brushed my teeth, got dressed, then kissed my girlfriend goodbye and took off for Kingston. When I arrived at the doctor's office, lots of seamen were already there. I checked in and took a seat beside them, waiting for my name to be called. A few minutes later, it was and I went in for the examination. At the end, the doctor told me to come back in a few days for the result and also my job letter. I then left his office and boarded a bus back to Port Antonio, went home and told my parents how everything had gone. I left my passport at their house and my vacation continued in a good spirits.

The following week, I went back to Kingston to get my medical report and hopefully my job letter. I went into the doctor's office, and he started going through the report with me; suddenly he said something very distressing. "Mr. Burke, you had a problem here." I got very panicked and asked, "What's the problem?" He responded, "You had a parasite in your stool." I asked if I would still get my employment letter.

He said, "No, your medical has to be cleared first."

I then asked him if the problem could be treated. He said that yes, it could and wrote me a referral to a private doctor in Port Antonio.

I went to the private doctor the following day, hoping to beat the seven days that was left before my job letter was expired. The doctor talked to me about the problem and prescribed some capsules. I took them for a few days and then retook the stool test three times as required by the company doctor. By the time I went back to Kingston with the result, my employment letter was two days expired. Nonetheless, the doctor took the results and told me he would fax it to the office in Miami and that I should call him in a week's time to check whether the new employment letter had been sent. He then drew a line across the one that was expired and asked if I wanted to keep it. I took it from him and left his office feeling down. I was back on the rocks again, with much more responsibility than before and just hoping that when I called his office the following week, I would get a positive answer.

On the bus back to Port Antonio, lots of things were going through my mind. I wondered if I was going back to America, how I was going to take care of my child when it arrived and what I was going to do right then. My disappointment would certainly be a subject of gossip in the neighborhood; the bus was driving at its normal speed that afternoon but I didn't want to reach home. I did not know how my parents and my girlfriend were going to take it. However, in life I've always believed in never giving up, so I went home and told my parents what had happened. I then went to my girlfriend's home and that was the first time she'd ever seen me in such a sad mood. We talked about the situation; she tried to comfort me by saying that everything was going to be okay and that I must just wait out the week and then call the doctor's office before I started worrying.

By then I only had seven thousand Jamaican dollars left in my bank account. I had to start using it for my daily pocket money, with a responsibility on the way that was going to require more than that.

CHAPTER SEVEN

SURVIVAL BACK HOME

When I met Veron, she was living with her daughter, Petra, next to her parents in a single room rented from one of her neighbors. It was about one hundred square feet in size, with board walls. There was just enough space for her bed, a table, a stove and a dresser. She was working as a guide at an outdoor tourist attraction and was supporting herself and Petra from her salary. She didn't need money from me just then but eventually she would needed help.

One week had passed and I called the doctor's office to ask whether my new employment letter had arrived. It had not. I called the ship company later that day to find out if they had gotten the fax from the doctor, stating my medical exam had been cleared. They told me they'd received it and that I would get my employment letter in one week's time. After the phone calls, I went back to my girlfriend's place and told her what had happened. Her strong words of reassurance were always the same. "They will send it," she told me, "just hold on and listen to what they say."

More than three weeks passed and I was still on the rocks, making phone calls with no positive answers. I was running out of money and needed a job because evidence of the coming baby would soon start showing on my girlfriend's belly. As I watched and waited, my pockets were nearly empty and I could hardly afford to make phone calls to them. My girlfriend had to start giving me pocket money in the mornings so that I could still ride around town and buy a beer if I needed it.

One evening, I waited for Veron at the bus stop and walked home with her. We were having an ordinary conversation until we got into the house, where it started to sound like a family conversation. Veron said things to me that I used to hear my mother say to my father and it just clicked into me right then that I was now a man with responsibilities. She asked about my plans if it turned out I couldn't go back to work on the ship and how we were going to find money to support the baby. I didn't have any answers for her; I was just sitting there, listening.

She then said, "If they don't send your employment letter in two weeks, you have to go and find a job and you could move in and live with me."

"Yes," I replied, "that sounds good to me."

The following day I started asking around for jobs. It didn't take me long to find one because of my experience overseas. Soon I was hired by a hotel to work as a cook and I was back to making hand-to mouth money again. Still, I did not give up my hopes of going back to work with the ship company. The pay at the hotel wasn't much and it certainly wasn't what I thought I would be earning at the time in my life, had everything gone well. But, life is a gamble and you have to play it the way it dealt.

When I started working again in Jamaica, I showed the community a lot of guts and ambition. Lots of people in the neighborhood would gossip about anyone's troubles. The fact that I had started working back in my own country confirmed to them that I wasn't going back abroad. Lots of the young men who fell into that situation lost their drive and ambition by hanging around town and acting as if they had lots of money, satisfying their critics and hurting themselves in the long run. I wasn't willing to do that.

As time went on, I could afford to call the ship company more frequently, but the answer was always the same: "You would receive your employment letter in one week."

Veron's belly was getting bigger, which meant she had to start working less and start buying baby clothes soon. By then some of the clothes I'd brought back from America were worn out and the colors were fading, especially the shirts. The soles of some of the shoes were also worn through; I had to start lining them with plastic bags and cardboard whenever I wore them, to keep my feet from touching the ground. I was back to the struggles of a hard life but I wasn't giving up. With the pressures facing me at times and having no place to turn for help, I started stealing from the hotel I was working for; I couldn't see what else to do. I only took a little at a time because stealing wasn't something I grew up practicing. It wasn't something I wanted to do; however, the toughness of life can sometimes push you into the wrong directions one does what he or she has to do to survive. The little money I was making for pay was all going toward buying things for the baby—my responsibility as a man was to also put food on the table.

During the daytime when Veron was at work, sometimes I would go to my parents' house to hang out with friends in the neighborhood. Lots of them were asking me why I hadn't gone back to work on the cruise ship as yet. I would only tell them that I was waiting for my employment letter. Some of them would believe it and felt my pain, but some of them were just looking for information to spread around the community in a negative way. I was already hearing bad comments from a lot of people's mouths, including some of the guys I associated with, suggestions that I wasn't going back to work on the ship, that I must have done something wrong and how it was time for me to change the clothes I was wearing. Some people used to laugh at me as I passed their gate, saying things that made me uncomfortable; nevertheless, I never answered back. I just continued to call the ship company, hoping that the opportunity to work for them would came back my way. I never let the negative people and their comments get me down—that's what they were trying to do. I would always tell Veron what they were saying and she would always tell me that I shouldn't pay any attention to them—my opportunity would come back again.

As time went by, the hope for that opportunity was falling lower, and the need for money to care for her and myself was getting more severe. The phone calls to the company continued with the same negative answer: "You would get your employment letter in one week," Then another week would pass and I would get the same answer again. Still I didn't give up hope.

Sometimes at night when I went to sleep, I would dream of working in the United States. When I woke up, I realized it was just a dream with great meaning, to become the reality of tomorrow. Veron's belly was growing bigger and the responsibility forced me to find another job where I could make a better salary. There was a position open at the last restaurant where I had worked before going abroad. I applied and accepted the position and that made things a little bit better.

By then, months had passed and I didn't knew what to believe anymore—whether the ship company were going to take me back or not. While waiting and hoping, I decided to start raising some livestock.

Growing up in Jamaica as a child, I always heard elderly people say, "Never put all your eggs into one basket." At twenty-one years old, I had already known what that meant. If I were still working on the cruise ship, I could support myself and look forward to a brighter future. That wasn't happening, yet I still have to plant seeds that will blossom into brighter days—I didn't want to depend solely on the money I was making from my job.

I started raising some chickens and pigs on the property where my parents lived, hoping to start supplying local shops and butchers in and around the area.

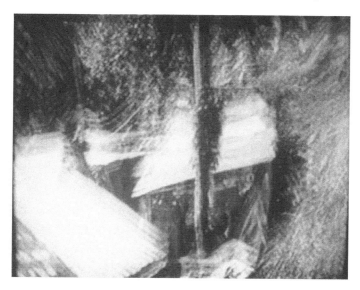

Above: my chicken shed. Built by my hands in 1995.

The chicken shed I built from mesh wires and bamboo and for the Pigpen, I concreted the bottom and railed the sides with bamboo. At that time, I had thirteen thousand Jamaican dollars to my name, which was equivalent to about three hundred eighty U.S. dollars in those days. Out of it I purchased one hundred young chickens, two grown female pigs, and fifteen bags of chicken feed, which should last the chickens for the six weeks' growth to perfection. My mind-set for the pigs was that in a few months, they would be ready for breeding.

I was working the evening shift at the resort and I would go to my parents' house during the daytime to take care of my livestock; when I couldn't make it there, my nephew Duwane, looked after them for me.

Anyone who'd ever been involved in raising chickens knew the risk of losing some during growth. Out of the hundred I'd bought, seventeen of them died. That took away a huge part of my profit. However, I never had negative thoughts about it; that was just a part of life. The eighty three which thrived and grew to perfection made me back the money I'd spent and a small profit in my pocket. As I finished selling them off, I put another set in and, as time went on, extended the chicken shed to start having chickens ready for slaughtering every three weeks. It got to a point where a deep freezer was necessary for storage. I could not afford it right away but was still able to manage business well enough.

By then Veron was in the late stages of her pregnancy and was requiring a lot of comfort and attention. I was there for her. I would still call the ship company once in a while, still hoping to go back and work for them; I was also thinking of building another chicken shed to try and establish myself in the business while getting closer to becoming a father.

In October of 1994, about four o'clock one morning, I woke up to the sounds of someone in pain; Veron had gone into labor. Without immediate access to transportation, I walked with her to the hospital, which was only about a quarter mile away. I spent a little time there with her, then had to leave, not because I didn't want to stay, but typical of hospitals in some third-world countries, there wasn't enough space to make it convenient for fathers to stuck around and see their loved ones gave birth.

I visited her at about 8:00 a.m. that same morning and she was still in labor. However, by later that day when I went back, this time she wasn't alone; a beautiful baby girl was lying there beside her. We later named her Tamoya Toni Burke, born on October 27, 1994.

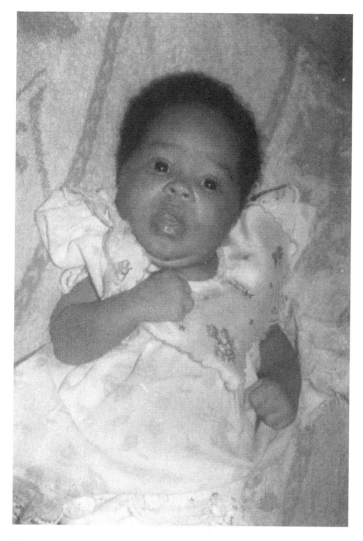

Above: Tamoya Toni Burke, my first daughter, at six weeks old

With Tamoya arriving on the scene, we now needed a bigger place to live; the one rented room was no longer big enough. During Veron's pregnancy, she had leased a house lot from the same lady she was renting from. We bought some cheap boards and started building a small studio house. Our plan was to have it finished before she gave birth but it wasn't. After she was released from the hospital, she had to live in her mother's house for a few days. In the meantime, I put all the labor that I could into our little house and finished it.

When we finally moved in, half of the concrete floor was still left to be poured; we covered that spot with cardboard and put the bed over it. We were comfortable living the life that faced us while looking forward to better days.

Babies require lots of attention and mothers need time to heal. I had to wash Tamoya's dirty nappies by hand for a few days, as well as Veron's clothes. I made sure everything was close to her hands whenever I was out of the house. That included water, which I had to carry from the main pipe, where most of the neighboring homes were drawing theirs.

My daughter brought forth happiness to my heart and also the realization that I now had someone to take care of and to prepare a future for. At work, we were doing lots of business, serving different tour companies coming to Port Antonio for rafting on the Rio Grande. I was making good money, enough to feed the hungry mouths that were living in that little shack we called home. Nonetheless, the pride of a man is not to settle for less.

January 15, 1995, had come and gone—it had been over a year since I had come back home. I continued calling the ship company whenever I could afford it. However, the answers remained the same. "You would get your job letter in one week's time," but that seven days would never come until one evening, God sent forth a disciple in flesh and blood and my experience with him over the next few days proved to me that everything in life happens for a reason and that every man's road is paved in different directions, for longer journeys and with different struggles.

One weekend at the resort where I was working, we had a function for three hundred people, including the prime minister of Jamaica and a number of business tycoons from all over the Caribbean. There was a lot of work to be done in the kitchen, so the boss man hired an additional cook to come in and help us make the jerk chicken and the jerk pork.

The Friday evening leading up to the prime minister's function, I went to work. I was the head chef on duty, along with my assistants, prepping for the following day. About 4:30 p.m., a tall black man walked into the kitchen. He was about six feet four inches tall, slimly built, seemed to be in his early fifties and walked with a limp. It was the first time I'd ever seen him but in spirit he'd already known me.

CHAPTER EIGHT

DELIVERANCE FROM EVIL AND
THE SAVIOUR WHO FOUND ME

In the kitchen, we had just a few areas for prepping. I was working on a broad table with a built-in wooden cutting board on top, using only one side. The man walked up to the next of the table and said, "Hi, Chef. I am the one the boss got to do the jerk chicken and the jerk pork. Can I work on this side of the table?"

"Yes," I replied.

He then asked me for the pork and the chicken. I showed him where they were and he started with the pig. He asked me if I had ever deboned a pig before.

"No."

He said, "Okay, I am going to teach you how to."

As he started, he looked at me and said, "Chef, you look like someone I had worked with before. You look like someone I knew and when I first arrived here this evening and saw you, my spirit took to you. You remind me of my brother."

I smiled and said, "Yeah, what's your name?"

He told me to call by him Jerky and I said, "Okay."

A few minutes after that he said, "Chef, the boss man told me to ask you for anything I want to eat."

"Okay," I replied and told him that we had some stewed pig's trotters and boiled dumplings left over from lunch.

"I will take some of the pig's trotters but not the dumplings because when I ate them, my stomach burns. Instead of the dumplings, could I get boiled potatoes?"

"Yes," I replied, then asked my assistant to prepare it for him and also to make enough to serve later as the starch on our entree dinner plates.

At one point, I was cutting some carrots; suddenly the man stomped one of his feet on the ground three times, then looked at me and said, "Boy, do you know that you should be abroad working now? Your job is out there on the cruise ship waiting on you but the girl and her mother mess you up." I immediately looked up to his face, frightened by what he had just said and I started wondering about what I'd just heard. His teeth were as white as chalk; his face got serious and his eyes were blood red, bulging at me. I looked at my assistant to see if he'd heard what the man had just said to me, but he looked as if he hadn't.

I continued working, feeling a bit different, not knowing how to react to what I had just heard. It was true that the company gave me six weeks of vacation, but over a year had passed and I was still there making phone calls to them and holding on to promises that would never came. For the rest of the evening he was there seasoning the meat, we had normal conversations. However, I was wondering if I should mention back to him what he'd said to me earlier.

He finished what he was doing and was heading out of the kitchen. I ran behind him and said, "Sir, what were you telling me earlier?" He bent his back over, looked into my face seriously, then replied, "I don't want to hear anything from you. I told you the girl and her mother mess up your life. They fixed it so you cannot leave and go back to work on the cruise ship. The doctor told you had a medical problem, but nothing is wrong with you. Look at you. You are healthy. That's the way they set it up to happen. Work on it, work on it."

I asked, "What should I do?" and he asked me what I was doing the following day after the function. "Nothing," I replied, he then told me to come and see him at about six-thirty on Saturday evening at his jerk stand, where I later learned he was residing.

That Friday night when I got home from work, as I walked into the house, I told Veron about the man and what he'd been telling me about my life. I repeated everything he'd said and she was stunned. Then I told her I was to go and see him the next day. She smiled and said, "Go. It must be the Lord who sent him for you."

I went to bed that night thinking about my future and what this man had said to me. The following morning, I reported to work at 7:00 a.m., the boss man was depending on my leadership in the kitchen to make the prime minister and his friends happy. Later that morning, the jerk man walked in, said hi to everyone and started making the jerk meat. Throughout the entire day he would always ask me for whatever was needed: nobody else. When the function was almost over, I asked him where in town his jerk stand was, so I would know where to find him. "In a local neighborhood," he replied, then gave me the directions.

At about 6:00 p.m. that Saturday evening, I rode to his jerk stand and parked my bike. He looked at me, then laughed and said, "Chef, sit down."

I took a seat on a large stone and he sat on one beside me. For a while, neither of us said a word to each other. A few minutes into the moment of silence, he said, "Chef, I know you came to hear something, man, just hold on a little." I nodded my head yes while looking in his face. He then opened his jerk pan and gave me a piece of jerk chicken neck to eat. Then he lit up a spliff full of ganja weed and started smoking. He smoked half of it, then put the rest aside and started looking at me. His eyes were bulging and shiny, lined with red. His facial expression was severely serious and he started talking to me.

He said, "Chef, do you remember when you started working overseas—your family wrote to you in a letter, stating that since you'd left Jamaica, your ex-girlfriend had been sleeping in your bed every night? You asked them to stop her from coming there, then they wrote back saying they couldn't and that you would have to do it yourself?

Well, when they finally told her and didn't immediately stop her, that gave her enough time to do something to your bedroom so that when you came back from the cruise ship and spent your first night there, you wouldn't be able to leave and go back abroad." Tears started pouring down my face as I listened to my past life unfold in front of me by someone whom I nor anyone of my family members had ever been acquainted with.

He stopped talking for a while, then he said. "Chef, you knew about the cow somebody had stolen from your father a few months ago? One of his friends did it." He even stated the guy's name. In fact, someone had recently stolen one of my father's cows. "Could you get it back for him?" I asked, but he could not. Amazing as all this was to me, he had yet to finish talking.

He continued by saying, "Chef, on this earth there are three ways in which a person can hold another down," and he told them to me. He then asked if I had any pants at home that I hadn't yet worn. "No, but I have ones which I had only worn about four times," I told him.

"Go home and bring those trousers back to me. Later tonight I want to take it to a cemetery to see what they had done to you."

I rode home immediately and told Veron everything he had said to me and that he wanted one of my newest pair of pants. She told me to take the pants to him and I did just that. The pair that I took was the same I'd worn when I went for my medical exam over a year ago. He took them and we sat and talked for a while, this time having normal conversation until I decided it was time for me to go. When I was leaving, he told me to come back the following day at the same time, and I couldn't wait.

On Sunday evening, I went back to see him. As I parked my bike and walked up to his jerk stand, he looked at me and smiled, then said, "Chef, they hold you two ways, boy, but they left me with one. I am going to free you and send you back to your job overseas. You fell into the right hands. You fell into the right hands, boy." Before I left, he asked, "When can I come to your parents' house, where you were living?"

"Anytime," I replied.

"Okay, we'll go there this Tuesday morning because there is no sense in making up the bed if the room is dirty," he said. He then told me a list of items I should bring with me when I was coming back that Tuesday.

The next morning, Monday, I rode to my parents' house before they left for the field to tell them that the following day I would be coming there with a stranger. They were curious to know who this stranger was, so I told them everything that had happened in the past few days, and they too had no problem with him coming. After I attended to my chickens and pigs, I went back home to spend part of the day with Veron and our newborn baby before going to work in the evening.

Tuesday morning, I left home at about seven-thirty, rode straight to the seaside and did as I was instructed. From the seaside, I rode to his house and got there around the time he'd asked me to, with all the items he'd told me to bring. I knocked on his door and his girlfriend answered. "Wait outside until he finishes his breakfast," she told me. I took a seat in the yard on a stool and while I waited, many thoughts were going through my mind, wondering what the people in my community were going to say about me if they found out about him. While thinking, his girlfriend reappeared at the front door and said, "The man said you should not worry, everything will be okay." A few minutes later, we rode out of his yard; I was on my red bike and he was riding a black one, carrying a black shoulder bag.

When we reached my parent's gate, I told him this was the place. He grunted and smiled, then parked his bike under the tangerine tree and We walked down into the yard. My sister Davine was washing dirty laundry and singing. Natasha, another of my sisters, was sitting on the verandah. As we approached the verandah, Jerky pointed at her and said to me, "Chef, don't you know they messed up that little one's hands?" I was stunned to hear him say that because since Natasha was about three years old, almost every year, her hands broke out into sores, but that day they were clean, with no sores on them.

We went into the house and straight to my old bedroom; Tony spun around three times and said, "Chef, this is it."

"Yes." I replied.

He laughed and told me to remove the piece of carpet from the floor and to get a small bath basin and two chairs. When I did that, he asked, "Can I light a fire in the middle of the verandah step?" I hesitated before answering, thinking that people passing by the gate would see the unusual fire; however, I told him to do it. He immediately reached into his shoulder bag and took out a plastic container of gray powder and a candle, then we walked back to the verandah. He used some of the powder to make a pile on the middle of the step, then stuck the candle into the pile of powder. He whispered some words to himself, then lit it.

We returned to my bedroom and he turned the two chairs so that they faced each other.

"Sit down," he said. Then he took a seat on the other facing me. He then reached into his bag and took out a Bible, which he handed to me, and said, "Open it anywhere."

I opened it to the book of Solomon and he told me to read a chapter. I read and read until he stopped me, then he placed a candle on a saucer and lit it. As the flame burned higher, he held the candle up in front of me in his left hand, then placed his right hand on my shoulder and started praying for me.

At the end of the prayer, he quickly stood up, stomped his feet on the floor, then he spun around three times and started pounding my body with his hand. His face was looking different from the one I knew and he started speaking a different language, one that I didn't understand, as if he were communicating with the other side. When he stopped speaking that strange language, he started praying again. In the midst of the prayer, he reached into his bag for bottles of different liquids and started rubbing them on my head. All of this lasted for about fifteen minutes.

He then asked me to take my clothes off. While I was doing that, he was pouring the other items we brought into the bath pan and told me to stand in it. Next, he poured some of the different liquids that he was rubbing on me into the water. I could tell some of them were different oils by the way the water looked. He opened the Bible again and started reading silently; then he prayed and started talking again in the language that I didn't understood. Suddenly he stopped talking and took out a piece of cloth from his bag and started to bathe me with the mixture in the bath pan. When most of the water had finished splashing off my body, he told me to step out of the bath pan, then he lifted it up and poured what was left slowly over the middle of my head. He then took a can from his bag and sprayed a sweet-smelling perfume all over my body, then told me to put my clothes on and not to take a shower for three days and also not to make love for that same period.

I finished putting on my clothes and he told me to leave the room and not to come back until he called me. I walked out into the bedroom next to mine and stood at the back door, listening to him stomping his feet on the floor and talking in the language that I didn't understood, louder than ever.

At one point, I heard him call three names, but I can only recall the last one. I remember him repeating the name three times: "Neneman, Neneman, Neneman," and at that time, I saw a shadow walk by me at the door. He shouted out loudly, "Chef, come in quickly."

When I entered the room this time, the two chair backs were now touching one another. He told me to sat on one of the chair backward and he did the same on the other chair, so now we faced each other. This time he prayed for about two minutes. Two candles were now burning in the room and third still at the doorstep.

He looked at me and said, "Chef, you want to go back abroad, huh?"

"Yes," I replied.

He said, "Don't you worry, boy, I am going to send you back. Do you have a document from the ship company with your name on it?"

I answered, "Yes."

"Where is it?" he asked.

"With my important documents," I replied.

"Get it to me right now," I opened my briefcase and took out my old contract, which I had signed when I started working with them. He looked it over and lit the fourth candle and placed it on a saucer with some kind of powder sprinkled around it. He then placed the saucer on top of the two chair backs according to how they were positioned and told me to hold up the letter and read a paragraph through the burning candlelight. I held it up behind the fire and started reading through the flames. When I reached the part that included my name and the date I started working for the ship company, he quickly reached into his bag, took out a little bottle and sprayed some of what was in it on the candlelight; in that split second, I saw the flame of the candle shaped into an airplane taking off with wings spread, just like I was at any airport.

He laughed and said, "Chef, did you see that? You're gone again, you're gone again, boy." He then put out the candles and continued, saying, "Chef, you are going to travel the world and you are going to be rich. Now go as wolves do among sheep."

I laughed when he said that and asked, "When should I call the ship company again?"

"Thursday morning at nine-thirty" he replied and then started packing his shoulder bag. When he'd finished packing, I asked, "How much money do I owe you?" He replied, "Chef, you don't owe me anything, man, just remember me."

I said, "No, seriously? I have to give you something, man."

Then he said, "Okay, give me seven hundred dollars, when you have it," and he left the house.

I walked out of the room feeling like a new man because of what I had just experienced—these rituals performed by another man, who was flesh and blood like me. It was unbelievable and the experience left me with a positive feeling that my future was now freed from the past.

After that, I spent some time in the yard taking care of my chickens and pigs and later that day, I rode home to my girlfriend's house.

From the moment I got off the bicycle at the gate and started to push it up the hill, I could see Veron looking through her window; she couldn't wait to hear what had happened. As I entered the house, I started telling her about the miraculous experience that I'd just had, and she was as happy as I was—I could see it on her face. That Tuesday was also my day off; I stayed home and cooked dinner for us. She used to love my cooking.

On Thursday morning at nine-thirty, I went to my cousin's house to call the ship company as the man told me to do. When I dialed the telephone number and the secretary answered the phone, I told her who I was and asked if I could speak to the executive chef. I had never spoken with him before; however, that morning I had remembered that, a long time ago, my friend Desmond told me his name and said that he was in charge of the kitchen department. The secretary told me to hold, then said his line was busy and asked whether I wanted to wait for him or call back. I told her I would wait and in about three minutes the executive chef came on the line. I told him my name and he asked for my employment number. When I read it to him, he asked, "Where are you calling from?"

"Jamaica," I replied.

"What!" he said. "Glenroy, weren't you supposed to be on a certain ship now? I am looking at your records here and saw when you signed off one ship and you were supposed to return in six weeks' time. What happened?"

I told him what had taken place with my medical clearance and the employment letter that was promised week after week but never arrived.

"Okay, Glenroy," he said, "you will receive your new job letter in two weeks."

I thanked him, hung up the phone, then went home and told Veron about the positive conversation that I'd just had with the company. She laughed and said, "It seems that everything the man told you were true." The following day, I told my parents all that had taken place and they too were amazed and happy. With the vision of an airplane that had appeared in the candle's flame, they too were optimistic that it would take their son back to America USA.

Days went by and I started to feel more confident about going back to America. At nights during that time, we would lie in bed having conversations similar to the ones had in the weeks after we'd first met; me on the left side, Veron on the right and beautiful Tamoya in the middle. Veron's older daughter Petra slept on two joining chairs locked to the side of the bed so that she wouldn't fall to the floor. Anxious to see the changes that were needed in my life, the days were moving slowly. Over a week had passed, but I'd been told it would take two, so I would just wait until then.

After eleven days on a Monday morning, I went to my parents' house to take care of my chickens and pigs. At about ten-thirty, I went up to the gambling house to hang out with friends. I was wearing a red shirt with white stripes and buttons in front, gray shorts that I'd bought in California (the zipper was broken, but the shirt was long enough to cover it) and a pair of brown shoes that I once gave my father but had to take back. At about eleven-thirty a Federal Express van drove up. It stopped in front of the shop and the driver asked, "Is there anyone here by the name of Glenroy Burke?"

One of the guys said, "No." He said this because at that time, the country was growing in the favor of crime that a person could just stop and asked for you and in minutes you could become a story in the newspaper. A brother-in-law of mine was also there. He looked into the van and knew the driver from past experience and whispered that to me and I stood up and told him I was Glenroy Burke. I walked toward the van and he asked if I was expecting a letter from abroad.

"Yes," I answered.

"From whom?" I told him the name of the ship company. He then handed me a cardboard envelope with a piece of paper attached, which I was to sign and gave back to him.

The van drove away and I took a good look at the company address on the envelope. I didn't even bother to look behind me into the gambling house or to tell the guys I was leaving. I just turned right and walked toward my parents' gate with the envelope resting on my chest and both hands under it, still looking at the address to be sure that it was really the letter I was waiting for, the one that I hoped would take me out of those old clothes and put me back into new ones.

Before turning into the yard, I heard one of my friends shout, "Yes, Shrimpy! You had gone again?" but I just looked at him, laughed and continued walking. As I stepped onto the verandah and opened the envelope which contained two letters, one of them read that I should retake my medical exams in two weeks and the other had the information of the Airliner Hotel in Miami where I should stay when I arrived. I was so happy when finished reading—I ran from the verandah, jumped on my bike and rode away to my girlfriend's house. I sat for a while when I got there, waiting on the right moment to break the news to her. It wasn't long before I opened the envelope and showed it to her. That was a moment of rejoicing and happiness in our little house. She read the letters aloud as I listened carefully and from that moment on we started focusing on the day of my medical exams.

The next morning I told my parents and discussed the necessary steps had to be taken from there on. They too were very happy and I could hear mother whispering to herself, "Lord, I hope what happened the last time doesn't happen again." They told me not to tell anyone my business, which I had already learned by then, but it was still a good advice from them.

As the days leading up to my medical were passing one by one, I was more confident than ever, feeling like nothing could stop me now. When the day finally came, I took the physical exam and there were no problems this time. A few days later, I opened my awaiting arms to receive my new letter of employment from the doctor, which read that I should arrive in Miami by June 3, 1995. I had dreamed of Miami many times over the past year and four months. Now the opportunity that I'd fought for was back in my hands and I only needed to get my visa at the American embassy.

The Wednesday after receiving my job letter, I went to the embassy to apply for a seaman's visa. The letter was due to expire in ten days, which would be Saturday of the following week, more than enough time to get the visa and left Jamaica.

That morning I joined the line at the American embassy with every piece of paperwork that was required, hoping to walk out of there later a happy man. However, it did not go that way. The system at the embassy had recently changed and I never knew until then.

Previously, if you went to the American embassy with an employment letter to apply for a seaman's visa, you would get it the same day. However, what I was told that Wednesday morning wasn't at all encouraging and presented yet another challenge.

When I went upstairs to make the appointment, the man gave me an interview date to come back six weeks later. I looked at him and said, "Sir, I have a ship's letter here and I am supposed to be in Miami by Saturday of next week."

He looked back at me and said, "Sir, there is nothing I can do for you. They recently changed the system. Your best bet would be to come in at 1:00 p.m. and talk to the walk-in officer."

"Thank you," I said, then exited the embassy at about nine-fifteen that morning.

I waited in the parking lot until one o'clock. It had been a weary morning session and I was hoping that the afternoon would change the mood; if only I would get the visa after explaining the situation to this officer.

The hour finally came and I walked up to the embassy gate, showed the police officer my pass and he let me in. I took a seat downstairs in a big auditorium where lots of people were also waiting. At one point, I decided to check my papers to make sure I had everything that was required. I looked and couldn't find my two visa pictures. I was sure I left home with them earlier in the morning; even when I was waiting outside, I had the pictures with me. I started to feel panicked, looking around the floor, but they weren't there either. I immediately ran back outside to look where I had been sitting and they weren't there on the ground. I quickly went over to one of the photographers who took visa pictures in front of the embassy and told him that I needed two pictures taken immediately. He asked what I was applying for, I told him my situation and what had taken place in the morning hours. He told me that from what he had been seeing and hearing in the past few days, my chances of getting the visa was slim but that I should still try my luck, and if I didn't get it, I should return and see him.

I went back inside and headed straight upstairs where my future was going to be decided. I took a seat on a single chair and moved closer to the windows as the counselors called us one by one. When it was my turn, I went up to the window, the immigration officer asked what I was there for. I told her I was supposed to join a cruise ship in Miami within the next few days, then gave her my employment letter. She didn't even look it over before gave it back to me and said, "Mr. Burke, today we are only dealing with emergency situations. This is not an emergency. You will have to call the ship company and have them send you another letter." I didn't even say a word in response to her, just walked away from her window and back into the hardship of life on my homeland. The fight, however, wasn't over as yet because I was still holding the letter of employment in my hand.

As I walked slowly toward the gate and exited the embassy, I approached the photographer who had told me to come back and see him if things didn't work out. I said, "Man! I didn't get the visa."

"You have five hundred dollars?" he asked. I told him yes; then he reached into his pocket for a roll of appointment stamps and stuck one onto my passport with a date stating I should return back to the embassy in two days' time, which would be Friday.

I left the embassy that afternoon walking slowly down Oxford Road to Halfway Tree Road, where I would board a bus back to Port Antonio. The moment I got home and told Veron what had happened, she was more disappointed than I was; but once there's life, there's hope, she told me. That same evening, I rode to the countryside to tell my family about everything and to look after my chickens and pigs. By the way I walked down into the yard, they knew it wasn't a happy Glenroy coming. I explained what had taken place and they too were disappointed.

That same evening, I sat down with my brother-in-law, Wayne, and talked with him about my next attempt back to the embassy, that coming Friday with the same employment letter that they already used to deny me. His thought about it was that the people at the visa office would remember me. His words weren't much encouraging to my situation, but they were true. Nonetheless, I made it clear to him and also to my parents that I was going to take my chances.

I went back to my girlfriend's house and for a good portion of the night, we lay side by side talking about the coming Friday, fearful they would remember my face and what their reaction would be. We also talked about the type of clothes I should wear to have a much different appearance than on the last visit. From that night on, the stressful thoughts of whom I was going to face at the counselor's window was all that was in my head.

Come that Friday morning, I was on the first bus that left Port Antonio heading to Kingston. When I got to the American embassy, I joined the line and it was just a matter of time before I would be called inside. The "red seam" police officer (those with red seams, rather than blue, down the sides of their trousers) to whom I showed the appointment on my passport didn't recognize me, though I remembered his face. I went inside to the auditorium where I took a seat beside many others who were also waiting on the counselors to let the first group upstairs.

When that time came around and I was climbing the stairs, I was outwardly showing confidence but inside I was really trembling. I got even more nervous when I entered the room and sat on yet another one of those chairs and it was just a matter time before the counselors started calling, "Next."

The chairs were in a row up leading to the windows; when the applicant in the first chair was called, the rest of us would move up one seat closer. As I got closer to them, thoughts of the previous Wednesday filled my mind and by the time I got to the final chair, I looked at window number 1, the same lady who had denied me the visa two days prior was there with no one standing in front of her. If she said, "Next," I would have to face her again and if she remembered my face, this time she could do more than just deny me. Nevertheless, when Moses was sent to request the release of the Israelite children, if he had fear he could never communicate with God, he knew his fate against who he was chosen to face, since he had known their strength against man. This was a new chosen journey for his life! So it was for me and so negative thoughts were overcome by the strength and determination that had sustained me since I was a little boy who always knew the future would be brighter. Luckily I was called to window number 2 and received a bright good morning from the counselor. I replied back in the same manner, then bravely handed her my employment letter. After reading it, she asked, "Glenroy, do you like working with that cruise line?"

"Yes, ma'am." I replied.

"Were you in Aruba the previous year, when some guys were busted for bringing drugs on board their ships?"

"No, ma'am."

She then said, "Glenroy, come back and pick up your visa next Monday." I thanked her and was walking away when she stopped me and said, "Glenroy, I forgot that Monday is Memorial Day in America. It's a federal holiday, so the embassy will be closed. Come on Tuesday."

I left her window feeling very happy within myself and grateful to have good news to ease the minds of those who cared and worried about me. I enjoyed the weekend with my family and the following Tuesday morning I made a reservation for a plane ticket but couldn't purchase it until I know for sure that I would get the visa. At about eleven-thirty that same morning, I boarded a bus to Kingston, with the intention of picking up my visa. When I arrived at the pickup window and spoke with the receptionist, I was told the visa wasn't ready and that I should come back the following day. I went home disappointed and was wondering if I would be denied for trying to reapply with the same letter that had been previously rejected. I went to bed that night thinking about it but was still able to dream.

I dreamed of a huge soursop (*Annona muricata, a tropical fruit*) farm, where all the trees were green with lots of soursop in them. As I woke up, I told Veron about the dream and also told her that Mother used to tell us as kids that whenever we dreamed of green plants, it meant disappointment. Later that day, I went back to Kingston, filled with the ominous feeling had from the dream and when I reached the embassy. I went to the pickup window; they told me the visa still wasn't ready and that I should come back on Thursday.

On the way back to Port Antonio in the loaded bus, I thought over and over of the whole situation, until I finally decided to let events take their course. It wasn't in my hands anymore—having come through the experiences of the previous few weeks, I felt that nothing could stop me now and I went to bed with that confident thought on my mind.

While lying asleep that Wednesday night, I had another dream. I was in the mountains, under a big tree with lots of honeycombs on it. Honey was dripping on me while the bees flew around. When I woke up the morning, I was feeling very confident about my chances because my mother had always told us that whenever we dreamed of honey, positive things could happen. That Thursday was my second-to-the last chance, as the employment letter would expire in two days.

At about 10:00 a.m. that morning, I kissed Veron goodbye as she watched me from the front door walking down the stony hill, heading to the embassy with one thing on my mind: I have to get my visa. When I got there, I approach the visa pickup window with the same positive thoughts from the dream and this time my passport was handed to me. As I turned around to walk off, I opened it to see if I'd gotten the visa and a big smile came on my face. The stamp was there, but instead of the seaman's visa for which I had applied, my passport had been stamped with a B1/B2 visa, which allowed me to travel freely to the United States. That filled me with even more joy as I headed home.

That evening, I hitched a ride in an open-back pickup truck to Port Antonio. The cool island wind was blowing as great thoughts were going through my mind. It was sweet knowing that my family would see me later that evening but the following day, they would remember and imagine me walking in beautiful Miami.

When I got home and showed my family the visa, they were all happy. My girlfriend Veron was crying and I could tell that mixed tears were falling from her eyes. Part of her was happy that I had fought the battle and came out victorious; however, to live successfully I would have to go where life takes me, which made another part of her sad, knowing the following day I would be gone, leaving her and beautiful Tamoya behind.

As Veron's tears fell, I was making plans about the chickens that were ready for slaughtering, what she might do with the money she would make when they were sold and how to seek out more markets. The two pigs I sold to a butcher to help purchase my plane ticket.

That same evening, I showed a few guys the visa, guys that I knew had the same, just to get some ideas of what to expect traveling on a B1/B2 visa instead of a seaman's. From what they were telling me it was much harder—you faced a lot more questions from customs and immigration and sometimes you had to show proof for the answers given. You were also required to travel with at least five hundred U.S. dollars in your possession. Some of the guys were telling me to take back the visa to the embassy and explain that they had granted me the wrong one, but others were telling me to take my chances and go to Miami. The last person I visited was my good friend Desmond Myers; we had worked together on the same ship during my first contract and he was on vacation at the time. We had a brief conversation that Friday morning about what had taken place in my life over the past few weeks, and I asked him what he thought of me traveling later that day on the visa. He encouraged me to go; I shook his hand and bid him goodbye. Before I could go through his gate, he called me back and gave me some money. As I walked out of his sight, I took it out and counted it.

The money he gave amounted to forty-one U.S. dollars, including twenty-one one-dollar bills. I hitched a ride back to Port Antonio and picked up my plane ticket at the travel agency. After leaving the agency, I was walking slowly down Harbor Street. As I got to the corner, in front of the CIBC Bank building, I saw the man who had renewed my future riding by. I stopped him and told him I was leaving for Miami that afternoon; he tapped me on my shoulder and said, "Chef! I know, man. Just remember me, man."

By the time I got back to my girlfriend's house, it was almost time to leave for the airport; I did one final check to make sure I had everything intended to travel with, including the little money. It wasn't much: only the forty dollars that my friend had given me, plus forty that Veron had borrowed from her mother. I had twenty, for a total of one hundred and one dollars, which wasn't even half of the amount required to have while traveling on the new visa.

I put all the money together, placing the small bills in the middle, then I put it in my front pocket. Within minutes, the taxi driver was at the gate, blowing his horn and it was time for me to go. I kissed Veron and baby Tamoya goodbye, then grabbed my little bag and headed out to the Norman Manley International Airport, where I boarded a plane to Miami, intending to report to the ship company's office.

CHAPTER NINE

BACK TO AMERICA

The employment letter I was carrying from the ship company, I had to hide in my briefs because I didn't have a seaman's visa to prove to immigration and customs that I was really going to work on a ship. If I let them see it, they would think that I was intending on working with it on a B1/B2 visa. The letter containing information on the hotel where I was supposed to stay also had to be kept hidden.

The plane ride from Jamaica was smooth and I was hoping everything would go just as smoothly when I arrived in Miami. That moment would soon face me as the Air Jamaica jet touched the ground at about seven o'clock on the evening of June 2, 1995, a Friday evening I will never forget.

When I arrived at the immigration checkpoint and stepped across the line, I handed the officer my passport. He opened it to the visa page and asked, "Mr. Burke, what is your purpose of traveling?"

"To shop for my daughter and family," I replied.

He then asked, "Are you still working with the ship company?"

"No," I told him. He asked where I was going to shop.

"At one of the flea markets in Miami," I answered.

"How long are you staying?" I told him about three days.

He stamped my passport and said, "Mr. Burke, have a nice trip."

I walked off and headed downstairs, where there was still customs to be dealt with but was I prepared for them? Only time would tell.

When I got to the customs line, I saw a single finger raised in front of a serious face, calling me over. I walked up to him and said, "Good evening, sir."

He replied with manners, then asked, "Can I see your passport?"

I gave it to him.

He then asked me to open my bags on a table. I did so. Next he looked at my picture on the visa, then looked into my face and said, "Glenroy, this picture doesn't look like you. Your face had lost some weight."

I looked back in his eyes smiling and said, "It's me, sir. As you can see the visa is newly issued."

"Where are you going?" And I repeated the same story that I'd told the immigration officer upstairs. He asked at which market I actually planned to go shopping. I told him I was going to the flea market on U.S. Route 1, which was the only one I knew because that was where I'd bought my chain.

"Where are you going to stay, Mr. Burke?" I told him the name of the hotel that was on the letter from the ship company. "You already made a reservation?"

"No," I told him.

"You don't know where you're going to stay then."

I smiled and said, "Yes, that's where I am going to stay."

"How much money are you carrying Mr. Burke?"

"Five hundred dollars, sir," since that was the required amount.

"Take it out and let me see it," he said. Hearing him say that, I was looking right back at Jamaica, knowing I was only carrying one hundred and one dollars in my pocket. However, I never hesitated or trembled. My journey was just beginning, with new eyes that had seen the flame of a candle take the form of an airplane that would take me beyond him and straight into America.

I pushed my hand into my front pocket and took the wad of money out, then held it up in front of him and said, "Here it is, sir." The mistake he made was that he didn't take the money out of my hand but just put his finger on the stack and flipped three of the bills, two twenties and a ten. All the one-dollar bills that were in the middle fooled him, assuming they were all big bills.

He then said, "Glenroy, pack your things and go." A big load was lifted from my mind, but despite feeling so relieved, I kept my composure, picked my bags up and exited the airport.

I got into a taxi and told the driver where I was going. On the way, in the car, I pulled the waistband of my pants and took the two letters out, which were kept hidden from customs and immigration. We drove for about ten minutes and were there. I paid the driver, then walked up to the receptionist at the front desk and I handed him the two letters. He read them as I watched, hoping he wouldn't ask me for a seaman's visa because if he found out that I didn't have one, then I couldn't stay there on the company expense. However, all the possibilities of him finding out did not affect my confidence. I was traveling on a new road, and standing in front of the hotel receptionist on that Friday night was as far as it had taken me. Where else would I go as the road continued?

I would soon find out.

After reading, he asked for my passport. I gave it to him, hoping that he wouldn't look at the visa. Indeed, he did not and the journey continued that Friday night and paused in room 42 at the Airliner Hotel, at about a quarter past eight, where I rested and meditated for a little, while lying on my back across the bed.

After a little relaxation, I went to the dining room for dinner, which was covered by the ship company. I finished dinner at about nine-thirty, then I walked around the hotel for a while until I decided to call Veron and tell her about the trip. I purchased a phone card and called her from a payphone. After that, I went back to my room, took a shower, and went to bed.

I slept well that night and the following morning had breakfast, I was also one of the first to be in the lobby, waiting for the ship company van to take me to the office. At about eight-thirty, it showed up. The driver asked if anyone was going to the office. I stood up and said, "I am, sir," then got into the van and took a seat. When we got to the office, I did what everyone else was doing, filling out the necessary paperwork to join a ship. Later that morning, my name was called to go inside. I confidently walked in and sat at a desk, where an attractive young woman entered my information into the computer.

I answered all the questions asked; however, as she continued to document my information, I knew something was going be wrong because she needed to see my passport. She looked at the visa and said, "Glenroy, this is not a seaman's visa; I can't employ you on it."

I asked, "Then what are you going to do?"

She replied, "We have to send you back home to get a seaman's visa."

I looked straight into her eyes and asked, "Are you going to give me another job letter to take back to the embassy?"

"Yes, Glenroy," she answered, "we will give you a letter and a return plane ticket back to Miami."

I said, okay and then told her about the six weeks of appointments that the embassy was giving applicants the last time I'd gone there. She left the desk and when she returned, she told me they will also give a letter of reference to take with me. I thanked her and before leaving the office, she said, "The van will take you back to the hotel, then you must come back here on Monday for your paperwork. I will also make reservation for you to fly back to Jamaica that same day."

I returned to the hotel feeling that I had accomplished what I'd came to Miami to do. I spent the weekend there thinking about going back to Jamaica without even bringing back a gift for my girlfriend and my daughter but I was happy because I was carrying great news that would make them happy too.

The following Monday morning, I went back to the office and picked up my papers. As I got the package, I opened the letter of reference and read it. It couldn't have been better with the company seal at the bottom. I then went back to the hotel and got ready to catch an afternoon flight back to my country of birth on June 5, 1995, with a return date back to Miami for June 22.

I departed Miami that evening in great spirits and landed in my country feeling the same way. Two days later, I went to the embassy to apply for the seaman's visa since I only have seventeen days at home with my family. The interview went well and the counselor told me to come back and pick up the visa in two days. When the time came and I went back, the stamp was there, but this time there was a mistake on the visa. My passport number had been incorrectly copied onto it. But otherwise it looked good and I was going to travel on it.

During the few days I had at home with Veron, I finished slaughtering all of the chickens and sold them. Now it was up to her to decide if she was going to continue raising more while I was away. As it got closer to my departure date, I would sometimes worry about traveling on a visa with the wrong passport number but a part of me was confident that no one would notice it. My departure date came and I flew to Miami without any problems and was soon back at the same hotel again.

A few days later, the company flew me to California to work on the same ship that I started out on. I was to work with the same chef who had pressured me before and who was so mean that he transferred me to nowhere on my first contract. That thought took over my mind from the moment I walked into the galley and saw his face again. I could only hope that during the next ten months, I wouldn't have to endure more of what I'd already suffered at his hands.

That Sunday evening, when I started working, I realized I was the only Jamaican in the main galley and would have to hold my own against men from all over the world, with no one to watch my back this time. I was once again placed at the sauce station as the head sauce cook. Things started out well for me—I gave it my best as I usually do, now more than ever because I had my daughter Tamoya to take care of. The pay still wasn't much, although it was a raise from four hundred and fifty-three dollars to four hundred and seventy-four dollars per month.

As time went on, a few Jamaican cooks started to join the ship and the atmosphere in the galley started to change. I was a little happier because now I had some of my own countrymen to talk to, including some with whom I'd worked before.

I called Veron on a weekly basis to make sure she and the baby were okay and I sent her money each month to make sure food was on the table. A few months after I signed on to the ship, it was going to dry-dock in San Francisco. I decided not to go because of my experience there back in ninety-three. The ship's generator had been turned off and conditions on board were very uncomfortable. Instead I signed off in California and spent the time with one of my friends and enjoy myself until it was time to go back on board.

Above: Me, right and my friend Desmond, left,
at San Francisco on dry dock in 1993

By then the reality of the responsibility left back at home was facing me and making it harder to save money. I tried to limit my enjoyment in Mexico and kept focused on my job, which gained me a lot of respect in the galley; even the executive chef from the company office would soon take notice.

One week in San Pedro, we were doing a special lunch on board for some travel agents. At one point I saw a strange man walking through the galley with some senior officers. I asked who he was and one of my friends who had been with the company for over ten years told me that he was the executive chef. For me it was amazing to see the man to whom I'd explained my situation to on the telephone from Jamaica months ago when I was badly in need of his help. Before the line was opened for service, he tasted the sauces and looked at the spaghetti carbonara, which I had made. He then turned to the chef in charge of the galley and asked, "Who is the sauce cook? The chef told him I was and he came over, introduced himself, shook my hand and congratulated me on my sauces. Throughout the serving of lunch, he stood nearby, talking to our chef and admiring our work on the line. At the end of the lunch, I went outside to call my family; on my way back, I ran into him on the gangway. He again asked me my name. I told him, then we shook hands and he walked away. When I went back to work that Sunday evening, the chef called me into his office and told me that the executive chef had recommended that I get a raise in pay and a promotion from assistant cook to cook. That was in September of 1995, a few months after I had signed on. I was encouraged by that promise to work harder, now that it seemed I could climb the ladder. However, as time passed it became clear that actually getting the promotion and raise of pay would require more than I could give.

Over a month had passed and I didn't see any changes in my pay. I started to question the chef on a weekly basis, asking if he had sent the paperwork for my promotion to the executive office. He continued to tell me that yes, he had and my response was always "Okay." Nonetheless, in life, as one grows, we learn, so by then it was clear to me that the color of a man's skin could shadow the results of his hard work.

When I was tired of asking him the same question over and over, I told him that I wanted to stop doing sauces and to move to the night shift so I could hustle with the cabin stewards in the evenings and make some extra money.

Before changing my shift when shame was shadowing his ignorant face, he recommended me for employee of the month, which also kept as secret since I was never invited to have my picture taken with the captain. Nonetheless, it put an extra two hundred dollars in my pocket, and then I started working the night shift as a prep cook.

My new shift now began at ten o'clock at night and I would prep right through until breakfast began the next morning, then help to serve breakfast until it ended, usually at 11:00 a.m., sometimes a bit later. My sleeping time would be from whatever time breakfast ended until 5:00 p.m. each day. At five-thirty, I would start working with a cabin steward, continuing until 9:30 p.m. Those would be my working hours for the next several weeks.

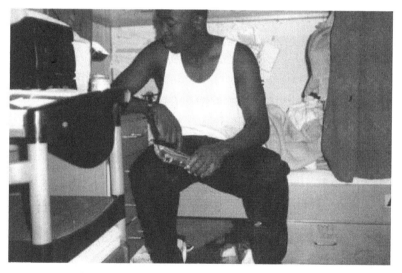

In my cabin, a tired Glenroy just returning from cabin work,
having time only to change clothes and start my prep shift

Starting my prep shift

While doing prep work at nights, our eyes would get dim and our beds seemed very far away, not in distance but by timing. Lots of guys would fell asleep standing over bags of carrots or onions to be peeled. I never let the pressure get a chance to take a hold of me; where I came from in life was all I meditated on during those hard nights and I sang Bob Marley songs to keep me happy. I worked that shift for a few weeks until the chef moved me to another station where I worked as the head crew chef. This new shift stopped me from doing cabin work but I did manage to save some money out of it.

Working the crew mess hall was an easier position; the greatest of it all was the experience of preparing and seeing the kinds of food that my fellow crewmen from other countries liked to eat and also how they ate it. Nonetheless, it wouldn't be long before I was called upon again to prepare sauces in the main galley.

By then my contract was coming to an end and being so conservative this time, my money added up to much more than I had on my first contract.

With the result of responsibility and a mind-set that God made man for who we are, I called Veron one week and she told me her boss wanted to rent the restaurant at the resort where she was working.

She asked if I was interested. "Yes," I told her and so I started making plans for it. I spent a few hundred dollars buying some of the supplies needed to run a restaurant and because of that I asked to stay on the ship a few extra weeks in order to make back that spent money. My contract finally came to an end on May 20, 1996. On that day, I went back to Jamaica with two thousand one hundred U.S. dollars in my pocket; still, I did not get the raise in pay or the promotion from the company.

I got home feeling happy and excited to see what it would be like to start my own business. The deal I was getting with the restaurant was very good, so I immediately sent the ship company a letter, requesting a leave of absence; then a few weeks later, I opened my own restaurant at Summerset Set Falls in Portland, which featured a great menu.

Months after we'd opened, Veron and I broke up. I moved out of her home and rented a one-bedroom apartment in town. Nevertheless, we would still be around each other every day at work, as she was still a part of the restaurant and my baby's mother. The reason for the breaking up was that I found out while I was away on the cruise ship, her actions at home did not matches the conversations we were having on the telephone.

With Veron and me working on the same property and already having a child together, we were still having fun which resulted in her becoming pregnant again. Another baby was on the way that would pull us back together.

As time went on at Summerset Falls, business wasn't the way I expected it to be, so my immediate thoughts were to go back and work with the ship company again. However, my mind wasn't quite ready. While lingering over my decision, another opportunity came to work in Cape Cod, Massachusetts, through the H2B visa program. I gratefully accepted it; this time I would be leaving with Tamoya running around and Veron carrying my second child, making the decision a little harder. Nonetheless, in the end, our children needed all the resources required to survive and develop properly, both physically and mentally—the things I never had as a child. I knew then that all kids need the compassionate love of a father around them. But in order to work for a living, it isn't always possible to be there night and day. Such is the case with poor families around the world and to depart again, I did so with all the love in my heart for them and I carried it with me, on May 6, 1997, when I flew to Massachusetts to provide us with a brighter future.

My H2B visa, on which I traveled to Massachusetts on May 6, 1997

That year, I worked as a cook for six months at an upscale hotel on beautiful Cape Cod. For the first time in my life, I was working on the mainland in America and feeling free. My nights were no longer spent rocking with the motion of the ship and I could now sleep comfortably.

At the hotel, there were huge challenges in having to perform in a new environment. But by then my experience and knowledge gathered over the years quickly caught the eyes of my bosses and coworkers as they watched me perform at my station. However, a man is without strength if he can't acknowledge his surroundings; sometimes we would be reminded of where we had came from and how we'd gotten to be working there.

I was making eight dollars and fifty cents per hour, which was very good for me. It was the kind of money I had never made before and I could save most of it, with the fact that Veron was still operating the restaurant in Summerset Falls. Her belly was growing again; soon we would need baby clothes, only this time at a limited budget since we could use the ones that Tamoya had outgrown.

My working station was in the pantry. On weekends I would also flip omelets in the dining room. The shift was from 6:00 a.m. to 2:30 p.m., which left me with lots of spare time in the afternoon. I decided not to sit around because of the job availability in the area, an evidence of how it should have been when I was a child growing up in Jamaica. Where there are working opportunities, there are brighter prosperity and a happier nation—a worldly method for peace.

I started a second job at a Pizza Hut; as the summer got busier, I started working in different areas at the hotel. This was much to my advantage, since I had already learned that, when working on a visa, you have to perform well to be rehired the following year, so I was making sure that I secured my opportunity in due time.

One of the areas where I'd begun to work was the pool house grill, which meant that I would have to go to work in the mornings, prep my menu and then take it to the pool house on a golf cart. I had never driven one before and only practiced once in a car. Feeling ashamed to ask someone to teach me, I decided to try teaching myself. I'd taken up so many challenges in life and this was just another one. I started out driving slowly until I became more familiar with it, then I increased speed. My experience driving the golf cart would be of greater help to me later in learning to drive a car.

Time went on and I was having lots of fun on Cape Cod. However, it hurt each time I called Veron, unable to be there by her side and knowing that the only comfort I could provide her with was to hear each other's voices on the telephone. She was working less and needed more time to rest, as her belly was growing bigger by the day.

By the fall of 1997, the result of working those two jobs was evident in my bank account and knowing that pretty soon I was going to be sent back to Jamaica, I started meditating about some things I wanted to do when I went back.

Veron gave birth to our second daughter on November 4, 1997. We named her Salenas Tameka Burke.

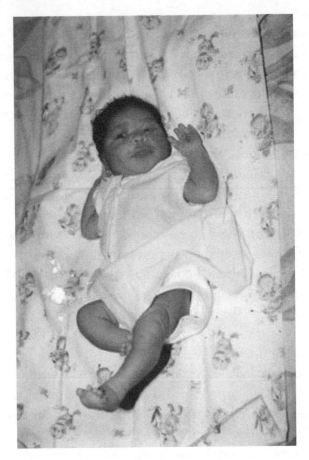

Baby Salenas Tameka Burke, eleven days old

Despite the arrival of my second daughter to the world, my social life in America was getting more exciting; I was partying and meeting different people. I wasn't as shy as I used to be, even with the hard memories of being a lonely poor boy growing up with no one to talk to when I had needed a friend. That fear which had grown in my mind that I would never be accepted was slowly going away but would never be completely gone.

There are so many sides to a person, the good and the bad, the brave and the cowardly. My braver side was coming out, which made communication easier; I was partying with lots of ladies and would soon to get involved with one whom I'll call Terry (not her real name) and that was when the real fun started.

As my time in Cape Cod was coming to an end, Terry and I were getting closer, spending nights and days together; it was quite clear our feelings were getting stronger for each other. She didn't have a car but once walked in the pouring rain to come see me. That night, I asked one of my friends to take me in his car to go pick her up. We made plans to meet in a parking lot; when we got there, she was soaking wet. Even though she was twenty-one years old, I still couldn't be seen picking her up at the house where she was staying. As we got back to my place, I put her clothes in the dryer, turned up the heat and kept her comfortable and relaxed for the night.

By then my six-month contract was almost over. The hotel held an end-of-season party for the staff, which took place on the eve of my flight back to Jamaica. Terry and I spent the hours leading up to the party together; I made her lunch, which was Jamaican stewed peas and white rice, then we went to the party, as she was also a coworker.

We had a good time mingling with the crowd, then after the dinner she gave me a bundle of roses which she gathered from the table vases accompanied by a cassette with a single song. The chorus was "How do I live without you, I want to know" We then went to the 400 East Club with most of the coworkers. We had fun there and spent the final moments together and on November 12, 1997, I flew back to Jamaica. With love in my heart, I was going to see my daughters and their mom, but if roses also meant love, then I was carrying another in my hand from Terry, who already told me she loved me. After clearing customs at the Norman Manley International Airport in Kingston, that was as far as the roses could go. I threw them away but couldn't throw away the times and memories spent together.

Growing up, I was confused by some of the many things that happened in life. I can remember asking Mother many times for clarifications. She always said and I quote, "You are growing up. You will know." Those memories hit me as a twenty-four-year-old man. With a confused mind, I left the airport for my hometown of Port Antonio, where Veron and my daughters awaited.

Later that evening, when I arrived in the community, as the taxi reached the front gate, I could see them all at the front door looking out for me. I was amazed at how much Tamoya had grown over the past six months and as I was climbing the hill, I could hear Veron asking her, "Who is that coming?"

"Daddy, Daddy, Daddy!" she kept on repeating. I felt so good. I just walked up to her, lifted her in my arms and kissed her. As I walked into the house there was little Salenas lying in the bed, innocent and asleep, just seven days old. I lay down beside her, gave a soft hug and a gentle kiss, then I hugged and kissed Veron and I felt warmly welcomed by everyone.

I relaxed for a while, playing with the kids and telling Veron about Cape Cod, then enjoyed dinner with them. I was happy to be back at home but was already missing someone in another part of the world, whom I had to call to tell I'd arrived home safely.

After dinner, I took a shower at my mother-in-law's house (she had a pipe with running water), then I got dressed and walked down into Port Antonio town, to a phone booth where I called her from. As the phone rang, she answered it; we talked for a while, then I went back home. That night I fell asleep beside my kids and Veron, feeling like a responsible man but not knowing how long I was going to be around.

The following evening, I went to the countryside to visit my parents and family as I usually did. Everyone was so happy to see me coming from America but this time happier than ever because I'd brought home over five thousand U.S. dollars to put into the bank and I had a valid visa in my passport and could travel to America whenever I wanted.

My family welcomed me that evening—all gathered around me in the yard with big smiles on their faces. However, some of them were still in farm clothes and they were still working at the plantation. The old board house behind them still looked the same, weathered by hardship. It seemed that I was their only opportunity for some changes in their lives. I talked happily with them while my mind reflected on America, where lay the opportunity to provide a better life for them and myself.

Before I had left Cape Cod, the chef at the hotel told me he wanted me to come back and work for him the following year. Since that promise wouldn't come to reality until six months later, in the meantime I still needed spending money for my household and didn't want to take it from what already saved in the bank because life has its rainy days.

I went back to Summerset Falls to operate the restaurant again and was having no problem feeding my family. Day after day, however, I would receive phone calls from Terry; she would cry sometimes about how much she missed me and ask when I was coming back. As those questions continued, I was remembering the good times we'd shared in a great country. My nights eventually became a time for thinking as I lay beside my daughters and Veron, of what the future held for me and what decisions to make. I would miss the little ones again, Tamoya and Salenas—I would always love them. Life's pathway was calling Daddy and he would be gone again but I didn't knew how to explain it to their mother.

One day in a phone conversation, Terry and I talked about whether, if I came to visit, she could find a place for us to stay, get a car and if possible a job, since she wasn't working and had none of those for my convenience. She said yes. While we were discussing those things, I was purchasing a two-way plane ticket back to America to see her. This time, more than ever, I didn't know what to expect, yet inner courage and strength had taken me past vicious phases before. As it was in the beginning when I first started traveling on visas, so should it be in the end. This time around, I might be coming back to Jamaica with a new status.

During the final days of phone conversations with the girl from the Cape, I asked her if she would marry 1me when I came to visit. She said yes. I also asked if she had gotten the necessities we'd talked about. She said that she had. The answers brightened my spirits a bit and I couldn't hide it any longer from Veron. It was tough to tell her that my journey was taking me away again and that I would be leaving her and the kids soon and didn't know when I would return. (A man's destiny is in a man's journey, such shall he find.)

I told her that I was going to visit some friends. She was upset but in the end helped to make my decision. The gravel that once squeezed the bottom of my feet in Jamaica had now turned to asphalt as a young man approached a new journey; On December 5, 1997, I kissed her and the children goodbye and boarded a plane back to America, traveling on a B1/B2 visa. On a warm Friday afternoon, I departed beautiful Kingston to land on a cold night in Massachusetts. Tamoya was three years and little over a month old; Salenas was so young that her head had barely felt the sunlight of Jamaica. She was just a month old, so hard to leave behind but I left in search of a brighter future for them.

Chapter Ten

Marriage in the American Melting Pot

When I arrived at Miami International Airport, I faced some of the usual questions and already knew how to answer them and that made it easy to clear immigration and customs. Unfortunately, I was only given one month in the country.

My connecting flight landed at Logan International Airport in Boston, Massachusetts, at about 6:00 pm. As I was about to exit the airport, there she was standing at the door, waiting for me. We hugged and kissed as we stepped outside into the cold New England weather.

I asked her where she'd parked the car; she replied that she hadn't got one yet.

I then asked if she'd found us an apartment and to my surprise she said, "No."

"Where are we heading to now?" I asked.

"Let's take a taxi," she answered.

We got into one and I repeated, "Where are we going?"

She answered, "To my dad's apartment in Chelsea, just north of Boston. About a fifteen-minute drive from here."

When we arrived at the complex, she paid the driver, then squeezed a door buzzer at the entrance. We were allowed inside, went up the stairs and down a hallway. By then my heart was pounding! Not because of fear, but rather pride, knowing I wasn't in the position as yet to give suitable answers to the questions good fathers would ask to ensure that their daughter or daughters would be happy. In fact, I was heading into his house when I should be taking her into mine, as a sense of responsibility.

We stopped at a door and were greeted by a man who seemed to be in his early sixties and a woman, who was Terry's stepmother. She introduced me and their response was friendly. I walked inside, sat down and was offered a hot cup of coffee by her father. As I accepted it, he asked whether or not I would like cream and sugar. Nervousness caused me to decline those, although I would have preferred them; so I drank the coffee black and strong. While I was drinking, he started asking me some personal questions, which I answered as best I could.

As darkness cast its shadow over Boston, Massachusetts, I started to feel hungry for my native Jamaican food. There was none to be had but I was ready to adapt to a new culture in a great country. I whispered in her ear, "What are we going to eat?" She replied she didn't know. I asked if there was any restaurants close by. "Yes." she said and we walked to a Burger King close to the Mystic Mall.

Hungry from the journey, I ordered two grilled chicken sandwiches for myself and Terry ordered what she wanted. While eating, I felt quite concerned about the current situation and asked why she had lied to me before I left Jamaica by saying that she found an apartment and a car. She answered with all sorts of stories but that was all right. I am a man and had to create a life for us but I also needed time to settle in.

I asked her where we were going to sleep; she said we'd stay at her dad's place. As I continued talking to her about getting our lives together, I realized she didn't have much in the way of assets and in the days to come, I would also learn that the thirty-one dollars she had in her pocket when I landed at the airport was all she had to her name. She had no job and was looking for a place to stay, just as I was. She did have a valid driver's license, which was very important. I'd brought back thirteen hundred U.S. dollars with me, which would pave the way for us.

We walked back to her father's apartment on that cold December night; I sat down in the same sofa where I'd sat in all evening. As the night grew later, her stepmother brought us a blanket and the couple went into their room. Terry immediately took a shower and came back in her nightgown. We made love on the living room floor and slept right there. All through the night, I could tell whenever someone got up to smoke a cigarette. In the morning, I went to the bathroom and took a shower. Again I was offered a cup of coffee by her dad; I accepted it even though I was hungry for a hearty Jamaican breakfast.

At around midday, my girlfriend and I went to a restaurant for lunch. Walking down the streets, we were holding hands. We stopped together when the traffic was passing and stood close together at the stoplights, waiting on them to change before crossing. We were very much in love by then.

While having lunch, we talked about some of the things we needed, such as finding work and housing. I had visited a few places in America when I was working on the cruise ship but Cape Cod was the only place I knew well. I suggested we go back and she had mixed emotions as to whether we should go or remain in the Boston area. My thought was that our first priority would be to find a place to stay and a car to move around; if we could find those in Boston, then we could also find them in Cape Cod. I was pushing for that because since I was a little boy, I'd never liked big cities.

After lunch, we walked around the Mystic Mall for a good portion of the afternoon, then we went back to her dad's apartment. With the thought of the living hall floor on my mind, I knew the coming night would be just like the previous.

We slept on the same spot and woke up on Sunday morning with the same needs. Around midday, her brother came to visit and to meet me. He was a fine young man I thought and after we talked for a while, he decided to help us find a place to stay. He left the apartment at about 3:00 p.m. and returned about an hour later with the good news that he had found us a motel room. It was walking distance from their dad's apartment and the rooms were going for thirty-five dollars a night. We went with him to look at it; the location was not at all impressive. But with no other choice, we spent a third night at her dad's apartment and then on Monday morning, we checked into the motel.

The inside didn't look much better than the outside; still, we had heat and it was a shelter over our heads. We went out for dinner that evening and returned at about eight o'clock. On Tuesday morning, we went to her dad's apartment for coffee and to make some phone calls. She called some of her friends, telling them we were thinking of moving back to the Cape and what some of our needs were. At that time, I only had two phone numbers of friends that I'd met at the hotel over the summer. One was Jamaican and the other a Puerto Rican; both were living on Cape Cod. I told them I was in Boston and that I was planning on moving there. My Puerto Rican friend told that he was taking his mom to a Boston hospital the coming Thursday and suggested that if we would travel on that day, he could give a ride back. "I will think about it and call back," I told him.

Later on in the day, we went for lunch. Evidently it was costing me a lot of money eating out with no income generated. I ordered lunch only for Terry and after, we went to a supermarket, where I got a loaf of bread, a few tins of chicken sausages and a quart bottle of Coca-Cola. We also went to the liquor store and got a bottle of Jim Beam whiskey. When we got back to the room, I made dinner from the items I'd bought and ate until my belly was full. We later took a few drinks of the Jim Beam and we played cards to entertain ourselves, since there was only a radio in the room.

After the card game, I mentioned to her that I was only given one month to stay in the country and that the only way we could be together would be if I stayed in America and the only way for me to stay legally was if we got married before the current stay on my visa expired.

"Let's do it now," she responded.

At the end of the conversation, I counted the money I had left, with the intention to purchase her wedding ring the following day.

It added up to eleven hundred and sixty dollars; however, I wasn't worried because before leaving Jamaica, I'd put my mother's name on my bank account so she could send me money if I needed it.

The following day we went back to the Mystic Mall to look around, this time mainly in stores that sold jewelry. We ended up purchasing two gold rings and then slowly walked back to her dad's place. From there, I called my Puerto Rican friend since the following day would be Thursday; he confirmed that he was still coming and on that day, we rode in his car to beautiful Cape Cod.

The trip was energized by shared conversation of the past summer. Nevertheless, in the midst of jokes, I told him we were thinking of getting married. He was surprised and asked whether or not we thought we were ready. We both answered, "Yes."

"Where in Cape Cod are you going live?" We didn't know but hoped it wouldn't be in the cold. While talking, I asked him if he knew any friends that would have an extra bedroom available. He said no, then took his cell phone out and started making calls on our behalf; we did not get back any positive answers but were still traveling on hope.

At about 6:00 p.m. that Thursday evening, the car drove across the Sagamore Bridge. We were now on Cape Cod and certainly in need of a place to stay but whose door could we knock on for an honest and positive answer? Only biblical stories match the result. I felt like Joseph, when his son was born and no one could protect him from the blade of Herod but one. Nonetheless, he was protected and was untouchable for a worthy cause; and so shall it be.

We visited some people whom we knew but after a few minutes of talking with them, it was time to go again. We also checked out a few motels that offered weekly rentals but there were no vacancies for us. It got to the point where Terry had no choice but to ask the lady for whom she'd worked as a babysitter the previous summer if she could spend the night at her house, with a black man from Jamaica. The lady agreed to let us stay. I thanked her plus my friend who had been very generous to drive us around all evening until we finally found a place to stay.

When we walked into the house, I greeted the kind strangers, then headed downstairs, to what I would later learn was called a basement. It was a very cold room but was clean, neat and at least there was a bed. I laid my suitcase down and started meditating as I sat on the bed, with both cheeks resting in my hands. After she'd sorted out herself, I asked her if she was hungry. She was and I asked where we could find a restaurant within walking distance. She said the closest place was the same club where I used to pick her up the previous summer. We walked there, had dinner, then returned to the house and went to bed.

That night, I asked her how much an old car might cost; she gave me some figures, then said that one of her friends had told her about one she had for sale. We borrowed the house phone and called to check if she still had the car. Indeed she did; we asked about its condition and how much she was asking for it. The price was three hundred dollars, and so the following day, we went to look at it. When we got there, we jump-started it; it needed a new battery but otherwise it was running well. The woman kindly took the cost of the battery out of her asking price and sold the car to us for two hundred and forty dollars.

That same Friday, we got it registered and insured. By later that evening, while driving around, we saw smoke coming from under the hood. We stopped to check the problem and had to take it to the mechanic the following day. I paid another one hundred and thirty dollars to take care of that problem with still another facing us: a warm place to live.

Around midday that Saturday, we bought a copy of the *Cape Cod Times* newspaper, stood at a phone booth in East Harwich and looked through the classified section. We dropped quarters as needed, making phone calls until we found a room at a motel in West Yarmouth. and moved out of the basement that same evening.

By then I only had about five hundred dollars left and the room was going for one hundred and five dollars per week with no cooking facilities. I paid for a one-week stay and got a key to room 35. As we opened the door and walked inside, I turned on the heat to warm up. Later that evening, we went to the Kentucky Fried Chicken in Hyannis for dinner and bought enough to take home for the following day.

That night, we lay in the room watching cable television; she was choosing the channels. The programs were funny; however, fun comes through responsibility and so we started talking about her getting a job since I wasn't allowed to work on my visa.

The following Monday morning, we drove around on a job hunt. Terry filled out about ten applications and landed a job the same day as a cashier, making seven dollars per hour and by the next day she'd found a second. Now when I kissed her goodbye some mornings, I wouldn't see her again until eleven-thirty at night.

During those days alone at the motel, I would wonder sometimes about what was next for me. All day until she got back home at nights, I would be watching television, but the remote control would always be stuck on only four channels: CNN, Court TV, the History Channel, and ESPN, from which I developed a love for American sports, such as basketball, baseball, football, hockey and many more.

The Friday of that week was exactly two weeks since I'd left Jamaica and I hadn't yet called Veron to find out how things were going. I walked to a store, purchased a phone card, went to a phone booth and called her. I asked about the kids and if she was spending the money that I'd left her wisely, in order for them to survive until I could afford to send her more. I also gave her a message for my mother to come to her house the following week for a phone call from me.

By then Terry and I were making plans for our wedding, inviting friends and looking around for a dress and also a suit.

With all the spending it took to arrange the wedding, the money I had was almost gone and only a hundred dollars were left in my pocket. In my first phone conversation with my mother, I asked her to send some money via Western Union and told her about my plan to get married. She replied, "Son, do what's best for your life." That I did on December 28, 1997, the day when at the tender age of twenty five, I said, "I do" to Terry. Immediately after the wedding, we started preparing the immigration paperwork to file for a work permit and to become a United States resident.

The New Year of 1998 began with me feeling the need of a job. One night, we were visiting my Jamaican friend and brother-man, Mark. My wife and I drove by a restaurant that looked very busy. While drinking and talking at his home, I mentioned it to him. He immediately said, "Let's go and check it out." And we did so. I spoke with a waitress when we got there, who directed me to the manager. I told him that I was there to apply for a job in the kitchen or any position they had available. He told me he have an opening for a prep cook and asked whether or not I could use a kitchen knife professionally. I answered by telling him a little about my work experience and was offered seven dollars an hour to start the following day.

My wife dropped me off at work on the way to hers; the moment I met the owners, I could tell they were genuine people and this would be proven over the course of time working with them. At the end of the day, my wife picked me up on her way back from work. As I sat in the car and we kissed, she asked about my first day. It had gone well, I told her.

With both incomes, we could now afford a suitable place to live, one that had at least cooking facilities. By the help of one of our friends, we found it the next day and moved in instantly. This place was located in the town of Dennis Port, a rooming house, where we had to share a bathroom with other tenants. The good thing about it, however, was that it was walking distance from my workplace and had cooking facilities. The rent wasn't too high, so I could now afford not only to send Veron some money to take care of the kids but also enough to maintain her as well.

Walking home from work in the afternoons, I would take the shortest road to make the journey easier on my feet. However, one evening I was forced to start walking the longer routes because of a dog attack. I got so scared when the huge animal attacked me in rage and forced me to step off the main road and into a personal property. In fear, I had no choice then but to break the property fence to defend myself. The animal then turned back as it sensed danger coming toward it and ran right back to the front door of the house, where I saw an old lady quickly open the door to let it in. That dog may have stopped me from walking on that road but he didn't stop me from loving America or from keeping my dreams alive. Nonetheless, from that day I was exposed to a different ideology of life, that tough hate exists on the shortcuts. I was so different from that lady that her dog needed protection from me. Only when danger was coming back at it that she opened the door to let it in.

As the months passed by and the summer season of 1998 approached, I was still interested in working back at the resort where I had worked the previous year. If rehired, I would need a car, since the distance from Dennis Port to the resort was about ten miles. I mentioned this to my wife and she started teaching me how to drive properly to apply for my driver's license. Meanwhile, all of the paperwork for immigration had been filled out and was ready to be submitted to the office.

In teaching me how to drive, she didn't have to do much because I already had some experience with the golf carts the previous year at the hotel. It was mainly a matter of staying in the lane steadily and using the signals correctly. When I was comfortable handling the car, she took me to the registry of motor vehicles for a driving test and I passed on my first try.

By then my twenty-sixth birthdays had already gone; I celebrated it for the second time in my life, this time in America. That night, we invited lots of friends and enjoyed ourselves. At about 9:30 p.m. my wife called me upstairs. When I reached the room, she started crying.

I asked, "What's wrong?"

"I'm pregnant!"

I said, "Yeah!" but I did not know what else to say just then.

However, I was confident that everything was going to be fine; she called her father later on to let him know he was going to be a granddad. After that night, she made it clear to me that when the baby arrived, she didn't want to continue living in that house, where there was not much privacy. "We have eight months to make preparations," I answered.

April came around and she made her first visit to the doctor. It was that day when I realized the expense of having a child in America. Neither of us had medical insurance or a well-paid job; however, I was on my way to finding one. I went back to the hotel and applied for a job, this time in the dining room as a busboy. I was hired but not to start immediately. At the same time, we were also looking around for an apartment and calling state offices every day in search of medical insurance. The first thing we needed, however, was another car for me to drive to work. We bought an old Chevy Nova that ran well. Then one day I made another call to a state office and we got medical insurance. This took a big weight off our shoulders, leaving us only to find an apartment and it wouldn't be long before that happened.

One day, we drove by an apartment complex with a phone number posted on the building. We called and when the phone was answered, I learned that something important was required that neither of us had. That something was credit. We explained our needs to the lady and she offered to meet with us. When we met, she seemed sympathetic to us as a young struggling couple. She told us to bring her pay stubs from our jobs and a reference letter from where we were living. As soon as we'd presented these to her, she asked for twelve hundred dollars as deposit. At that time, we only have six hundred, but my Jamaican friend, Mark, become a Good Samaritan and loaned me six hundred dollars from a credit card. He asked me to pay him back in two months, with one hundred dollars interest.

When we got the key to the apartment and looked at it, we realized how much furniture was going to be needed, despite not having the money to buy any. Again, more than four eyes were looking out for us, including Mark, who called me one day in reference to a local motel in Hyannis that was selling out most of its furniture and appliances. He took me there in his pickup and I bought most of what we needed; my bosses also gave me some furniture for the living room and a few days later, we moved in. Our life was now more like that of a married couple, and we felt ready to move forward.

By then the hotel had reopened and I started working as a busboy. My wife also got a job at another hotel as a hostess, so the summer season started out looking fruitful. As time went on, we were able to start saving money, enough to have a few parties at our new apartment with only close friends invited.

I would accompany my wife to every prenatal checkup and awaken with her most nights to comfort her through her groans and pains. September 15th of that same year was the date set for my interview with immigration. My wife accompanied me there. She sat close beside me and held my hand tightly as we went through tough questioning. In the end, I was made a permanent resident of the United States and returned from Boston that day a very happy man. Nine months after I'd left Jamaica, my status had changed and I was now awaiting the birth of my third child in less than three months.

The conference season kept me busy at the hotel. So did the baby crib I had to put together one night. Evidently it would soon be occupied, as the young soon-to-be mother, located a spot for it in the bedroom, decorated by her favorite colors of fabric. Bit by bit and day by day, she added them to the sides and smiled as she explained the meanings of them to me. I would listen keenly and shared smiles but hers were slowly turning into severe pain at nights. A husband's love could only comfort her to a certain extent. Then on November 24, at about 7:30 a.m., she woke up to new signs from her reproductive system. I hurried her to the doctor and then straight to the maternity ward at the Cape Cod Hospital.

I spent the first nine hours beside her hospital bed, trying to comfort her as she cried in pain. With no option left, at about 8:30 p.m. the doctor began surgery to deliver the child by C-section. One hour later, on November 24, 1998, a screaming Samantha Lyn Burke entered the world. She was my third child and more responsibility that would encourage me to work harder.

Samantha Lyn Burke

When my wife woke up from her surgery, she asked for the baby, who was now in the nursery. I pushed her bed into the room; she touched Samantha and smiled. I then pushed her to another room where she would be staying for the next three nights. Later on, the kind nurses brought a long chair into the room, which I would sleep in for next three nights, watching over my wife.

That experience gave me a chance to see the pain that mothers go through to bring a baby into the world and sometimes the pain that they bear in giving birth later becomes a burden when the father or fathers who had pleasure in the beginning do not stand up to their responsibilities in that child's life. It is a shame when that happens.

The following day was the country's Thanksgiving celebration; the hotel was usually busy for that event, so I had gone to work. All day, however, I wasn't happy as my mind constantly was on my wife and little Samantha, whose eyes weren't yet open. I hurried out of work that evening with my wife's Thanksgiving dinner: turkey and mashed potatoes with lots of gravy, accompanied with other items in a takeout box and, last but not least, a bundle of roses. When I got to the hospital, she couldn't eat it but could only drink cranberry juice. She must have been hungry I imagine but it was too soon for solid food, as she was still recovering and in pain. (That's why kids need to respect their mothers; at birth they come out as a living being, but they never see the pain that mothers bear to bring them here.) After spending a few hours with her, I went home, took a shower and then went back to the hospital to spend the night.

Three days after giving birth, she was released from the hospital. A few days later, she started experiencing problems with her incision; it wasn't healing properly, so we went back to the doctor and she was readmitted into the hospital.

That day when the elevator stopped on the floor where she was going to stay, as we stepped out and were walking down the hallway, she burst out into tears. I said, "Honey, what wrong?" She whispered in my ear, telling me that a dearly loved member of her family had died on that floor in the same direction where we were heading. The nurses saw her discomfort and wanted to know what was wrong; she told them about her relative and they asked if she remembered the room. She pointed it out and they made certain not to put her close to that one. She stayed in the hospital for about five days, receiving medical treatment and I was there with her day and night, playing my role as husband and father. When she was released again, we went back home, and our lives returned to normal.

As the New Year of 1999 approached, our plan was to purchase a new pickup truck; we made stops at many dealers to get a feel for prices, then on President's day in February we made one final stop and purchased a V6 extended cab Dodge Dakota Sport, a 1999 model. In fact, I am still driving that truck. That achievement in itself started the year on a positive note for us, since it was a plan that came through. (It's always a good thing to approach every New Year with a plan to achieve, and saving your money is the key.)

167

The pickup truck that we purchased in 1999

It had been over a year since I had seen Tamoya and Salenas and I started having sleepless nights thinking about them. The money I was sending couldn't help my feelings; it never added up to the love I had in my heart for them. They needed to see me at least once in a while but I still wasn't sure when that trip would be. It was finally made after an emergency phone call from my family, just hours after I was awakened from a dream. It would be a trip to see them and to bury a loved one.

Lying asleep one Saturday night, I dreamed of my family back home. When I woke up on Sunday morning, I asked my wife whether or not it would be okay with her if I were to go to Jamaica for a week. She didn't say yes but wasn't opposing the idea.

After breakfast, we sat in the living room watching television. At about eleven o'clock, I felt like doing something. I said bye to my honey, then left the apartment to go to a nearby beach, intending to clean the truck. When I came back, my wife asked if I was okay. I answered, "Yes!"

"Your sister called while you were away."

"Which one of them?"

"Arlene," she replied.

"Well, what's the news?"

"I will tell you in a bit, honey."

The moment she said that, I instantly remembered my dream and knew something bad had happened. One minute later, she finally told me that my beloved paternal grandmother had passed away. I loved her very much. She showed me so much love as a boy growing up and I still remember her cooking.

The following day, February 27, 1999, I booked a flight and departed for Jamaica. My kids were there at the airport to meet me. I greeted them with lots of kisses, then we took off for Port Antonio; this time I would be staying with them at my parents' house.

When we arrived home and I walked into the yard, my family was there waiting. My sisters and brother were all excited to see their little brother who once walked the burning sand with them, coming home from America, this time as a conditional resident. However, the look and expression on my father's face was something I was not used to seeing. It was the look of a man who had just lost the loved one who had brought him onto this earth, my dear grandmother.

While sitting with everyone on the verandah, the first things they all wanted to see were my green card and a picture of my wife and daughter. By the following day, I rented a car to take my family around as we all mourned through the sad days.

There is a time and place for everything, or what society said. Nonetheless, the proper time and place for a man shall produce what God made him as. He shall be an evidence of fulfillment under his name, not under mankind. Such legacy of righteousness brought forth the pride to drive in my community, carrying an American driver's license and enjoying the respect I received from the elderly people who had watched me grew up humbly in poverty and pain. Yet I was able to elevate myself out of hardship and perhaps become an example to other young men and women in the world.

We went through the days leading up to the funeral in the traditional way. At night, the entire community gathered at our home, sharing our grief while playing games, drinking rum and cooking. Moreover, it was a very sad time for those who loved my grandmother, as the ninth night since she had died approached. Traditionally it was and still a sense of old African doctrine, filled with love, left behind from loved ones from the motherland. It continued until daybreak. On the following day, her body was laid to rest at a community cemetery in Windsor District, Portland, Jamaica.

That Sunday evening, hundreds of people were in the cemetery and as I was looking around, I saw a face I knew, a face that had lived with me since I was four years old. There was a man there at the burial ceremony who looked just like the ghost I had seen when I was a boy. I immediately went to my father and said, "*Baudon*, do you remember when we were living in John's Hall District, when I told you I had seen a ghost in the house?"

"Yes," he replied I then said, "Do you see that man standing over there? He looks just like the ghost."

My father looked at me and said, "That's his son."

With my cousin Warren (right), at the cemetery,
the day we dug a grave for my Granny

After the funeral, my father and I made plans to remodel the old board house into a concrete structure. However, earning the money to make such an improvement was a responsibility that rested on my shoulders and it was constantly on my mind while spending the final days with Tamoya and Salenas. I would then return to United States carrying that prideful burden, as I usually did.

When I returned to America and arrived at Logan International Airport, my wife and daughter were there waiting for me. This time when I walked out of the airport, I wouldn't have to worry about where I was going because our pretty black truck was parked there waiting to take me to our apartment in Dennis Port. After I got home, I hooked up the video camera to the television and showed my wife some of what had happened on my trip. Whether or not she had found any of the footage to be interesting, I didn't know but later that night, I noticed some changes in her behavior and soon realized she had found new friends while I was away.

It was now March of 1999 and time for me to reapply at the hotel, this time to be a waiter. I was expecting to be making more money and was looking forward to having a good summer.

As time went on I noticed my wife started spending more time with her friends than with me. I asked about them and what was going on. That led us to start arguing. She would always take the baby with her and I didn't like it. If she'd gone by herself, it wouldn't have hurt so bad; I would still have my baby to play with but she never saw it that way.

Some nights, I would go to bed with her not being home. That was when the respect for each other started fading away. This continued until one night after I'd come home and was sitting in the living hall, watching television. She showed up by herself at about eleven-thirty. I asked about Samantha. "She's with my friend!" she answered. For a brief moment, she stood there looking at me, then started crying. In tears, she told me I had to go and that we weren't together anymore.

"Here's the car key and I will keep the truck!" she said. I tried dearly to talk her out of it, but she wouldn't change her mind. I had to move out in two days.

The following day, I packed my bags and without even saying goodbye to Samantha, I went out the door with nowhere to live. This change of life instantly presented a very hard time for me; nonetheless, an awaiting Good Samaritan was kind enough to offer me his bed on nights when he would sleep at his girlfriend's. When his bed wasn't available, I would spend those hard nights in the town of Chatham, park by the bushes and tried to fall asleep in a small car. However, mankind's body shall also shrink to his situation when life takes us on bumpy roads. This went on until I moved in with a few friends in the town of Brewster but it was only for a few days until I found a motel room in Harwich. The rent was seven hundred dollars a month; this was added to the responsibilities of my wife's apartment, Samantha and also my two kids back home. I couldn't do it by myself, so I had to get a roommate to cut the rent in half.

During that period, I would call my wife day and night, trying to talk the situation over but she wouldn't answer the phone. She only did only about once or twice a week. I would have to beg to see my child and whenever that happened, I tried to talk her into getting back together but the word "yes" would never came out of her mouth. As a man, I accepted the situation, knowing that what happened was a part of life. Remaining focused on my job and taking care of my responsibilities was all what mattered now.

Over two months had passed since Terry and I had separated. It was looking more like there wasn't any chance of us getting back together, since she was about to go and live with one of the friends she'd chosen over me.

Before leaving, she asked me to take the truck and buy her a new car; I couldn't afford a new one, but I did get her a used car.

I called the company immediately after she handed me the truck key and was told that there hadn't been any payments made over the previous two months and the insurance policy was also about to be cancelled. I quickly paid off the past dues as life took me forward.

Terry gave the apartment up to one of her friends and moved with Samantha to the Boston area. It hurt me very badly and I would often share conversations about what I was going through with my roommate. He was a native Jamaican who resided in Florida but was in Cape Cod working for the summer. He always gave me good advice, as mankind experiences similar obstacles in life, just at different times.

He was telling me about a resort in Florida where he worked and encouraged me to apply for a job there. I could make good money, he told me. It was definitely something to think about since the winter of 1999 and 2000 was approaching. If I stayed on Cape Cod, my expenses would be more than I could earn; in the end I took my friend's advice. I applied for the job in Florida and was hired.

With very little experience on the highways, in a few weeks I would be off to take up the challenge of driving from Cape Cod to Key Largo, Florida, then visit my family in Jamaica before I started working.

I spoke with my parents and some family members about what the main purpose of the trip home was. I wasn't blind to either the poor circumstances left behind, or them. The conversation was about starting a small business, to be operated by some of the family members. We all agreed upon the ideas, so I started shopping around New England for cheap clothes and shoes. When I'd bought enough, it was time to begin the drive to Florida.

Three of us were taking the trip all in separate cars. Before we left, I made sure to take my friend's address and phone number in Florida, since he was leading the way. I also wrote down the route we would be traveling on to get there. Anything could happen and I wasn't yet an experienced driver.

At about five-thirty on a Friday evening in November, we drove out of Harwich, with my truck loaded with all that I had to my name. We left the chilly Cape Cod wind behind as we headed out to a warmer region in America.

My friend and the other guy took the lead and I followed. At about 8:30 p.m., they exited the highway. I didn't knew they were turning and wasn't prepared, so I had to continue driving, knowing that Route 95 South was the line on the map, in case we didn't see each other again. I was the only one carrying a cell phone and one of the others had my number, so I could only hope he would call. With or without them, however, I was driving to Florida. Now it was just a sense of nerve and not panicking.

Entering the state of New Jersey, I was low on gas. I exited into a service station to fill up the tank. I mentioned to the attendant where I was going and asked if I was on the right route. He confirmed that I was okay and again I fastened my seat belt and got back on the highway. As I settled into my lane, I called a friend in Florida, who has driven that route many times; he told me to call him if I have any problems and to just stay focused. "Okay, man, no problem."

At about eleven-thirty, my cell phone rang. It was my driving partners calling from a payphone, wanting to know where on the road I was. When I described some of the places that I'd passed and some signs that lights up in the distance, they realized I was far ahead of them. Since we should be a team, I stopped by the road and waited for them. When they caught up, we drove until about 2:00 a.m. before stopping at a rest area in Baltimore, where we slept for a few hours in our cars.

By 6:00 a.m. Saturday morning, we were back on the road; we drove all day until about 10:30 p.m. We made another stop in Florida, slept in our cars until about 2:30 a.m., then started driving again. Our next stop was in Fort Lauderdale, Florida, at my friend's apartment. We arrived at about five-thirty on Sunday morning.

Coming off a long journey tired and dirty, I took a shower and slept for a few hours on their sofa. Later that day, I called my family in Jamaica to tell them I was in Florida and would be coming home later that week. Then the following day, I drove to the resort in Key Largo, completed my paperwork, mainly to secure my living accommodations with them; it was very important. Later that week, on November 17, 1999, I went to Jamaica.

After arriving at home that evening, I talked about the tough times I was going through with my immediate family; they showed their sympathy. At the same time, I was encouraging them to start advertising the merchandise for sale right away. We soon were doing well selling the clothing. Meanwhile, I was looking for a car and when I found one, my brother Tony and I purchased it together and immediately put it on the road for taxi service, with the agreement that Mother would save my half of the money while I was away.

The thirteen days spent home with my family were very relaxing. The vacation took a lot of things off my mind; I had the best of time with my kids. And most of all, I made Mother and Father proud to have a car parked at their gate, owned by our household, for the first time in our lives as a family. I returned to Miami on November 30 and started working immediately.

In the bar at the restaurant where I started
working in Key Largo, Florida, in 1999

It didn't take long to fit into the pace of the restaurant; when I did, I held my own as a strong worker. I was making pretty good money to cover my bills. I also found a second job at another hotel, serving breakfast. The extra income would allow me to save a little.

I would still call my wife at least once each week to make sure my daughter was fine. In late December of that same year, I received a phone call from her, she was crying; I asked what was wrong. She said the man she had been living with wanted her out of his house and she had nowhere to live with Samantha. I couldn't let that happen; I was still a father and a husband. Immediately I started looking around for an apartment in Florida. I found one in the town of Homestead, then sent her some money to purchase a bus ticket and come to Florida so that we would be back together as a family.

When they arrived, I didn't have any furniture, not even a bed. However, I did tell one of my friends ahead of time and asked if we could spend the night at his place. This was all right with him and the following day we started looking around for furniture; we found a few pieces and moved into our apartment later that day.

As we got settled in, we started talking about the things that had happened between us and tried to put the past behind. After a few weeks, when she got used to the complex and started meeting new people, mainly my friend's wife, we started experiencing some of the same problems we'd had in the past. The two women became so close that in a short time, my wife started spending night after night at her new friend's place with my baby. The other apartment was so close that I could look at it from my mine.

From my apartment (left), I could see into my
friend's place, across the driveway (right)

Despite all the time my wife spent with her friend, I never went over there to bother her. Sometimes late at night, I would go out on the verandah to look across the way, hoping in my heart to see her walking out with my baby to come home but that never happened. I would just go back to bed feeling lonely and thinking of what the following day would bring.

My household situation wasn't getting any better and meanwhile in Jamaica, things weren't going the way that we'd planned it to be. My family's efforts weren't good enough to make the business succeed. Some thought that since I was in America, I didn't need anything. Phone calls to the family weren't making me happy anymore but the love for them was still there.

The year of 2000 was moving along slowly, as domestic problems took hold of my life. It was becoming too much to bear, so on May 4, I took a break for three days and went to Jamaica to visit my kids and family. My arrival this time was different from previous. I was going to see a family who failed me by not carrying out our plans; they had, I believed, failed themselves on the road to success. There wasn't any money in the bank from the merchandise sold nor from the car that was put on the road to be operated as a taxi.

After the visit, on my way back to the airport, I rolled the car window down letting the fresh Jamaican wind blow over me, as my confused mind headed back to America. It was so confused in fact that when I arrived at the airport, the plane had already gone and I was scheduled to work at four-thirty that afternoon. *What to do now, Glenroy?* I asked the lady at the desk about other flights to Miami that might get me there in time for work. She replied that the only other one was leaving at 5:30 p.m. and the only available seats were first class. The second-class ticket I was carrying wasn't transferable and over five hundred dollars more was needed for the first-class ticket. Luckily I had my debit card and made the purchase from it. This gave me a chance to experience flying in first class and it was much different from the rest of my flying experience.

As soon as I arrived in Miami, I called my workplace to let them know why I hadn't shown up on time. It was no problem with my boss because he knew that when I am there, my presence was felt. From there, I took a taxi to Homestead.

I got home and sat on the verandah for over an hour. I didn't have my key and my wife wasn't home. As she arrived from the passenger seat of her friend's car, we started arguing, even louder than usual. After that evening, I made myself a more humble man at home but at work I was questioning lots of people about working opportunities they may know of across the country. I had to leave Florida. Life's journey had taken me into a place where temptation overcame love and the only enjoyment left then were my days spent with Samantha; I cooked, fed, and took good care of her. I even remember the exact spot by the front door where we used to spread a blanket every day and after lunch, Samantha and I would lie there until her mother got home.

With my daughter, Samantha at home in Florida, May 2000

As the pressure at home got tougher, things at work got better. I was told of a hotel in upstate New York; I immediately applied for a job over the phone and was hired. Now life was forcing me away from home but I couldn't leave my wife without a car and I had no money to purchase another. Nonetheless, a road that is blessed is a journey to continue. Such journey shall periodically bring forth frights; none more so than the accident I had one evening.

As I entered my place of work, a golf cart came crashing into the passenger side of my truck. (The door still has the dent.) Her insurance company paid enough for the damage; I added another fifty dollars and was able to purchase Terry a Ford Taurus. Once we licensed and insured it, I started packing. Then one morning in July I loaded my truck, leaving only one Nike sweatshirt hanging in a closet, before driving away. I kissed my baby Samantha goodbye, then bid her mother farewell with a sad feeling in my heart. Whatever happened from there on, I would deal with it, but I would surely take care of my daughter and help in any other way I could, no matter what.

I reached the hotel in New York about five-thirty the following afternoon and started working the next day.

In the dining room of the hotel in upstate New York where I started working in July 2000

Lying in bed the first night in upstate New York, I reflected on the times my wife and I had spent together and what the love had melted down to. The shelter which once covered our heads, true love, now turned to sins and had become a dwelling place for those who hate. I didn't have any control over what had happened; I had tried hard! I even took her to counseling but her friends' voices were more important to her than the counselor's advice. Still, life goes on.

The employee housing at the hotel was very accommodating. I had my own room with cable TV and could watch my favorite programs when I wasn't working, mainly *Comic View*. The money was also good. It was enough to pay my high bills but wasn't enough to save a dollar. However, I could provide for my children, a value more than saving.

As the end of the fall season approached, my next decision was whether or not to work at the hotel year-round or go to a winter resort in another state where I could make more money. While sharing conversations, two Jamaican guys who had been working for the company before I got there were encouraging me to stay, so I took their advice and stuck around.

The author in upstate New York, in the winter of 2000-2001

That winter in the Catskill Mountains was the coldest I'd ever experienced but I tried to stay inside and keep warm. As the New Year of 2001 approached, I started telling myself that I couldn't continue to work and live from hand to mouth. The bills were very high and I was willing to work much harder if the jobs were available, in order to save money.

In March of the new year, I sat with one of my best friends, talking to him about the life that was facing me; I mentioned that I was thinking of going back to beautiful Cape Cod, the place I knew best.

The same night after our conversation, I signed on to my computer and started checking out hotels where I could work and make the most money. I downloaded an application from one and submitted it the same night. The following day, I called to find out if they were accepting summer applications for servers in the dining room. They said, "Yes," and I told the person that I had submitted an application the night before. He told me to call him back in a few weeks and I couldn't wait for the month of March to go by, including my twenty-eighth birthday, so I could call him and get a positive answer to start packing my things.

As soon as April came around, my clothes went into my bags and one day in that same month, I packed my truck and bid my friends goodbye. I then drove onto Route 87 North, to Route 90 East, to 495 South, on to Route 6 East. I exited Route 6 at exit 11, at 11:00 a.m., and drove straight to the hotel where I was going to work; I was back on Cape Cod.

The hotel provided me with housing, a motel room which I was to share with another employee. I moved in the same day and started training the following morning. At the end of the breakfast shift, the dining room manager put my name on the tip sheet to be paid as an assistant server instead of getting the hourly training pay. I guess they did love what they saw. By the time my training was over, I was already recognized as a good worker and I was only going to get better.

As the summer moved on, the working hours became very long, but it was important to work hard so I could do what I needed to. With what I earned, I could now go ahead with the plan my father and I had made to change the old board house into a concrete structure. I sent my parents some money and my father added what he had to it and start building. I was very happy to know that soon my parents would be living in a nice house and when I went to visit them, I could sleep in it with pride.

By the end of the season, I'd achieved the goals I'd set when returning to Cape Cod. I did save some money and decided to keep the job seasonal. I told that to my boss, then went back to Florida to work for the winter season where I had worked before. I did this to be closer to Samantha but would be living in the hotel housing.

I drove back to Florida in late November, worked for a while, then went to Jamaica to spend the Christmas holiday with my family and friends. I had a wonderful time celebrating it in the traditional way, by playing music and dominoes all day Christmas. We killed a goat to make curry and also mannish water *(which is a delicious soup made from the head and tripe of the goat)*. It was very special for me because it was my first Christmas with them in five years.

I flew back to Miami two days after Christmas and started working immediately. The property was still the same but in the restaurant, things had changed a lot. New managers with different mind-sets had taken over. They divided workstations in the dining room differently and not equally and because I wasn't one of their favorites, I wasn't making much money. If I had settled for that kind of treatment, it was going to affect my kids but I was determined that they should never suffer as long as I am alive, free and strong. I didn't even bother to stay there through the winter season; I just coped with the situation until February 22, 2002. I then went back to Jamaica to spend time with my kids, with the intention of going back to Cape Cod for the summer and working at the same resort where I had been the previous year.

When I went back home, I bought a car to drive around and spent over six weeks with my kids. I took them to school and many different places. I was also helping them with their school assignments and reading stories to them before they fell asleep at night.

Tamoya (right) and Salenas in their uniforms, ready to go to school

I had a wonderful time with my kids; I flew back to Miami on April 10, drove straight to Cape Cod and started working three days later at the same resort. My hopes were very high at the beginning of the season because the previous one had gone so well. However, one afternoon in May, three weeks after I started working, an act of cruelty was perpetrated on me by someone in the kitchen. I went to the emergency room at the Cape Cod Hospital for medical treatment and when I returned to work the following day, I was fired for my honesty.

The deed took place on May 9, 2002. I went to work that evening, and I was offered something to eat by one of the cooks who wasn't of my color or race. I accepted the offer because there shouldn't be any borderlines between mankind, as to whom we can accept food from or associate with. We are all one people and we should live that way. Such wasn't the reality in the kitchen that evening. When I started eating and took a few bites, I realized that my body was consuming something that wasn't prescribed for human consumption. The managers in charge did not even give themselves a chance to hear my side of the story, so I was terminated the following day.

I went through the rest of the summer unemployed, then went back to New York to work for the winter season, heading into 2003. During that winter, I thought about the many things that had happened in my life for the past three years or so. The bills were still up to my neck and I was still the only one my family could stretch their hands to in times of need. This I discussed with one of my old-time friends who was still working there; I also talked to him about taking another chance with my family and starting another business to help their situation. He liked the plan, which was to get back into selling clothes and shoes. But this time, I wanted to do it in a more official way.

I called my family soon after and talked to them about it. I even selected who I wanted to be in charge when I was away. This was fine with everyone who would be involved. After talking with my family, I started shopping around for cheap merchandise. I spent most of the winter doing that and when I was done with the shopping, my next step was to secure a job in Cape Cod for the upcoming summer season. I made some phone calls to different hotels and when I found a position, I packed all my stuff and shipped it down to Jamaica. A few days later on March 6, 2003, my thirtieth birthday, on a cold, snowy winter morning, I drove down from the Catskill Mountains, on through the small town of New Paltz, then picked up the highway and I was on my way back to Florida once more, intending to board a plane to Jamaica.

The drive that morning did not last for long. As I entered Route 84 West in Newburgh, I drove into a huge snowstorm that lasted the entire day. I parked my truck in front of a gas station and sat in it until about five that evening; with no change in the weather, I checked into a motel. The road was too icy for me to drive and my truck didn't have four-wheel drive. I celebrated my birthday watching the snow fall and then spent the night in a motel room by myself with two big beds. I occupied one, with a six-pack of Budweiser beside me and I drank four of them before falling asleep.

The next morning, at about five-thirty, I started driving again—very slowly at first since there was still a lot of ice on the road. I had to be careful because life is too valuable to be driving fast under bad conditions. Further south, the weather improved and so did the speedometer needle.

By 10:30 a.m., I was cruising through Virginia, admiring the great landscapes of America and listening to a radio broadcast of a testimony from the inspectors who were in Iraq searching for weapons of mass destruction. By midday, I was deep into the Carolinas, driving across bridges that carried the names of men who had fought bravely and in their own belief, for this great land of America. At eight-thirty that night, I was entering Georgia. I drove until about 10:00 p.m., then stopped for the night in a motel close to the Florida border. Early the next morning, I started driving again and before midday, I arrived in Homestead, at the apartment of some friends. I spent the day with them and flew to Jamaica the following day to spend five weeks with my family.

I was very busy on my vacation; this time getting things together. When everything was in place, we opened a shoe and clothing store close to the center of Port Antonio town. It looked as good as any other stores in town. I felt good about it and so did my family.

I had two nephews whom I kept a very good relationship with, Duwane and another I nicknamed "Dave," who is the son of my sister who is to remain unnamed in this life journey.

Over the years, I watched them grow up into adults and they left school with the same level of education as most of my family members did. With no economic growth and no hopes of prosperity in Jamaica, without proper leadership, their level of education could not provide them a means of living to make their family hold their heads up higher. Knowing the struggles I had been through at their age, I purchased another car to use as a taxi service, which Dave was going to be driving. My other car that I'd bought on the previous trip home, Duwane would have, using it for taxi service also. With the cars and the store, we were all excited and looking forward to great things.

This type of business is very common in Jamaica; over the years of living there, I saw many people make a good living from it and elevating themselves to a better standard of life. That was something my family and I talked about in the process of putting the business together. We agreed upon the amount of money that each of the nephews should take home from the cars and give to my sister Davine. All that was supposed to happen when I was gone was laid out for those who were in charge and the rules were supposed to be followed. When everything was in place, I packed my bags once more and departed Jamaica on April 15, 2003, to continue my journey that lay ahead. Nonetheless, I was about to face the fact that when the shepherd is away, the sheep go astray. My family's hope and effort to let the business thrive would only last until I was gone.

Chapter Eleven

Family Betrayal

As a little boy growing up in Jamaica, I remember seeing people leaving the island for foreign countries and then their parents and family members would continue living in the same circumstances in front of my eyes. I would often wonder why they were away in a better country and couldn't help their family needs. I never understood the reasons for this. However, sometimes I would hear my parents and big sisters gossiping about a neighbor's business. My young mind had an idea of what they were talking about but it wasn't mature enough to face the reality of what it can feel like to ignore your family. It's a feeling that a kid with a healthy mind doesn't want to experience. But in life, only time can tell what will happen next and it took me thirty years to experience that bitter, deeply painful feeling.

When I landed in Miami, I drove back to Cape Cod and started working at a hotel in Brewster. On the first day, when I was introduced to the food and beverage director. Surprisingly enough, he wasn't a stranger (but his mind-set was). He was the same man who had terminated me from the other hotel where I was working the previous year. It was nerve wracking to shake his hand but I could look in his eyes, just concerned about what working with him this time was going to like. However, I was there to work hard and in life, if you try to be on the right side at all times, then you can face your worst enemy with confidence. That gave me the strength to work comfortably around him.

In the early weeks after returning from Jamaica, I would call my family regularly to find out if things were going well with the business. Already the news wasn't good but my confidence that it would work was telling my mind that blood is thicker than water and that businesses needed time to grow. Before I'd even sent another shipment, the phone calls started to make me sad. Almost every day, a different family member would call to tell me about what others were doing but never blamed themselves. One of the cars was having mechanical problems before I left and was about to be taken off the road because of people doing what they wanted to do with it and not what we had planned. The other car, which was a very good one, was making lots of money but Dave, who was operating it, wasn't taking the money to Davine to save. His concern was only for himself and those who were behind him in his doings.

I called Dave one day to talk about the arrangement we'd made before I left Jamaica. He told me he wasn't making any money, trying to fool me, saying that every other taxi drivers were but he wasn't. I told him if he didn't stick to our plan and take the money to Davine, he would have to stop driving the car. He said he would do better.

Around then, I started to feel the pressure of being on the losing side again but I tried not to let it affect my job. My blood pressure was rising, high enough to start affecting my driving ability and every time I called home, it would go up more and more. It reached its peak one evening when I called my daughters and little Tamoya asked me if my nephew Dave was still driving my white car. I told her, "Yes," and she said, "Daddy! Today when I got out of school, I was waiting for a taxi to take me home. I saw the car coming, stepped out onto the road to stop it and he didn't pick me up." She would later say to her mother, "Imagine, my father has two cars on the road and I couldn't even drive in one of them." It hurt me a lot and I would express that hurt to Dave the next day when I called him.

After talking to Dave his mother offered to buy the car and I said no, I later called my parents and talked to them about the situation. I remembered her voice as a little girl growing up, when we slept together on the same floor as poor sisters and brothers but couldn't remember the mind that those words were coming from. Had it been so corrupted from then? I thought about it all night and by the following morning, I just decided to put everything behind me and move on with my life.

I called my parents later that day and explained my conclusions to them, as to where we now stood as a family. I also talked to everyone involved in running the store and told them to close it down when they wanted to and do whatever they wanted with everything that was in it. While there is life, there is hope. I then hung up the phone. I thought about it from time to time but whenever sad feelings appear, I always found someone to talk to who could cheer up the mood a bit; a little encouragement always helped.

As the summer of 2003 was boiling down, I had barely saved any money but my kids were all right. I was fighting back from the loss of everything, both my family and my money. This I would have to deal with for the rest of my life. However, there is always a part of our heart that offers forgiveness and only life can lead us into forgiving.

The upcoming winter of 2003 and 2004 brought forth more important things to think about. One, I was turning thirty-one years old and needed to be settled in one location. In order to make Cape Cod that location, I would need a suitable second job since the one in Brewster was seasonal. I found one at a boatyard in Chatham, cleaning, waxing and painting boats.

Working at the boatyard

With the help of one of my cousins, I found a year-round apartment in West Harwich, which I shared with one of my friends to cut the cost in half. As time went on, family members would still call to mention something about the business but I wasn't interested anymore, so the conversations would be cut short.

By February of the new year, my main focus was on the upcoming summer with the intention to stop working at the hotel in Brewster and find a job at a local restaurant. By April, that had happened; however, that wasn't the only good thing that took place in the month of April. I also filed an application with the immigration office to become a United States citizen. I had been living here for almost seven years and knew it would bring joy to my heart to become a citizen of this great country. It would allow me to take my kids on the road that I had been paving for them while I was physically away. (I wanted to give them the benefit of a good education that can never decay.)

The future plan I had for my children is the same dream I have for every other around the world. I would say to them, "You are all champions, no matter where on earth you are or what kind of life faces you. Work hard at your education in order to succeed. Raise your trophies and show that you are all winners but let those trophies be the great marks on your examination papers. Education is the key. If you obtain it, you will have an easier walk through life and there will always be a better world out there awaiting you."

It had been over a year since I'd last spoken to my parents and family, except for two of my sisters, Davine and Judy. I never got back the feeling to call anyone else and I still didn't know when that feeling will come back.

I approached the summer season of 2004 thinking of what I wanted to achieve. My major concern was still my children; I'd been missing them every day, just as I knew they missed me. Tamoya was almost ten years old and she needed a father in her life for more than just financial support and occasional visits. It hurt that I could not be around her on a daily basis to help correct her mistakes, to show her love as a father and to answer some of the basic questions little girls ask when growing toward maturity.

Talking to her mother on September 9, 2004, when Hurricane Ivan threatened to strike my homeland of Jamaica, she told me Tamoya was excited and wanted to experience the hurricane, having no idea how dangerous the winds can be. I could only laugh, remembering how I felt the same way when I was a boy in 1988 and Hurricane Gilbert struck Jamaica.

The nation, however, did make a speedy recovery because of good leadership in our cabinet. On September 11, 2004, the last call I made to Jamaica was at about 3:00 p.m. My kids and all whom I asked for were safe. Nonetheless, I could see the result from the storm on television here in the States; Jamaica had been hit by Hurricane Ivan, and the recovery wasn't going to be easy, as the country was facing huge economical difficulties. I could only hope that those who could help would extend their hands to those in need.

Aftermath of Hurricane Ivan, which struck on September
11, 2004, causing the deaths of eighteen people

After the disaster, I thought I could no longer see myself living
away from my children. In that same time, those thoughts continued
to strengthen my will of responsibilities, with strong hopes of getting
to a comfortable place in life, where my road wouldn't be rocky
anymore and where my dream of stopping looking at myself in
pictures with my children and start living with them again would
become a reality. Then they could share the love of their father that
had been missing for so long. "Tamoya, Salenas and Samantha," "I will
always love you and we will be together soon."

Top right: Daughters Tamoya and Salenas celebrating their birthday in 2003; Top left: Daughter Samantha at two years old; Center right: On vacation in Jamaica, playing with my daughters and my niece and nephew, Paul and Tashana; Bottom left: Tamoya and Salenas at Salenas's graduation in 2003; Bottom right: Samantha as a baby eating a meal

Chapter Twelve

The Fulfillment

The promises that were made to me through the strong encounter of the 14 and of the 17, to the anointment from Jerky, who renewed my future, the mental toughness taught to me by my parents, grandparents and the many different people from around the world whom I have encountered and shared rich stories of each other's pasts and our hopes for the future. Over the years, many topics were discussed and many answers were given. For me, they all summed up life's values for which we live. Those values of believing we all can achieve were forming building blocks in my head, which was about to lay a new foundation in life. If the base is solid, the building will be stronger—that strength I applied to my mental thoughts in moving ahead for the calendar year of 2005.

My two daughters arrived in the USA on May 16, 2005. It brought great joy to my heart when I picked them up at the Logan International Airport in Boston. It was the fulfillment of a promise I made to myself from the day I chose the USA as my home, that someday my children would become United States citizens and grow up in a safe environment. Joyful it was for me and a huge change for them to come into their new country and to adopt the principles of this great land.

It was the reality of a dream to awaken in the same house with my children and watch them go off to school. However, the words of wisdom from my father to me as a boy growing up were echoing in my head: "Glen! Every man's pride in life is to own his own home and so you must when you grow up!"

The first Thursday night my daughters and I spent together in a long time, I sat in their room telling them stories of my past. They loved to hear them and of course, other stories that kids at their age enjoy listening to. I bit my lips at one point, without leaving any evidence for them to see, when the subject had changed from fun-loving stories to the reality of life, which was facing us as a family.

The apartment was way too small for us and before their young minds could get confused about our living conditions, I made our current situation clear to them and told that it was just a part of life's struggles but that they should just cooperate with me for a while and take up a little responsibility too, like just keeping their room clean. They laughed and before kissing them good night, I made them a promise that in six months, we would own our own home.

That promise come to pass on November 17, 2005. I purchased my first home in America. Watching the kids running around was a fun feeling and brought a pride every father should share. We would play games, mainly badminton with both of them teamed up against me and most times, I would let them win. The biggest win, however, was the value in what a father and his daughters were doing, playing together— those are always great memories for a child and a great part of life's legacy that we take into adulthood with us.

Friends and family commended me on buying a home, which gave a great feeling. The joy of it all, however, was that I had just taken another step up life's ladder and as a believer in the faith of Jacob, I know I will claim another.

Despite the recession our country was heading into, I never thought of the negatives or looked back; as a nation we strive together in good times and in bad times. A different economical standard meant different thoughts. My mind then immediately reflected on what John F. Kennedy said. I quote: "Ask not what your country can do for you—ask what you can do for your country." To represent those strong words of wisdom, I set out to pursue a career as a marine technician with the same company I was working for. When I told the boss man I would like to become a technician, he didn't hesitate to give me the promotion. By his response, I guess he was watching my attitude over the past few months. I was spending a lot of time in the mechanic shop. First I started sweeping the floor every day, which was my smart excuse to be over there and to watch and talk to the head mechanic about the trade. Gradually I became his assistant and we started working together.

As days of working with Rog went on, I realized that he wasn't just a great technician or a great teacher, but a genuine man and would later become a father figure to me. We made a good team immediately and on those days, we would share conversation about our pasts. He and I had a lot in common; some of those similarities would come out in conversations we had on our spare time at work. His childhood days growing up on Chestnut Street in Philadelphia take me back to my childhood in Jamaica.

Rog and I would talk about life in depth, some topics on economics, some on law, governmental issues and of course, the attitude of some leaders who put themselves in front of citizens to whom they govern. With my brain motivated by a past president's speech, this created a clear pathway which became the road I drove on. Six months later, I was enrolled at a New Hampshire Technical College to cover a course in being a marine technician through Mercury University. The course was rather challenging but dedication overcomes the challenges, which makes it fruitful; the fruits my family and I would digest in the months and years to come. In June of 2007, I received my certificate from Mercury University, another piece of paper posted on my wall of life to represent me in the fields of work.

The visions of mankind are all for nothing if we can't turn them into dreams and then dreams into reality; all of mine were adding up, and the calling to fulfill them was knocking on the higher steps of life's ladder. As sweet as being a marine technician was, it still wasn't sweet enough to shadow the memories of the conversation had with my mother, when I was eleven years old. Neither could it shadow the promises made to myself, of owning my own restaurant, when I started food and nutrition in high school. Those dreams were about to be fulfilled and the reality of them has now come to pass.

In March of 2008 my friend Rog was driving on the main street of Route 28. He spotted a place for rent and as he arrived at the boatyard, we started talking. He urgently said to me and I quote: "You know what, Shrimps! I saw a place down the street for rent and I think it's a restaurant."

"I will check it out later," I replied.

That evening when I got out of work, I drove to see the place he was talking about—indeed it was a vacant restaurant. I applied for it immediately but my application was denied in favor of a person who wants to use it for a flower shop. Nevertheless, I never took my eyes off of that spot and three months later, it was up for rent again. I reapplied, and this time my application was accepted.

I went to bed that night under deep meditation, thinking of my next step in the United States of America. Before my eyes were closed and my head lay to rest, I could not shy away from what had gotten me to this stage in life. From the mental toughness of the past that structured the will of my body to move forward; the words and miracles of Jerky in front of my eyes, the encouragement from Rog, who always believed I could become whatever I wanted to; all those values that I'd carried were my agenda which became a stepping stone that conquered negative thoughts as I moved forward to fulfill another one of my dreams.

On August 18, 2008, the Jerk Café was born on Cape Cod, Massachusetts, USA. At about 7:00 a.m., a prideful Chef Shrimpy turned on the lights and opened for business. As fast as the lights beamed on was as fast as my mind reflected on some great words of wisdom I'd learned in eighth grade from my teacher Mrs. Hanson: "Only the best is good enough." The reality of those words took effect on the first cup of coffee served and has become one of our motto, as our eyes bore witness to what was to come occupying that spot.

Business is challenging: the long days standing, the late nights going to bed, thinking of what I could do to make the following day better. We all know! Businessmen always think of making more money and that's absolutely right—it's job creation, which means economic growth and prosperity for any nation. The answer, however, were the values of my mother. Those silent words of wisdom she use to utter, meant a lot to business principles. She used to say, "Never watch the noise of the market but the end-of-day sale. One on one penny, fill a bucket." Which means never listen to the critics or the finger pointing or who thinks you can't do it. Smile with that one penny you save each day and that bucket will automatically be full. However, your responsibility is to grow that penny into more and more.

As time went on, in the early weeks of running the business, I realized that there's no getting rich quick in business and the challenges of maintaining my pride as an American entrepreneur would take a lot more effort. I learned this after seeing the people who were supposed to be my partners in crime start losing effort, backed by a negative mindset that business should be better already. This attitude continued until one night when I went home and was told that I was on my own with the business.

Listening to these voices made me start thinking of how I was going to do it, especially with the mere fact that I could not afford to hire anyone as yet. I was left to meditate. The journey has gotten to a crossroad. To be challenged by the foundation of mental toughness, fundamentally sunk into the brain already, automatically made me stronger and ready for the next day by myself.

Many things happen for a reason, or what the elders usually said, mainly Mother. That next morning at work, it proved even more truthful. My restaurant has an open kitchen: the dining room and cooking area are separated only by a counter which hosts the cash register, a working cooler and a steam table. This convenience gave me the leverage to greet the customers, cook their food, run the cash register and do my dishes at the appropriate time. Indeed it was challenging, but a man's strength and stamina has no boundaries. The result of positivity will never stay silent or be blinded. Multitudes will follow in his footsteps, such effort out of man, will stand firm for generations to come.

Day by day, the revenue was climbing, which made the mind more comfortable and freed up spaces in the brain to hold more thoughts. Around that same time, a longtime friend of mine came by; without me saying anything to him, he already acknowledged my situation and offered to join me in brotherhood. I accepted his generosity and so he started working with me a few hours per day.

When he first started, everything was fine until he found out I was desperate in one sense: the lack of help and communication from my immediate family. It wasn't long after he discovered it that he started playing his games too. He used to come to work at 7:00 a.m., then all of a sudden, he started showing up at 8:00 a.m. That went on for a while until some days I wouldn't even see him and when I did, it wasn't only him by himself, it was him and a bag of stories which made no sense. After listening to him a few times, I had no choice but to show leadership on my side. I read him his rights one day and that was the end of him at the Jerk Café. Immediately after he left, I stopped serving breakfast and stuck to lunch and dinner.

By late September, the *Cape Cod Times* newspaper came to the restaurant to do a story on my cuisine and background. The article was a success for the restaurant; nonetheless, the attention of the press wasn't over. By December of 2008, another company did a YouTube video, which was also shown on the local TV channel in South Yarmouth. This video made my restaurant very popular and is still online at *thejerkcafe.com* with thousands of viewers.

As the early months of 2009 came around, I was getting more comfortable in the business and many thoughts started going through my mind, mainly the days I spent in food service and management class in Jamaica. I started remembering the lecturing of a former teacher; many of his teachings had nothing to do with the curriculum he was following. Rather, it was his own practical knowledge that he was handing down to whom could receive. (It was enough to make a human better, as I live through life's experience).

One day in class, my teacher had been telling us about the many dishes that existed, which mankind adapted as part of their menus in whatever cooking establishment they represented; in today's world and that of yesterday, how did they come about? Around the same time those thoughts hit, I also remembered the Friday night in the kitchen on Navy Island, when my saver found me. He taught me then how to make Jamaican jerk sauce and it was time to make the promise I made to him become a reality.

From the morning I opened my restaurant, in the back of my head, I already knew it was time to establish my jerk sauce. Listening to the daily comments from the little cup that accompanied each meal served was encouraging. The taste, flavor and consistency left the customers taste buds wanting more. With the growth of my clientele, I sent my jerk sauce out to a university in New York state to begin the process which would culminate in my being able to market it.

Around that same time, we attracted the attention of the local media again. We were approached by *Cape Cod Magazine*, which wanted to do an article on the restaurant.

A few months later, the jerk sauce research process was successfully completed. I then approached a nutritionist in the state of Vermont, and in July of 2011, the promise through Jerky that I made to myself had come to pass. However, labeling and designing work needed to be done and that could never have happened without the help and support of a beautiful young intern from Russia.

It was on May 20, 2011. I was in the restaurant preparing for lunch when I saw three people walking by; they stopped, open the door and asked if I served breakfast. "No!" I replied. But they were still interested in having something from the lunch menu. I highly recommended to them my signature jerk pork and jerk chicken. The young lady wearing the green blouse ordered the pork with a beautiful smile on her face. While they were eating, she asked, "Are you hiring?"

"What position are you guys interested in?" I gave them applications and they filled them out right there. Without bias, I asked, "Who wants to start working tonight?"

"I want to," the one in the green blouse said.

"Okay, come to work at five p.m."

Around that time of the evening, I was doing my usual routine, getting ready for my evening customers. When I looked through the glass, I acknowledged her coming from across the street. She had the figure of a model; her legs curved the way a man likes to see them, with a stride to back it up and her beautiful long hair flowed behind her. She was breathtaking from first sight and for the rest of the summer, every step I took, she was beside me. Through the values she brought to my company, all my labeling and designing work was accomplished and in July of 2011, Chef Shrimpy's Jerk Sauce was in bottles with proper labeling to sell across the world.

Chef Shrimpy's Jerk Sauce

A unique concoction that makes every meal taste better

It's not the heat, it's the flavor!

Our jerk chicken meal served at the Jerk Café daily

Our jerk pork meal served at the Jerk Café daily

A tip from Chef Shrimpy to your home

Method of Preparation

Use three teaspoons of Chef Shrimpy's Jerk Sauce per 1 lb. (453 g) of fully thawed pork or chicken, massage thoroughly into the meat.

Marinate for at least half an hour, then cook to your method
of liking, on the barbecue grill, the stovetop, or in the oven,

For pork on the grill, you'll want to cook
it for at least forty-five minutes

And for chicken, at least thirty minutes.

Of course, that depends on how high the flame is.

For Chef Shrimpy, once the golden brown color I look for is
achieved, I turn the grill down low for it to cook slowly.

Your end result should be chicken and pork with
a tender and juicy taste of a lifetime.

Chef Shrimpy's jerk chicken and jerk pork for your home

Our jerk sauce can also be used to season your roast beef, your veal, your turkey, your seafood and all the many things you cook at home.

Getting the jerk sauce through the process makes me feel proud that dream became a reality. If one works hard for what they desire, we can all achieve our dreams. Moreover, my achievements have no limits, so I did not stop there with my creations. I would move on to create Chef Shrimpy's Mignonette Sauce for sale.

Chef Shrimpy's Mignonette Sauce

Chef Shrimpy's Mignonette Sauce—use it for all your shellfish needs! Goes best with raw oysters, little neck clams and shrimp cocktail.

Method of preparing your shellfish
Wash oysters and little neck clams thoroughly.

Make sure you have the right knife to shuck them with.

For your shrimp cocktail, put a pot with water
on high flame and bring to boil.

Chef Shrimpy always adds bay leaves, cloves and onions to
the water for flavor; add your shrimp to boiling water.

Cook for a minute or two at boiling point.

Strain off, then put to cool in refrigerator.

Pour Chef Shrimpy's Mignonette Sauce in a bowl, then dip as you eat.

You'll keep wanting more.

Facing life's struggles on earth has taught me that it's never who we are, but it's who we can become. Those valuable thoughts of mine remind me of the men and women of the past who created some of what became today's greatest necessities. They could have limited their genius minds to one invention and could have easily fed their family and have a good life on earth. However, they chose the other road, knowing there invention wasn't only to serve their needs, but they were leaving behind values that would serve mankind for generations to come. That concept of thought was one that fills my body, with the beliefs that greatness continues, that records are made to be broken and that there will be generations that follow mine. So within the next six months that followed my second creation, I would move on to create ten more food products, including six fruit salad dressings, a pickle, a pickled onion, Chef Shrimpy's All-Purpose Seasoning and Chef Shrimpy's Poultry Seasoning.

Chef Shrimpy's All-Purpose Seasoning

A blend of herbs and spices that adds a satisfactory aroma to your kitchen.

Use to season all of your meat needs and also your vegetables.

Chef Shrimpy's Poultry Seasoning

Chef Shrimpy's Poultry Seasoning—use it for all your poultry needs and make your taste buds tingle.

Chef Shrimpy's Sweet and Sour Pickles make your mouth water for more.

Chef Shrimpy's Pickled Onion—the secret is in the taste. You add it to your roast beef sandwich, chicken sandwich, pork sandwich, turkey, or if you are a onion lover like me, add it to most things you are eating—that how good it is

Chef Shrimpy's salad dressings are a wonderful choice for your favorite salads and are great for your health too. These delicious dressings are a honey base combined with fresh berries and vegetable oil and contain zero percent trans fat. Chef Shrimpy's salad dressings contain only the best ingredients available today. I make them in six delicious flavors, so you have a lot to choose from.

Chef Shrimpy's Cranberry Vinaigrette

Chef Shrimpy's Mango Vinaigrette

Chef Shrimpy's Blueberry
Vinaigrette

Chef Shrimpy's Raspberry
Vinaigrette

Chef Shrimpy's Strawberry
Vinaigrette

Chef Shrimpy's Blackberry
Vinaigrette

Chef recommendations for some of the salads we serve in the restaurant:

Tossed Garden Salad

Recipe

Lettuce of your choice: could be iceberg, romaine, whatever you like.

Tomatoes

Cucumbers

Red or yellow onions

Red or green peppers

Method

Wash all vegetables thoroughly.

Toss together in a bowl.

Add your choice of Chef Shrimpy's salad dressing, then place on your serving plates.

Optional: Prep your salad and let your family add their dressings accordingly.

These wonderful salad dressings can also be used as a marinade on any type of meat or poultry. Just by marinate into these lovely natural dressings and cook to your method of liking, then use your choice of dressing at the end.

Cook it like Shrimpy, bring sexy back to the kitchen.

Since we bring sexy back, we present our healthy natural drinks to accompany our healthy natural cuisine.

By the end of 2011 and the beginning of 2012, I acknowledged that I had gotten to the stage in life where marketing becomes a necessity. With my limited amount of knowledge in that field, I sought out professional help. I had very little money to my name; yet bleeding for success, I had been filing applications with negative results and making phone calls that have been ignored. Nonetheless, the sweat and tears were already donated, which was and still enough to produce a thin black line on the asphalt of life; the strongest shall be called Prince Solomon, as a witness for those who cried. (In the midst of wealth, mankind is suffering.) A temple shall bear evidence.

Mankind can be blessed to see images smiling in thy visions, with negative words of financial help for job creation, such faces would meet to confirm a result already overcome—wearing the same colors. With ears open, the promising words to help a life and a nation's economy through job creations; resulted in the chaff which the wind blows away.

I started making phone calls to my state house, senator and all the representatives that formed the political umbrella which covers my constituency, seeking information to represent my products and to create jobs.

Their great help as public servants led me into new directions, where I needed to focus my marketing strategies. One of those was the 2012 New England Food Show in Boston, where I had my products displayed and presented to domestic and international buyers and by the summer of that same year, I was also participating in the local farmers' markets in Cape Cod.

Chef Shrimpy at the 2012 New England Food Show

The greatest part of their help thus far was the journey that led me to the University of Massachusetts, Dartmouth on September 12, 2012. I was there in a marketing classroom to present Chef Shrimpy's Jerk Sauce as their marketing project for that semester.

I would be lying if I told you I wasn't nervous to do the presentation, since have never stepped foot in a university classroom before, much less speak to those intelligent students.

I was one of three entrepreneurs representing our respective products. The professor did me a great favor—before we addressed the first class, he asked me if I wanted to speak second. "Yes," I quickly responded. I got a chance to see the strategies used by the first speaker to present his product.

On my journey, I always knew I would get to these stages in life, since I lived to represent it in that manner and even though I was nervous, that concept of thought relaxed me as I took about thirty footsteps from the back of the classroom to the front to address the students.

At my opening statement, they asked where my accent was from.

"Jamaica, yea man!" I replied.

The entire class started laughing. They now knew that thirty footsteps were coming from a distance and where I was standing in front of them that morning was where this new journey had taken me. Smiles always prove confidence and so I wrapped up my presentation on that note.

The afternoon presentation was also wonderful and at about 2:45 p.m., a new aspect of my life's mission paused in UMass Dartmouth and would only continue when the semester was over. However, the old journey moved on as I drove back to Cape Cod to open my restaurant the following day.

Working with the students over the semester advanced my communication skills and with the exposure at the farmers' markets, I was invited to participate in the Chatham Seafood Throwdown held at the Chatham Fish Pier on October 27, 2012. I won the competition with a mix of recipes. Utilizing my mango vinaigrette, my all-purpose seasoning and my jerk sauce, I created a winning method that blew the judges away.

Chef Shrimpy at the 2012 Chatham Seafood Throwdown

October 23, 2012

The Jerk Café
1319-A Rt. 28
South Yarmouth, MA 02664

Dear Chef Shrimpy,

Thank you for your participation in the Chatham Fish Pier "Meet the Fleet" Seafood Throwdown on Sunday, October 21st. Congratulations on your winning 3-course tasting menu, of which all dishes included freshly caught skate.

Your enthusiasm and professionalism shined against the competition, and you were certainly a crowd favorite, not to mention sweeping the judges palates! The dishes you presented with the difficult task of wrangling whole skate were fresh, clean, healthy and superior. We, the Northwest Atlantic Marine Alliance (NAMA), would be delighted to ask you back for future cooking competitions of this kind.

NAMA is a 501-C3 non-profit organization effecting policy change in favor of healthy fish stocks and secure food systems & economies. You may have heard about our Fleet Vision project, or watched a "Who Fishes Matters" testimony on our website www.namanet.org, or tasted from another Seafood Throwdown at your neighborhood farmer's market. Maybe you hold a share in your Community Supported Fishery (CSF). Whatever the case, we are pleased that you are part of the community that respects sustainable fish practices.

Thank you again for your generosity, dedication, and overall support of NAMA's mission to think globally & fish locally!

With kind regards,

Shannon Eldredge
Board President

Chef Shrimpy's letter of recognition

At the end of the semester, I made a three-day visit to the university in attendance at the presentations. It was one of the greatest moments of my life, to sit in the classroom among the students, involved in the topic they were covering. I felt like a kid again who should've spent several years on one of those chairs. It had never happened because of life circumstances; nonetheless, we can never think we can't accomplish all of our desires. From childhood into adolescence, one goes through the stage of growth by the responsibility of our parents. From adolescence into adulthood is the stage where we should accomplish all our educational needs, the ones that are most important for our endeavored career. Achieving those values in life depends on our parents' well-being. Dreams come and go and some will stay until they are approached. So if our mother and father couldn't do it for us, then we can do it for ourselves. I never attended college for an education but was participating in another aspect of my life.

Thanks to the University of Massachusetts, Dartmouth, to the Commonwealth of Massachusetts, the professors and the students; a special thank you to the parents of the students too.

After the presentation at the university, life continued at the Jerk Café. As a child growing up, if Mother promised me a cookie, I would look forward to it. The same can be said for dreams and promises made to myself. They are all for nothing if I can't work toward fulfilling them. The result of my life's fulfillments have been based on the effort with which I approached my dreams. As the old saying goes and I quote, "If you build it, they will come." (Children, that is true)

They came one Thursday morning in December.

The phone rang at the Jerk Café. "Hello!" I answered.

"I am calling you from Phantom Gourmet," the young lady on the other side of line said.

"You have my attention," I replied.

"We would like to feature your restaurant on our network gourmet program, which broadcasts on my TV 38."

That I already knew since I watched it most weekends. "Come on down," I told her. We instantly set up a meeting and on December 13, 2012, we had a filming session at the restaurant.

By then I had become more comfortable with the media and with the continuous belief that I am a great chef; the time had come for me to show the world how good I was. And that I did, since it was a longtime dream of mine from the day I started food and nutrition at fifteen years old. (Children, dreams are for real—they are for real). The segment was broadcast on March 9, 2013 and can also be watched at *thejerkcafe.com.*

Chef Shrimpy (right), colleague Chef Marvin Lawrence (left)

The knowledge I gained through working with the university, advanced my marketing skills, which I intended to use as the forefront of my campaign to market Chef Shrimpy's line of condiments to the dinner table of every human being around the world. The Jerk Café will forever bear evidence of where the products are produced and it is a concept that will encourage brand trust because consumers will be more comfortable knowing the products are actually served in a restaurant. Our natural ingredients will make consumers grab our products off the shelves and not have to think about other potential products. Chef Shrimpy's line of products will model the condiment market and will forever be in buyers evoked set.

Between these walls in South Yarmouth, I stand evidence from the day the Jerk Café was opened. Seventy percent of my days was spent occupying my chair with my head turned to the wall, doing God's work. My spirit brightens when I talk to a customer, who over time may become a personal friend. Sometimes I try to stretch conversations to keep them there longer or just to look busy, knowing my next customer would sometimes be an hour later or my friends become my repeat dinner customers.

Those fruitful days in front of God produced a reward through self motivation, as blood, sweat and tears were shed to bear evidence of a road that must traveled by the guiding light of God and a fulfillment of time.

Through those pilgrimage days, knowledge was granted out of time seems wasted; to leave behind an abundance of food products, all which are blessed to nourish mankind as earthly food, as they will not starve for nutrients.

Besides smiling at the most frequent statement made on a daily basis (the one-man show), the legs bear the pain as I dance, cook and sing day by day to entertain mankind, in search of the full loaf of bread of life. Despite the fact that my loaf could never form into one, the journey shall not be disturbed by wants or needs, as the children's handbook must be completed in front of all mankind, guided by God's will and divine power to bear evidence of the fulfillment.

Chapter Thirteen

The Face Of Job And The Skeleton Of Wrath

The right hand which handed the four stones saw the 14 and the 17. These presented the message of fruitful times: four decades, one for each stone. A life lived and a journey trotted to the end. The words in this book will stand as an honest life in front of God, as a stepping stone for the next generation and building blocks as they live them day by day.

Every being serves his purpose on earth; every drop of blood is shed for a reason, every pair of lips whisper thy last moment; the earth has been robbed of its fruit, such is what blossoms into our children and should provide a fruitful pathway for them.

I thought of our children watching as the earth becomes fearful, that they questioned their young minds day and night in the midst of poverty, disease, war and disasters.

Their shadow bears their own reflection as they cast their eyes to the sun, whispering for a cure and without immediate answers, they live another day by hope, waiting for decisions made by mankind that sometimes never get down to them. Many of their crying voices have not been answered for too long, but their prayer has.

Every drop of blood is a sacrifice and shall stand as evidence of fulfillment. Our children's memories, for too long, have been focusing on the continuous blood that is shed every day instead of the garden of earth which they were born to dwell in.

I thought of their tears as their hopes and those tears are thickening in front of our eyes, now being answered by God as a sacrifice, as their garden is on the brink of bearing fruits for the next generation.

I thought of the many of the sacrifices have been fulfilled and stand as evidence in front of God and man. I thought the blood is now floating on the surface of the earth; it takes decisions from your heart to clean it up.

Mankind! I thought the stables are occupied again, we saw the nails in the arms as an evidence of sacrifice. I thought the cross is evident again; **if our hearts continue to be disobedient and our children continue to suffer under the hands of man, I thought it will be occupied again. The eyes of the blind may not behold it. I thought of the days of the final bloodshed stood at its peak. Blood will continue to be shed through unjust** of the continuous slathering of the fruit of life, as the final sacrifice and as an offering for the suffering of the children and shall stand as evidence for the next generation, (That of the 14 and of the 17.)

An answer for the urgent search will be evident soon but will also bear evidence of the fulfillment of bloody times, (That of the14 and of the 17.)

The rainbow is evidence as a sign of his covenant with mankind, which colors marveled as it stretches across the skies. I thought the power of the rainbow is like that of the thunder, of lighting, of the volcanoes, tsunamis, the earthquakes, the hurricane. (That of the 14 and of the 17.)

I thought of the wise man who built his house upon the rocks; locations will vanish in short time and will bear evidence as a fulfillment.(The children's tears are flooding the earth,) "That of the 14 and of the 17"

I thought the earth was trembling. The promise to the future, as a statue planted as a fulfillment of sweat and tears, which shall bear evidence and stand as a witness for decisions made to govern mankind.

Such shall produce again to bear occupancy and, if ever harmed that can be evident by God and man, will cause outrage across a nation, (That of the 14 and of the 17.)

Oh God, through the visions of the 14 and of the 17, 5002 show evidence of the seventeen and the sixteen, the seven and the seventeen, and the seven and the twenty-six. The cities will be occupied and our eyes will bear evidence of new tough decisions made by mankind, which shall stand as a fulfillment for the next generation, 000,062 will be scattered.

I thought a nation of reliable strength and spiritual background will be weakened because of selections. Such a decision will make another region unite for a while, then the war will be so bloody because of failed ideology left behind by mankind's mind, (That of the14 and of the 17.)

I thought of a region basin that has been cracked in recent years because of recent activities which will cause disaster resulting in mass casualties and bloodshed upon its people. "The wise man built his house upon the rock." (that of 14 and of the 17.)

Coming down is easier than going up; our eyes behold going up a success, but eyes will also behold going up, becomes a new coming down, that never thought of, (That of the 14 and of the 17.)

I thought of the performances of our athletes on the track, the course, the field, the court will marvel the next generation, we have risen to new events that seemed impossible yesterday. The dark walls of peeping holes evidences itself as the door which embodies the eyes that smile at the first will see a history of the twenties (20-21-22-23-24-25-26-27-28-29) left behind (189-degree turn) that shall stand as an evidence of the fulfillment. A disgrace in front of man is not a disgrace in front of God,

(That of the 14 and of the 17)."

Eyes witness the world rise in this belief, as God took mankind's journey to the highest level of competition, which will stand as a fulfillment for the next generation. The one to pass judgment or to judge will become a bearer of guilt in front of God. Such verdict of guilt or innocence will stand as a fulfillment in front of God that will build the case against one who will be immediately judged by him. Eyes will behold some the way they were made and not what they become. I thought the tears that fell from the eyes of the cripples will drown those who make such decisions in front of man. Who will be judged. The universe is active now more than ever and our faith has been tested in so many ways, (That of the 14 and of the17).

A genius lives among us, who lately brought out the best in the form of education. His granted knowledge goes beyond mankind and into the destiny of life—an ideology of learning—gathered through the simplest form of mankind's thinking—from creation, "common sense, it was the first form of education." As it was in the beginning— as redeem itself into this time. He should be left unharmed to continue his job and be protected. His contribution to life has been acknowledged by God; he is blessed. His legacy donated to the human race, will leave on imprint on life, which will never go dull. And it will stand as a fulfillment for the next generation, (That of the 14 and of the 17.)

I thought of gates that will be opened to release enemies who bear occupancy on their home properties; they will come to a crossroad on what side to choose, right or wrong, good or bad. Such result will be that of mankind's remembrance, from occupying the tunnels, which echoes the darkest sounds of immediate confrontation; with nothing left, mankind will fall asleep thinking of the games played without rules and the values of life, which have lingered for too long, now being adapted by the whispering sounds of life, which is protected by wrath, bitterness, destruction and hate, govern by an ideology which bears the shape of a 3 pronged fork, a steep slope, which water can settle on, but life can't survive there. Their answers will only come by their own actions since there is no other witness to bear evidence, (That of the 14 and of the 17.)

"An eye open vision, with feet standing"

A year in life's calendar, eighteen-year-olds' eyes, mind, soul, heart, and body, witness the strength of the strongest music; brought forth the strong caucus which shed the stain that is painted on the concrete of hardship, which bear evidence of sacrifice for any race strength. Such strength shall redeem itself again as the universe is made to produce; such death will stand as a fulfillment for next generation, whose caucus shall forever bear evidence of strength. Eyes and ears open to bear witness of speech read by leaders in reception. To ignore the caucus and put Gods being in you (who have done his work). The result of him will stand strong until the end of time, (That of the 14 and of the 17.)

The face seen, which bears the look of Job and skeleton of fright, has redeemed itself into forces unseen by the blind. Such a face is beautiful, such a skeleton is wrath. Two images adjoined present themselves in different forms, one of peace and one of wrath, (That of the 14 and of the 17.)

A PRAYER OF PRAISE AND JOY, GLENROY SOLOMON BURKE

YOU HAVE SHIELDED ME FROM THE FURNACE OF THE SUN, WHEN SHINETH UPON ME AS YOUR DIVINE POWER, WHEN MY ENEMIES CAME UPON ME TO DESTROY ME, YOU PRESENTED A WALL OF PROTECTION FROM THEIR WRATH. WHEN MY ENEMIES LAUGH FIRST, YOU ALWAYS SAVE MINE FOR LAST, JOYFUL BE UNTO WHOM OBEYS YOU, SUCH WILL ALWAYS FEEL YOUR PRESENCE. OH, GOD, I WILL CONTINUE TO PRESENT MYSELF AS A LAMB TO YOU; TO DWELL INTO YOUR COVENANT—IN YOUR HOLY NAME. AMEN.

A Prayer of Thanks by Glenroy Solomon Burke

Oh, God, you have held my hands on my journey, so tight, you will never let go. Through my tough and bumpy roads you saved my tires, through the hills and valleys, you lightened my load, through disasters and wars, you kept me safe. You have built blocks for me to stand on and I never miss a step; when I slip, you balance me. Through temptations, you *kept me calm You have blessed me with strength unimaginable and I used it in your favor. All dreams matter—carried and protected by you. When I shy away, you found me. When the energy has bled out, you strengthen me. When the journey was rough and I was searching, you overcame my doubts and put away temptations. Through thy obedience oh, God, I have trod the road thou prepared for me. The work is done and it's back in your hands to be handed out. It shall stand as a scale in your name. **LET IT BEAR YOUR SEAL OH, GOD.** Amen.*

This, in my own words, is my life's mission. My dream is to someday become **the Prime Minister of Jamaica.**